MORE PRAISE FOR *Before the Feast*

WINNER OF THE 2014 LEIPZIG BOOK FAIR PRIZE

"A village in the Uckermark, fully in the present, yet rife with legends. In *Before the Feast*, this village tells its own story—a novel as a compelling multi-voiced chorale put in prose."

—Leipzig Book Fair Prize Jury

"A book like few others. Politically well-versed and stylistically a work of art."

—Die Zeit

"Highly entertaining and full of chutzpah."

—Die Welt

"Switching among styles with a dancing virtuosity, Stanišić knits a dozen characters into a multi-stranded tissue of gossip, myth, and memory . . . In English, Stanišić makes a dream team with Anthea Bell, who translates with a pitch-perfect ear for every twist and frisk of his German."

—The Independent

"Episodic, impressionistic and whimsical . . . clever and funny."

—TIBOR FISCHER, *The Guardian*

BEFORE the FEAST

BEFORE *the* FEAST

SAŠA STANIŠIĆ

translated by **ANTHEA BELL**

Tin House Books

Portland, Oregon & Brooklyn, New York

Published by Tin House Books, Portland, Oregon, and Brooklyn, New York

Distributed by W. W. Norton & Company

Library of Congress Cataloging-in-Publication Data

Names: Stanišić, Saša, 1978- author. | Bell, Anthea, translator.
Title: Before the feast / by Sasa Stanisic ; [English translation, Anthea Bell].
Other titles: Vor dem Fest. English
Description: First U.S. edition. | Portland, Oregon : Tin House Books, 2016.
 | ©2015
Identifiers: LCCN 2016006742 (print) | LCCN 2016012861 (ebook) | ISBN
  9781941040393 (pbk. : alk. paper) | ISBN 9781941040409 ()
Classification: LCC PT2721.T36 V6713 2016 (print) | LCC PT2721.
T36 (ebook) |
  DDC 833/.92--dc23
LC record available at http://lccn.loc.gov/2016006742

First US edition 2016
Printed in the USA
Interior design by Diane Chonette

www.tinhouse.com

For Katja

For billions of years since the outset of time
Every single one of your ancestors has survived
Every single person on your mum and dad's side
Successfully looked after and passed on to you life.
What are the chances of that like?

The Streets,
"On the Edge of a Cliff"

I

WE ARE SAD. WE DON'T HAVE A FERRYMAN ANY more. The ferryman is dead. Two lakes, no ferryman. You can't get to the islands now unless you have a boat. Or unless you are a boat. You could swim. But just try swimming when the chunks of ice are clinking in the waves like a set of wind chimes with a thousand little cylinders.

In theory, you can walk round the lake on foot, keeping to the bank. However, we've neglected the path. The ground is marshy and the landing stages are crumbling and in poor shape; the bushes have spread, they stand in your way, chest-high.

Nature takes back its own. Or that's what they'd say in other places. We don't say so, because it's nonsense. Nature is not logical. You can't rely on Nature. And if you can't rely on something you'd better not build fine phrases out of it.

Someone has dumped half his household goods on the bank below the ruins of what was once Schielke's farmhouse, where the lake laps lovingly against the road. There's a fridge stuck in the muddy ground, with a can of tuna still in it. The ferryman told us that, and said how angry he had been. Not because of the rubbish in general but because of the tuna in particular.

Now the ferryman is dead, and we don't know who's going to tell us what the banks of the lake are getting up to. Who but a ferryman says things like, "Where the lake laps lovingly against the road," and "It was tuna from the distant seas of Norway" so beautifully? Only ferrymen say such things.

We haven't thought up any more good turns of phrase since the fall of the Berlin Wall. The ferryman was good at telling stories.

But don't think that at this moment of our weakness we ask the Deep Lake, which is even deeper now, without the ferryman, how it's doing. Or ask the Great Lake, the one that drowned the ferryman, what its reasons were.

No one saw the ferryman drown. It's better that way. Why would you want to see a person drowning? It's not a pretty sight. He must have gone out in the evening when there was mist over the water. In the dim light of dawn a boat was drifting on the lake, empty and useless, like saying goodbye when there's no one to say it to.

Divers came. Frau Schwermuth made coffee for them, they drank the coffee and looked at the lake, then they climbed down into the lake and fished out the ferryman. Tall men, fair-haired and taciturn, using verbs only in the imperative, brought the ferryman up. Standing on the bank in their close-fitting diving suits, black and upright as exclamation marks. Eating vegetarian bread rolls with water dripping off them.

The ferryman was buried, and the bell-ringer missed his big moment; the bell rang an hour and a half later, when everyone was already eating funeral cake in the Platform One café. The bell-ringer can hardly climb the stairs without help.

At a quarter past twelve the other day he rang the bell eighteen times, dislocating his shoulder in the process. We do have an automated bell-ringing system and Johann the apprentice, but the bell-ringer doesn't particularly like either of them.

More people die than are born. We hear the old folk as they grow lonely and the young as they fail to make any plans. Or make plans to go away. In spring we lost the Number 419 bus. People say, give it another generation or so, and things won't last here any longer. We believe they will. Somehow or other they always have. We've survived pestilence and war, epidemics and famine, life and death. Somehow or other things will go on.

Only now the ferryman is dead. Who will the drinkers turn to when Ulli has sent them away at closing time? Who's going to fix paperchase treasure hunts for visitors from the Greater Berlin area, in fact fix them so well that no treasure is ever found, and the kids cry quietly on the ferry afterward and their mothers complain politely to the ferryman, while the fathers are left wondering, days later, where they went wrong? Those are mainly fathers from the new Federal German provinces, feeling that their virility has been questioned, and once on land again they eat an apple, ride toward the Baltic Sea on their disillusioned bicycles and never come back. Who's going to do all that?

The ferryman is dead, and the other dead people are surprised: what's a ferryman doing underground? He ought to have stayed in the lake as a ferryman should.

No one says: I'm the new ferryman. The few who understand that we really, really need a new ferryman don't know how to ferry a boat. Or how to console the waters of the lakes. Or they're too old. Others act as if we never had a ferryman at all. A third kind say: the ferryman is dead, long live the boat-hire business.

The ferryman is dead, and no one knows why.

We are sad. We don't have a ferryman any more. And the lakes are wild and dark again, watching, and observing what goes on.

THE FUEL STATION HAS CLOSED, SO YOU HAVE TO go to Woldegk to fill up. Since then, on average, people have been driving round the village in circles less and straight ahead to Woldegk more, reciting Theodor Fontane if they happen to know his works by heart. On average it's the young, not the old, who miss the fuel station. And not just because of filling up. Because of KitKats, and beer to take away, and 𝔘𝔫𝔣𝔬𝔯𝔤𝔦𝔟𝔦𝔫𝔤, 𝔒𝔯𝔞𝔫𝔤𝔢 𝔍𝔫𝔣𝔢𝔯𝔫𝔬 flavor, the energy drink 𝔱𝔥𝔞𝔱 𝔱𝔞𝔨𝔢𝔰 𝔈𝔞𝔰𝔱 𝔊𝔢𝔯𝔪𝔞𝔫 𝔣𝔲𝔢𝔩 𝔰𝔱𝔞𝔱𝔦𝔬𝔫𝔰 𝔟𝔶 𝔰𝔱𝔬𝔯𝔪, with 32 mg of caffeine per 100 ml.

Lada, who is known as Lada because at the age of thirteen he drove his grandfather's Lada to Denmark, has parked his Golf in the Deep Lake for the third time in three months. Is that to do with the absence of a fuel station? No, it's to do with Lada. And it's to do with the track along the bank, which in theory is highly suitable for a speed of 200 km/h here.

The lake gurgled. At first Johann and silent Suzi, up on the bank, thought it was funny, then they thought it wasn't so funny after all. A minute passed. Johann took off his headband and plunged in, and he's the worst swimmer of the three of them. The youngest, too. A boy among men. All for nothing; Lada came up of his own accord, with his cigarette still between his lips. Then he had to lend a hand with rescuing Johann.

Fürstenfelde. Population: somewhere in the odd numbers. Our seasons: spring, summer, autumn, winter. Summer is clearly in the lead. The weather of our summers will bear comparison with the Mediterranean. Instead of the Mediterranean we have the lakes. Spring is not a good time for allergy sufferers or for Frau Schwermuth of the Homeland House, who gets depressed in spring. Autumn is divided into early autumn and late autumn. Autumn here is a season for tourists who like agricultural machinery. Fathers from the city bring their sons to gawp at the machinery by night. The enthusiastic sons are shocked rigid by the sight of those gigantic wheels and reflectors, and the racket the agricultural machinery kicks up. The story of winter in a village with two lakes is always a story that begins when the lakes freeze and ends when the ice melts.

"What are you going to do about your old banger?" Johann asked Lada, and Lada, who is no novice at the art of fishing cars out of the lake and getting them back into running order, said, "I'll fetch it one of these days."

Silent Suzi cast out his fishing line again. He had barely paused for Lada's mishap. Suzi loves angling. If you're born mute, you're kind of predestined to be an angler. Although what does it mean, mute? Saying his larynx doesn't work would be politically correct.

Johann gently tapped out a rhythm on his thigh. He has his bell-ringing exam tomorrow, and he's going to play a little melody of his own composed specially for the Feast. It's to be performed by striking the bells instead of making them swing. Lada and Suzi don't know anything about it. It's better that way or they'll make fun of him.

They stripped to their underpants, Johann and Lada, so that their clothes could dry, Suzi out of solidarity. Lada's flawlessly muscular build, Suzi's flawlessly muscular build, Johann's skinny ribs. Suzi combs his hair back, he always has a comb with him, a custom now verging on extinction. A dragon's tail on his forehead, the mighty dragon's body round the back of Suzi's neck, the dragon's head on his shoulder-blade, breathing fire. Suzi is as handsome as the stars of Italian films in the 1950s. Suzi's mother is always watching those films and shedding tears.

Grasshoppers. Swallows. Wasps. Tired, all of them, very tired.

Autumn is on the way.

Today was the last hot day of the year. The last day when you could comfortably lie on the grass in your underpants, with beetles climbing all over you as if you were a natural obstacle in the terminal moraine landscape, which in a way you are. If you come from here, you know that sort of thing: it's the last hot day. Not because of the swallows or the weather app. You know it because you've stripped to your underwear and you're lying down, and if you are a girl you've burrowed your toes into the sand, if you're not a girl you haven't done anything with your toes, you're just lying down. And, lying like that, you looked up at the sky, and it was perfectly clear.

Today—the last hot day. If by some miracle there should be another one after all, it wouldn't mean anything. Today was the last.

Lada and Johann watched Suzi and gave him tips, because he wasn't catching anything. Try under the ash tree, it's too hot for the fish here, that kind of thing. Suzi put the rod between his legs and gestured wildly. Lada understands Suzi's language quite well, or rather, he doesn't know it all that well but he has known silent Suzi for ever.

"We have all the time in the world," he translated for Johann's benefit. Johann looked at him enquiringly. Lada shrugged his shoulders and spat into the lake. Anna came along the lakeside path on her bike. Wearing a dress with what they call spaghetti straps or something like that. Johann spontaneously waved. He's a boy, after all. Anna looked straight ahead.

"What are you waving for?" Lada punched Johann's shoulder. "Let me show you how it's done." An excursion boat was chugging over the lake. Lada whistled shrilly. The tourists on board were moving under the shelter of their roof. Lada waved, the tourists waved back. The tourists took photos. Then Lada showed them his middle finger.

"That doesn't count, they're tourists waving. They'll wave no matter what," said Johann.

Lada punched him again. There's a wolf baring its teeth on Lada's shoulder. The wording on Lada's back says 𝕿𝖍𝖊 𝕷𝖊𝖌𝖊𝖓𝖉. The lettering is almost the same as in the ad for the energy drink.

"What are you staring at?"

"I'm going to get a tattoo as well."

"Hear that, Suzi? This wanker's going to get a tattoo. Fabulous."

One thing Johann has learned from knowing Lada is not to lose his nerve. To stick to his point. Letting people provoke you shows weakness. "Does that mean anything?" he asked. Suzi has a wolf on his calf as well.

Lada looked him in the eye. Spat sideways. "The wolves are coming back." He spoke very slowly. "Germany will be wolf country again. Wolves from Poland and Russia, they can cover thousands of kilometers. Wonderful animals. Hunters. Say: wolf-pack."

"Wolf-pack."

"Wicked, right? Such power in that one word! Suzi and I support the wolf." Lada grabbed Johann by the back of the neck. "This is just between ourselves, okay? We've brought wolves. From Lusatia. Because once there were wolves here too. Ask your mother. In the Zerveliner Heide, near the rocket base? We set them free."

Stay cool. Ask more questions. Sometimes Lada just goes rabbiting on like that to scare Johann. Suzi has turned round, listening intently. Johann cleared his throat.

"How many?"

"Very funny. I thought you'd ask *how*. Four. Two young wolves, two adults. Listen, you: it's no joke. Keep your mouth shut, understand?"

"Sure."

"Good."

Suzi had a fish on his hook. It put up a bit of resistance. A small carp. Suzi threw it back in the water again.

Lada got up. "Off we go to Ulli's, you guys. Suzi will stand us a drink." And that's what they did, because Lada is someone who keeps his word.

A CARP CAN FEEL ENVY FOR FOOD. WHEN THE other fish come to feed, it joins in. But from autumn onward, as the water temperature drops, it needs less and less nourishment.

Male hornets copulate with the young queens and then promptly die. The young queens settle down to wait for spring under moss, in rotten wood, in the dragonfly's nightmares.

In the Kiecker Forest, the old woods, the woodpecker chisels out the milliseconds of our mortality.

For autumn is here.

The wolf-pack is awake.

IT WAS EXACTLY A YEAR AGO, ON THE DAY BEFORE the last Feast, that Ulli cleared out his garage, put in some seating and five tables and a stove, hung a red and yellow tulle curtain over the only window and nailed a calendar with pictures of Polish girls leaning on motorbikes to the wall, partly for the ironic effect, partly for the aesthetics of it. A Sterni beer costs you eighty cents, a Stieri ninety, a beer with cherry juice is one euro fifty, and you can watch football on the weekend. The guys think well of Ulli because of all this, even if they don't say so.

We drink in Ulli's garage because you don't get a place to sit and tell tall tales and a fridge all together like that anywhere else, which makes it a good spot for guys to be at ease with each other over a drink, but at the same time not *too* much at ease. Nowhere else, unless you're at home, do you get a roof over your head, and Pils, and Bundesliga on Sky, and smoking and company.

We do have a restaurant too, Platform One, and it's not at all bad. Still, you don't want to get drunk in Platform One. You want to have dinner, maybe celebrate an anniversary, but try to get well tanked up while plastic flowers and tourists who come on bicycles are watching you. Now and then Veronika brings real tulips in. Try to get well tanked up while real tulips are watching.

Ulli's garage has a good smell of engine oil. Motorbike badges and beer ads adorn the door, and there's a shield with the imperial eagle on it and the words 𝕲𝖊𝖗𝖒𝖆𝖓 𝕰𝖒𝖕𝖎𝖗𝖊. It's a fact that almost no one but men come from the new pre-fabricated buildings. Sometimes there's trouble, nothing too bad. Nothing really nasty. Sometimes you can't make out what you're saying. In retrospect you're glad of that. Sometimes someone tells a story and everyone listens. This evening, it will be old Imboden telling the story over the last round. Imboden is usually a quiet but fierce drinker. His wife died three years ago, and it was only then that he began coming here. Ulli says he has to catch up after all those years of sobriety.

In the garage, and because of the Feast tomorrow, the talk was about earlier feasts, and how feasts in the old days were better than now. For instance, no one could remember a good, really satisfying brawl among grown men in the last couple of years. They used to be the norm. These days only the young lads fight. "Badly, at that," said Lada, laughing, but no one else laughed.

So now Imboden stands up to go and take a piss, but before he leaves the room—the garage doesn't have a toilet, but there's something like a tree in front of the prefab—he says, "Just a moment. This won't do."

For several weeks there's been a color photo stuck to the fridge. Ulli's granddaughter Rike is going through a phase. The picture shows Rike and her grandpa in a little rectangle, which is the garage. When Ulli put up that picture he took the naked Polish girls down. As a result the men called Ulli Gramps for a few days, but then they forgot about it and called him Ulli again.

Everyone can drink at Ulli's, even drink more than he can take on board. But when a guest can't lie down without holding on to something, Ulli gives Lada a nod, and Lada escorts or carries that guy out.

Everyone can talk at Ulli's and say more than anywhere else. But if he goes on talking and saying more, and Ulli has had enough of it, Ulli gives Lada the nod.

You pay less at Ulli's than anywhere else. But if anyone hasn't paid in full after a month, then Ulli gives Lada the nod.

Everyone can weep at Ulli's, out loud at that. But no one does weep at Ulli's.

Everyone can tell a joke at Ulli's that we don't all think is funny. But when a guy means something seriously that we don't all think is funny, Ulli gives Lada the nod.

Everyone can tell a story about the old days at Ulli's, and usually the others listen.

Old Imboden came back from having a piss, and Imboden told his story.

THE VIXEN LIES QUIETLY ON DAMP LEAVES, UNDER a beech tree on the outskirts of the old forest. From where the forest meets the fields—fields of wheat, barley, rapeseed—she looks at the little group of human houses, standing on such a narrow strip of land between two lakes that you might think human beings, in their unbridled wish to grab the most comfortable possible place as their own, had cut one lake into two, making room right between them for themselves and their young, in a fertile, practical place on two banks at once. Room for the paved roads that they seldom leave, room for the places where they hide their food, their stones and metals, and all the huge quantities of other things that they hoard.

The vixen senses the time when the lakes did not yet exist, and no humans had their game preserves here. She senses ice that the earth had to carry all the way along the horizon. Ice that pushed land on ahead of it, brought stones with it, hollowed out the earth, raised it to form hills that still undulate today, tens of thousands of fox years later. The two lakes rock in the lap of the land, in the breast of the land grow the roots of the ancient forest where the vixen has her earth, a tunnel, not very deep but safe from the badger, with the vixen's two cubs in it now—or so she hopes—not waiting accusingly outside like last time, when all she brought home was beetles again. The hawk was already circling.

She would smell the earthy honey on the pelts of her cubs among a thousand other aromas, even now, in spite of the false wind, she is sure of its sweetness in the depths of the forest. She is sure of their hunger, too, their stern and constant hunger. One of the cubs came into the world ailing and has already died. The other two are playing skillfully with the beetles and vermin. But rising almost vertically in the air from a stationary position and coming down on a mouse is still too much like play. Their games often make them forget about the prey.

The vixen raises her head. She is scenting the air for humankind. There are none of them close. A warmth that reminds her of wood rises from their buildings. The vixen tastes dead plants there, too; well-nourished dogs and cats; birds gone wrong, and a lot of other things that she can't easily classify. She is afraid of much of what she senses. She is indifferent to most of it. Then there's dung, clods of earth, then there's fermentation and chicken and death.

Chicken!

Behind twisted metal wires in wooden sheds: chicken! The vixen is going to get into those chickens tonight.

Her cubs are staying away from the earth longer and longer. The vixen guesses that tonight's hunt will be her last for her hungry young. Soon they will be striking out and finding preserves of their own. She would like to bring them something good, something really special when she and they part. Not beetles or worms, not the remains of fruit half-eaten by humans—she will bring them eggs! Nothing has a better aroma than the thin, delicate eggshells, because nothing tastes as good as the gooey, sweet yolks inside those shells.

It is never easy to get inside a henhouse. Even if no dog is guarding it, and the humans are asleep. She isn't afraid of the fowls' claws. But carrying eggs is all but impossible. Her previous attempts were failures, if delicious failures. This time she will close her mouth as carefully as she closes it on the cubs in play. This time she won't take two eggs at once but come back for the second.

A female badger slips out of the wood. The vixen picks up the scents of bracken and fear on her. What is she afraid of? Bats fly past overhead. Taciturn creatures, moving too fast for any joking, fluttering nervously away. On the outskirts of the forest a herd of wild pigs is holding a council of war. They are unpredictable neighbors, easily provoked but considerate. Their scent is good, they smell of swampiness, sulfur, grass and obstinacy. Just now they are deep in discussion, uttering shrill grunts in their edgy language, butting one another, scraping the ground with their hooves.

Their restlessness gets the vixen going. She trots off so as to leave those tricky creatures behind quickly.

The Up Above, roaring, brings thunder. It doesn't like to see the vixen out and about. It is threatening her. Warning her.

AND HERR SCHRAMM, FORMER LIEUTENANT-Colonel in the National People's Army, then a forester, now a pensioner and also, because the pension doesn't go far enough, moonlighting for Von Blankenburg Agricultural Machinery, is watching the sports clips on the *Sport 1* channel. Martina (aged nineteen, Czech Republic) is playing billiards. Herr Schramm is a critical man. He has objections to the program, he doesn't think Martina plays billiards properly. She sends her shots all over the place. They never go into the pockets, and that bothers Herr Schramm. Martina dances round her cue, and that's not right: it's not right for her to dance, it's not right for her to sit on the table and wiggle the billiard balls with her bottom, it's not right for her to be playing by herself. Because if you are playing by yourself it should be with the clear intention of sinking the balls in the pockets. The opponent you best like to beat, so Herr Schramm firmly believes, is yourself.

Of course, after every shot Martina has to remove an item of clothing, nothing wrong with that. But she could have done it somewhere else. *Sport 1* shouldn't have made a billiard table available to her, it should have been somewhere Martina knows her way around. Herr Schramm believes that everyone is good at something, and he tries to guess what that something might be in Martina's case. Clues are thin on the ground: she has full breasts, short fingers, shiny fingernails. Herr Schramm believes in talent, and Herr Schramm likes talent. He likes to watch people exercising their talents: he's an upright military man with poor posture and an empty pack of nicotine chewing gum.

He doesn't like to watch Martina. Martina still has her knickers on; they are black with a number 8 in a white circle at the front. Herr Schramm thinks that is witty. But it's not about her knickers now, it's about the fact that Martina plays so badly, as if she didn't even know the rules. And rules are the first thing you teach someone who doesn't really belong in a place.

Herr Schramm is a man who avoids conversations with strangers, and even with acquaintances prefers to talk about anti-aircraft missiles, bats and the former ski jumper Jens Weissflog, the most talented ski jumper of all time.

He thinks Martina has good calves when she bends low over the table. But when she takes off her knickers, drapes them over her cue, misses the white at her next shot and has to laugh at that into the bargain, Herr Schramm has had enough.

"I ask you!" says Herr Schramm. He switches the TV set off.

In German households, on average, there are more germs on the remote control than on the lavatory seat. Herr Schramm thinks about that "on average." It's all relative. Lavatory seats are larger than remote controls.

In his own household, thinks Herr Schramm, there are more disappointments about himself, on average, than about the world. With a sigh, he gets off the sofa and in the same movement pulls up his underpants from round his ankles. The rest of his clothes are in the bathroom. He searches their pockets to see if he has enough change for a packet of cigarettes. He does.

Herr Schramm sits in his Golf for a little while first. A tall, upright man with poor posture, thinking: on average. Martina (aged nineteen, Czech Republic). Bats hang upside down because their legs are too weak. They can't take a run and then fly away, like a goose, for instance.

His pistol is in the glove compartment.

Much that Herr Schramm regrets today was done of his own accord. Pressure is what Herr Schramm was good at. Standing up to pressure and exerting it.

He drives away. Maybe to the cigarette vending machine, maybe to the abandoned anti-aircraft missile department at number 123 Wegnitz, where he was stationed for seventeen years. A few cigarette ends or a shot in the head, he hasn't made up his mind yet which.

Maybe Martina has a talent for fingernails. What would that be called?

In Wilfried Schramm's household there are more reasons against life, on average, than against smoking.

WE ARE GLAD. ANNA IS GOING TO BE BURNT. THE
sentence will be carried out at the Feast tomorrow evening.
The children are put to bed in the hay with the calves, but they
don't sleep, they peep through the boards at what they'd like to
be scared of in their sleep, and when there's no more boiling
and hissing and crying in the flames the baker connects up his
fiddle to his portable amplifier and then there's fiddling, then
there's dancing, predatory fish are grilled until they're cooked
and soft. Anna is going to be burnt, and on such a night many
couples find their way to each other, they dance among sparks
and stars and security precautions, making sure nothing that
doesn't gain by the flames catches fire.

Autumn is here now. Ravens peck the winter seed corn
out of the body of the fields. They come down to settle on
scarecrows, they preen their plumage.

There's still time to pass before the Feast. We have to get
through the night, and the final preparations will be made
in the morning. The village cooks, the village sprays window
cleaner on glass, the village decorates its lampposts. Our car-
penter, who is dead now, spent a long time making sure that
the bonfire would stand steady. An interior designer brought
in from Berlin has offered his services instead, but if we let
him get at it, so the village thought, there'll be nothing but
problems; it's not just a case of where to put your sofa for a

good view, we have to make sure we don't have another disaster like the one in 1599, when four houses caught fire, and in all the commotion two notorious robbers escaped being burnt to death, so now a scaffolding company from Templin does the job.

The village provides itself with seats. The seating plan is a ticklish subject. Who gets to sit at the beer table in front, near the bonfire? Who has earned the merit of being near the flames? Who defines what merit is this year?

The village cleans its display windows. The village polishes up the rims of wheels. The village takes a shower. The fishermen are after pike today, the bakery is generous with its jam fillings. Many households will prudently lay in a double dose of insulin.

Daughters make up their mothers' faces, mothers trickle eyedrops in the lower lids of tired fathers' eyes, fathers can't find their braces. The hairdresser would make a real killing if we had a hairdresser. Apparently one is supposed to be coming from Woldegk, but how is that to be managed? Will he go round the houses like the doctor on his Thursday visits, or put up his chair and mirror somewhere central? We don't know.

Frau Reiff has invited guests to her pottery on this Open Day: she serves coffee, honey sandwiches and a talk about making pottery. Her visitors get beer tankards made by the Japanese *raku* method fired in her kiln, or maybe have a go at firing a vase themselves. Later there will be a band from Stuttgart playing African music. The musicians have already arrived. They keep saying how wonderful the landscape is, as if that were the village's own doing.

Zieschke the baker will be auctioneer for the sale of *Works of Art and Curios* again. Last year he did it with his shirt worn loose over his trousers and using a beer bottle as the auctioneer's gavel. The proceeds go to our Homeland House. We can already guess some of the items to be sold:

- *Antique globe (including Prussia): reserve price 1 euro*
- *Self-adhesive silicon Secret + bra: reserve price 2 euros*
- *Laundry basket with surprise contents: reserve price 3 euros*
- *Local Prenzlau calendar for 1938: reserve price 6 euros*
- *People's Police uniform (with cap, worn): reserve price 15 euros*
- *Brand new oil painting by Frau Kranz (painted the night before the Feast): reserve price not known*

Non-villagers can also bid in the auction, and they laugh at some of the items on offer, most loudly of all when they are no laughing matter. Or that's how it sounds, when some of them think they are cleverer than the story; they don't credit us with irony.

Our Anna Feast. No one really knows what we're celebrating. It's not the anniversary of anything, nothing ends or began on exactly that day. St Anne has her own saint's day sometime in the summer, and the saints aren't saintly to us any more. Perhaps we're simply celebrating the existence of the village. Fürstenfelde. And the stories that we tell about it.

Time still has to pass. The village switches off its TV sets, the village plumps up its pillows, tonight hardly anyone in the village makes love. The village goes to bed early. Let us leave the dreaming villagers in peace, and spend time with those who lie awake:

With our lakes that never sleep anyway.

With animals on the prowl. Under cover of darkness, the vixen sets out on a memorable hunt.

With our bells, which will soon be ringing in the festive day. These days, who can boast of still having a bell-ringer, and an apprentice bell-ringer too?

Herr Schramm weighs up his pistol in his hand.

Frau Kranz is awake too. What a pity, when many old ladies are snoring! She is out and about, well equipped for the night: flashlight, rain cape, she has shouldered her easel and is pulling the trolley with her old leather case behind her. Going through the Woldegk Gate, she takes a good slug from her thermos flask, which has more than just tea in it. Frau Kranz is very well equipped.

And Anna, our Anna. Tomorrow is her last day. She lies in the dark, humming a song, the window is open, a simple tune, the cool night air passes over her brow. In this last year Anna has spent a lot of time alone at Geher's Farm, surrounded by her family's dilapidated past: her grandfather's tools, her mother's garden, neglected by Anna but popular with the wild pigs, in the garage there is the Škoda, in which the cat has had her umpteenth litter of tabby kittens. There is a fallow field run wild under Anna's window. And tonight, on such a night as this, there are memories of a house that was once full, and the question of what has ever been good for her in the eighteen years she has spent there. On Monday Lada will come to clear the house out, in spring the people from Berlin will take it over, and Anna, on her own, remarkably indifferent to others of her age, Anna with her school-leaving certificate and her love of ships, Anna who shoots her grandfather's airgun out of the bathroom window at the wild pigs in the garden, Anna up and about at night, even tonight—come here to us, Anna. Come along the headland of the field to the Kiecker Forest, to the lakes, going all the old ways one last time, that's the plan, we young people of this village, from the new buildings and the ruins, we are glad. Anna is not alone, Anna is humming a tune, a sweet, childlike melody, we are with her.

The night before the Feast is a strange time. Once it used to be called *The Time of Heroes.* It's a fact that we've had more victims to mourn than heroes to celebrate, but never mind, it does no harm to dwell on the positive side now and then.

Over there by the ovens? The little girl with the log in her arms? She is the youngest of the girls called heroines. A child of just five years old, in a much-mended smock and a shirt too big for her, with pieces of leather wrapped round her feet. Her brother beside her is fair and slender as a birch tree. Timidly but proudly he throws the log that the little girl hands him into the flames. Their mother is placing flax to dry in one of the ovens, she will bake bread for the Feast in the other. The village is celebrating because war has stopped stealing and devouring, driving everything out and killing it, because harvest has kept the promise of seed time. Things could get exuberant, the bigwig from town isn't here: Poppo von Blankenburg, coarse, loud-mouthed, observing the law as he sees fit.

The village says prayers daily for a *to some extent*, for an *at least*. For the continued existence of the fish. For our own continued existence. The little girl and her brother and the sieve-maker's two boys, there aren't any other children here now.

This is the year such-and-such. Frau Schwermuth would know the date for sure. She is our chronicler, our archivist, and wise in herbal lore as well, she can't sleep either. With a bowl of mini-carrots on her lap, she is watching *Buffy the Vampire Slayer*, series six, right the way through. The Feast and all the upheaval make considerable demands on her: Frau Schwermuth holds many threads in her hand.

The little girl chases her brother round the ovens. Anna, let's call her Anna. A little while ago the ovens were moved from the village to outside the walls. The fire had sent sparks flying too often, the sparks in their turn had rekindled fire, and like all newborn things the fire was hungry and wanted to feed, it swallowed up barns and stables, two whole farms—although the Riedershof fire, people say, had nothing to do with the ovens. It was to do with the Devil. The Rieder family were in league with him, and the Devil had simply been taking an installment of the bargain.

The children's mother sweeps the glowing embers out of the oven with a damp bundle of twigs and puts a loaf into it, carefully, as if putting a child to bed. She reminds the children to keep watch on both the bread and the flax, it wouldn't be the first time that someone helped himself to what didn't belong to him. "Come and get us if you see strangers arriving."

Let's leave the picture like that: the girl's brother is combing Anna's fair hair with his fingers. The little girl stands closer to the oven, holding out the palms of her hands to the stove flap. Their mother sets off along the path back to the village, humming a tune.

Anna, our Anna, has a similar tune on her lips. She shivers; the night is cool.

Come along, we'll take you with us. To your namesake, to other people, to animals. To the vixen, to Schramm. Into a hunger for life, into the weariness of life. To Frau Kranz, to Frau Schwermuth. To the smell of baking bread and the stink of war. To revenge and love. To the giants, the witches, the bravoes and the fools. We're sure you will make a reasonably good heroine.

We are sad, we are glad, let us pass our verdict, let us prepare.

HERR GÖLOW IS DONATING SIX PIGS FOR THE
Feast. One of the six will survive. First thing in the morning
the Children's Day organizers inspect the place, and then the
children get to pardon one of the pigs.

What for, and what does pardoning mean?

The spits for the remaining five are set up behind the
bonfire. The children will be allowed to turn the spits. That
kind of thing is fun too.

The Gölow property. Stock-breeding. Products for sale:
honey and pork.

When pigs are being slaughtered in summer, in the heat
that makes all sounds louder, you can hear their screams
kilometers away. Many of the tourists who come to bathe
in the lakes don't like it. A few of them don't know what the
noise is. They ask, and then they don't like the noise either,
and they also don't like having asked about it. So far as we're
concerned the dying pigs are no problem, dying pigs are part
of what little industry we have.

Olaf Gölow walks across the farmyard. Barbara and
the boys are asleep. Gölow lay down to sleep as well, but
his thoughts kept going round and round in circles: about
Barbara's forthcoming operation, about the Feast, about the
ferryman's death, about the Dutch who have been in touch
again asking how things are going.

Gölow got up, carefully, so as not to wake Barbara. Now he is in the farm buildings, in the air-conditioned sweetness of his pigs and their sleepy grunts. He lights a cigarette, breathes the smoke in away from the pigs, turns the ventilation regulator.

Gölow is that kind of man, honest to the bone, you'd say. There are certain moments: for instance once, on a rainy day, he saw something lying in the mud outside the shed. There are certain ways of bending down, maybe they set off a reflex action, that could be it, a reflex action making you think: here's someone helping himself, look at the way he bends down. There are moments like that, something lying in the mud, an object, and Gölow bends down—broad-shouldered, wearing dungarees, a gold earring in his left ear—and picks it up. He takes his time, in spite of the rain, takes his time looking at it and squinting slightly, looking absent-minded. What's lying here with my pigs, what is it? Is it a nugget of gold, is it a pen, yes, it's a pen, why is it here? We're glad to see a man like that, we think of him as kind to his children and fair-minded when he presses the dirty pen down on his hand, draws a loop on his hand with it as well, to see if it works, yes, it does, and Gölow puts it in his pocket. Later he asks everyone: Jürgen, Matze, silent Suzi, have any of you lost a pen?

Then again: the ferryman owed Gölow money. Not a lot of money. Not a lot for Gölow. Presumably a good deal for the ferryman. And Gölow goes and buys him a coffin. He specially asks for a *comfortable* coffin. He spends two evenings doing research into coffins on the Internet. Barbara gets impatient:

why comfortable, what difference does it make? Gölow says the ferryman had a bad back. Some of the movements you make when you're rowing, when you're pulling on ropes, never mind whether you've been doing it right or wrong for years, in the end you need a comfortable coffin.

Gölow had known the ferryman for ever. He was already an old man as far back as Gölow can remember. Recently he went out with him several times, taking the boys with him. At last they're at the age when you can tell them scurrilous stories and they don't start blubbing, and the ferryman could tell stories that would really unsettle them. Kids love to be unsettled.

Gölow grinds out his cigarette. He smokes a lot without enjoying it. He always has that little tin in the front pocket of his dungarees, the one with the Alaska logo on the lid. He walks past the pigsties. Making notes; Gölow is making notes. With the pen that he found in the mud. We trust him to pick the six best pigs. Obama always pardons a turkey before Thanksgiving.

Obama; Gölow isn't very keen on him. Talks a lot of hot air. Out of all those American presidents, somehow, Clinton was the only one he liked. They sent him a letter once: the Yugos, Barbara and Gölow himself. That was in '95. Gölow had a Bosnian and a Serb working for him, and he had no idea exactly what the difference was. Then he found out that they didn't really know either. They both hated the war. They argued only once about the question of guilt, because there's always a one-off argument about questions of guilt, but they settled the question peacefully and then decided to watch only the German news from then on, because on that channel everyone was to blame except the Germans—they couldn't afford to be guilty of anything for the next thousand years, and the two Yugos could both live with that.

The two of them had been pig farmers at home, and knew a lot about keeping pigs. At least, they'd said so when they first came along. Pretty soon Gölow realized that they hadn't the faintest idea of pig-farming, but they were happy with the pay, and at the time Gölow couldn't pay all that much. On the black market. Of course the black market or it would never have worked, on account of the visas. Tolerance was the name of the game, they were tolerated here.

It's years since Gölow thought of the two Yugos, but on such a night as this. . . Anyway, the letter to Clinton. All the horrors had just come to light, the mass graves, the camps. And then the Serb said: they'll have to bomb us Serbs. If they only ever make threats it'll never come to an end. Only not the civilians. No one likes to think of bombed civilians. The Bosnian had no objection to that idea. Well, and then Gölow said: let's write the President a letter. They both agreed at once, although it was meant as a joke. The Serb dictated it, the Bosnian's German was better, so he translated it into German, then Gölow tried to guess what it meant and Barbara wrote it out in English. This went on until late at night, and in the end they hugged and wept and posted the letter, addressed to the White House. As sender's address the Serb had given his own before he got out of the country, to lend emphasis to their request. Next day he thought that was probably a mistake, because if they see that it's a Serb writing, he said, that's the place that they'll bomb first.

Gölow doesn't think anyone ever read it. But soon there was bombing, and then that died down.

We hadn't been too happy about the Yugoslavians. So soon after the fall of the Wall. Lack of work, and anger, and he goes giving them jobs. These days, it shouldn't sound the way it does. The village was surprised. His own father, old Gölow, formerly a pig-breeder himself, privately and collectively, was surprised. They'd always taken Gölow for a man who thought locally. Maybe he thought *too* locally. Of himself. But anyway, now he's made it to where he is. Employs thirteen men. Now, for the most part, Gölow is doing well.

Gölow in his office. Air like old socks. He puts the note with the six numbers into silent Suzi's locker. The lad can get those pigs out when the kids arrive in the morning.

A poster of Alaska on the door. All blue, blue mountains, sky, water, polar bears. Gölow would like to go to Alaska. Money wouldn't be the problem these days, but where would he find the time? And Barbara might—perhaps a long journey like that might not be good for Barbara at the moment.

A farm in Alaska would be quite something. With modern air conditioning you could even live on the moon. Kayaking, salmon-fishing, and the snow-covered mountains reflected in everything that can reflect them. Blue. Blue seclusion, peace and quiet. Lovely, all of it. Sleigh dogs. But that's not what attracts Gölow. There's kayaking here, too. There are other reflections. Reeds, there are reflections of reeds, and brown seclusion and peace and quiet.

It's the gold. The days of the gold-diggers. The new finds only recently, in an old gold-rush village called Chicken. What the Yanks call old is a joke to people in our parts. Chicken died out, like the gold-diggers' hopes of wealth. Seven people live there now, it's all but a ghost village. And then a Japanese finds twenty ounces near it.

Gölow as a gold-digger in a hat, on the Klondike River. When he was a child, he read Jack London. Of course that comes of childhood. He'd never set up as a farmer there. The rents and cost of living are much higher than ours here. Those Dutch people have offered Gölow half a million. It's ages since he had any time for reading.

We don't mourn the dead animals.

We don't complain of missed chances. Ghost chances.

The doctors say that Barbara's chances are fifty-fifty.

Gölow has been pardoning a pig before the Feast ever since he took over the farm in '92. The chosen pig isn't slaughtered later, either, it dies a natural death. Although what does natural mean for a pig bred for slaughter? In fact it dies an unnatural and improbable death. Also, pardon sounds as if pigs were criminals. Whereas the opposite is true. An animal, as Olaf Gölow knows, is always innocent; the laws of Nature don't understand the idea of punishment. An amnesty, more like.

With her wig on, Barbara looks a bit like that woman Governor of Alaska. And they both have greasy skin. Gölow likes that—Barbara's skin shines. He can't understand why she tries to correct it, but he doesn't interfere. However, why is shiny hair thought beautiful but not shiny skin?

The pigs snore. Gölow would have liked to be the auctioneer himself tomorrow. But that lot on the Creative Committee wouldn't hear of it. Cliquish, that's what it is. The auction has been Zieschke's business for years. Not that he's particularly bad at it, but the jokes. . . charming, yes, charming, but salacious too. Women, politics. The sort of joke you can make in private, perhaps, but not in front of guests! The laughter then isn't kindly laughter, it's the laughter of superior people and Gölow doesn't like it. He doesn't care for that kind of humor.

And just because Zieschke was already the auctioneer before the fall of the Wall. That's no argument. Why does everything have to be traditional? Gölow gives work to thirteen people. Zieschke gives work to two. Gölow trains his employees, Zieschke collects old recipes for bread.

Gölow crosses the farmyard, hands in his pockets. It's a quiet night except for the distant rumbling of thunder. Gölow imagines nights in Alaska as soundless. Simply imagining that sometimes helps him get to sleep, but not tonight.

We look forward to Olaf Gölow's contribution to the auction. It always turns out to be something surprising. Last year he raised mini-pigs in secret. He gave his boys one each, but he also gave one to the auction. They were so cute, the bidders were beside themselves. Three hundred and sixty euros and applause, the mini-pig went to a hotelier from Feldberg. Our own bidder retired after 100 euros.

Gölow wants to suggest two weeks in Alaska to Barbara. He will organize it all. The flight, good accommodation, a jeep with four-wheel drive. A bit of driving around and sightseeing, eating salmon, feeding sleigh dogs, looking for gold.

Gölow isn't going to sell up. Not while Barbara is alive, and certainly not to those Dutch people.

He slips into bed under the covers. He hears Barbara breathing. Gölow's thoughts circle in a blue silence, circle in his sleep.

AND HERR SCHRAMM, FORMER LIEUTENANT-
Colonel in the National People's Army, then a forester, now a
pensioner and also, because the pension doesn't go far enough,
moonlighting on the side, rubs the coin over the place on the
cigarette machine that others have rubbed before him. He
sniffs his fingers. They smell of lukewarm money-rubbing.

Herr Schramm puts the coin in the slot at the top of the
machine, the coin comes out again at the bottom.

The machine, beige with big black buttons, stands outside
the Pension Alpschnitter. The building used to be the dairy.
It was sold at auction in the early 1990s. Herr Schramm
had thought of bidding for it. But foreign visitors? Not in
his line. He'd been able to offer hospitality now better, now
worse, depending on the guest. Homemade jam for breakfast
was probably on the worse side. The Alpschnitters are from
these parts. Industrious folk. Rudi smokes. Herr Schramm
could ring the bell. There are no lights on.

Herr Schramm puts the coin in the slot at the top of
the machine, the coin comes out again at the bottom. Herr
Schramm mops his brow. He's sweating. He feels hot in
the wind.

Leipzig, '82. In the sauna after the officers' training course.
Pear schnapps in the outlet of the sauna. A dozen officers relax-
ing on the steps of the sauna like pears in a display window.

None of them saying a word. They could have made harmless small talk. Someone could have said, "How long do we have to sit around here before we get good and sozzled?"

Herr Schramm fishes his small change out of his jacket pocket. He pushes the coins back and forth on the palm of his hand with his forefinger. Doing that makes him sad. He tries a different one-euro piece. It comes back out.

Herr Schramm leans his forehead against the cigarette machine.

The top man in the sauna was General Trunov. The only one sitting upright, showing everything, his Uzbek prick wreathed with strong hair. He was naked except for a sword belt with a cavalry saber stuck in it. The blade lay against his thigh. Maybe cool, maybe hot. His adjutant, a pale Jew, kept pouring iced water and schnapps on the hot stones, and whipping the hot air through the room with a towel.

Herr Schramm kicks the cigarette machine.

"Hell," says Herr Schramm.

General Trunov wanted war. Because war called for battles. Because battles called for soldiers, because soldiers called for men like him to lead them into battle. Trunov was a devout man and made no bones about it. And like every devout man he knew what was his and what wasn't his but ought to be. He intended to defend the former and get his hands on the latter.

General Trunov wanted war, but judged by the modes and methods of those days he was a pacifist. He loathed nuclear weapons and chemical warfare, he didn't even really like artillery, nor diplomacy either. Man against man in the open field, that's what Trunov wanted. He wanted to sink submarines with his own hands. Lieutenant-Colonel Schramm was sure he could do it, too.

Herr Schramm puts the coin in the slot at the top of the machine, the coin comes out again at the bottom.

He had been sitting next to Trunov in the sauna. If he turned his head he could smell Trunov's shoulder. General Trunov's shoulder smelled of the successful defense of a bridgehead against an enemy three times superior in strength. Schramm smelled the grass of the steppe and horses' flanks, smelled Afghanistan, smelled dances with Uzbek village beauties.

Herr Schramm puts the coin in the slot at the top of the machine, the coin comes out again at the bottom. Herr Schramm gets his pistol out of the car.

After ten minutes Captain Karrenbauer stood up and groped his way, dripping sweat, toward the exit. Karrenbauer, the fattest man in the sauna. Dark curls, though. Skin and fingernails infuriatingly well groomed. Karrenbauer always wheezed as he breathed. Trunov jumped up, had already positioned himself between the exit and the Captain, hand on the pommel of his saber. The Jew dunked the towel in the drain outlet and began working the General over with it vigorously.

"Where you go, soldier?" called Trunov. He wasn't looking at Karrenbauer. He was looking over Karrenbauer's massive head, through the sauna wall, out to the interrogation cell, the Albertina library and on, far beyond Leipzig, through mountains, over plains, and as he didn't spot an enemy to look daggers at anywhere he finally saw himself in his bitter native land, riding along the cotton fields, through the valley of the River Surxondaryo, on his stallion whose name was All My Prayers.

He wanted to go out, Karrenbauer nervously replied.

"So tell me, soldier, why I let you out?"

Karrenbauer stammered, "I-I c-can't take it any more. M-my heart. I'm n-not supposed to. . ."

"You joking? I not ask about your anatomy. And I not ask why you no stay. I ask why you worth I let you out. Convince me you important, soldier!"

Herr Schramm is an upright man with poor posture. Herr Schramm puts his pistol to the temples of the cigarette machine.

In the new Federal German states people are more inclined, on average, to repair defective items themselves, whereas the people of the old Federal German states think first of buying a new item, then of finding an expert to repair the old one, and very few of doing the job themselves.

It did everyone in the sauna good to sense the heat of Karrenbauer's fear. Because it was the fear of a man who was as bad and as good as themselves, and because it was his fear and not their own.

Karrenbauer fell to his knees.

Trunov drew his saber.

Herr Schramm dries the coin on his trousers. Stands still like that, one hand on his pistol, the other, holding the coin, close to the slot. He looks along the main road. From here he could reach the outer perimeter in fifteen minutes. Anti-aircraft rocket station Number 123 Wegnitz. Stationed there for seventeen years. In the "jam factory." In the "textile mill." In the "milking shed."

Once mushroom-gatherers came. Schramm had just finished doing his round, and there they were by the fence: mother, father, child, another child, dog, mushroom baskets, weatherproof clothing. They'd ignored the warning notices, had wandered through the woods in the no-go zone for hours without being stopped by the guards and patrols, and now they were gawping straight at the installation. You could see half the firing position from there. The anti-aircraft battery. The starting ramp. The technology. They were confused, who wouldn't be? You go looking for chestnut bolete mushrooms, you find anti-aircraft rockets.

Schramm goes over. Afternoon. Mmph. The fence between them. So what have you got to say for yourself?

Says the father, "Looks like we've got a teeny little bit lost."

Schramm picks fluff off his uniform.

Says the mother, "I suppose we can't go any farther."

Schramm raises his eyebrows.

Says the little girl, "Are you a soldier?"

"No, I'm a forester," says Schramm, giving the girl a fairly friendly tap on the finger she's putting through the fence.

Says sonny boy, pointing to the starting ramp, "Is that a rocket, Comrade Forester?"

What do you say now?

Says you, "I'll ask you to vacate the grounds of the Wegnitz jam factory."

Schramm never again met such a vital man as Trunov, a man so much at peace with himself and the world. The smell of his shoulder. Trunov didn't let the Captain go out. Tapped the wooden partition between the sauna and the interrogation cell with his saber in time with Karrenbauer's heartbeat. "Tell me what you worth, soldier!" He put the sword blade behind the captain's ear.

"I'm—I can't—please, Comrade General. . ." Karrenbauer was sweating well, sweating phenomenally, his best visit ever to a sauna, the Jew swiped him one with the towel. Over the last few days they had all been drinking schnapps before and during and after lectures, had drunk from the outlet before the sauna, but when Trunov put back the arm holding his saber no one was drunk any more. Schramm jumped up and looked into the General's left eye with its little broken veins.

"Leave the man alone," he said. "You can't learn anything from a man sliding about on his knees."

Herr Schramm puts the coin in the slot at the top of the machine. The machine gives a satisfied click. It digests the coin, the display shows the amount of credit and the information, "Tobacco sold only to age 18 and over."

Herr Schramm says, "That's right."

The display says, "Proof of age required. Insert EC card with chip."

"No," says Herr Schramm. "No."

Lieutenant-Colonel Schramm escorted the mushroom-gatherers to the outer perimeter. There were plenty of mushrooms beside the path, but now they didn't know whether it was all right to pick them. So Schramm made a start and put a porcini mushroom in the little girl's basket. Then it turned out not to be a porcini after all. The mother took it out of the basket again without a word.

Karrenbauer crawled out, and Trunov kissed Schramm on the mouth like a brother. He insisted on visiting Schramm's department, so Schramm took him to see the anti-aircraft rockets. The workforce came to the reception. The General pinched everyone who had a bare neck affectionately on that bare neck. There was a state flag, a national anthem and a one-pot lentil dish. The anti-aircraft station at 123 Wegnitz ate lentils and drank for five days. The General wasn't interested in the rockets and rocket technology. The General was interested in the soil. He had a hole dug one meter deep, smelled the earth, climbed happily into the hole and said they must plant a vegetable garden there. Peppers, he wanted them to grow peppers. Comrade Trunov was interested in cultivation. And culture, he wanted culture every evening. The Radar Combo II played for dancing. Trunov taught the musicians a song from Uzbekistan. The workforce danced awkwardly at first, and then more casually. The Adjutant played a solo on the double bass. The General sang. The General danced with Schramm, whispered into Schramm's ear that Trunov wasn't his real name, and the only fear he had in the world was fear of those who appointed themselves judges of names. He slept in his boots, and the Jew shaved him while he dreamt. The anti-aircraft station at 123 Wegnitz had forgotten what it was like to be sober. The fifth night was hot. The garrison members on active duty undressed. There was dancing on the starting ramps. The battery commander, the loading gunner and several artillerymen wanted to fire at something, never mind what, but Schramm stepped in, and Trunov punched them all and then told them how once he had climbed the great cold-blooded Tian Shan mountain range on his stallion All My Prayers without dismounting. He asked the rockets if he could use them for that kind of thing, and the rockets whimpered, "No." He asked the soldiers what their lives were worth, but no one could say. In the light of dawn General Trunov was seen getting on a tractor with two young peasant girls and driving it east, with the Jew in the trailer, a typewriter on his lap, on which he was hammering out everything Trunov had ever said, even in his dreams.

Herr Schramm takes three steps back and shoots the cigarette machine.

JOHANN SLAMS THE DOOR. COULDN'T STAND IT at home any longer, Ma watching her soap opera again, and when he said he must go out at midnight to ring the bells she carried on a bit.

It's cold now. He'd been chilling out in the sun beside the lake today, winter's coming. Maybe he ought to call for the master bell-ringer? He always turns up late. It'd be kind of nice to ring in the midnight bell for the Feast at midnight itself.

Johann puts on his headphones (The Streets), goes past the old smithy. It once belonged to his ancestors (so Ma tells him, and she's boss of the village history, so she should know). Right sort of sound for that, the song he's listening to now. About ancestors. The unlikely way some of them have survived over centuries—wicked! Started life going and now you're part of it yourself. Johann Schwermuth, sixteen, virgin (working on changing that status), trainee (in retail trade, another year then he'll earn the basic wage), fantasy role-player, church bells, hip-hop.

He stops outside the church, wonders whether to go right up there, take a look at the village. The few lights in the land-scape aren't so great, it's the darkness in between, the Kiecker Forest, the fields. What he likes best is seeing the promenade and the boathouse for the ferry light up for a while, then there's nothing for some time, and after that you get to see a few lights from Weissenhagen and Milbrandshagen again. The black bits in between are the lakes. Two holes in the world (threatening, yup, you bet).

That guy the ferryman: wicked! Done for, you might think. Big hairy terrorist-type beard, fingernails and all that. But he wasn't really done for, not like a few others around here. If he said anything, then either you understood something that hadn't been clear to you before, or you didn't even know what he was talking about. Lada says there was a guy like that used to sleep under the bridge in town. We don't have a bridge here. People liked the ferryman and at the same time they were scared of him. Specially the passengers on the ferry. He somehow didn't seem to belong here. It wasn't that he didn't belong in the village, Johann thought, he didn't belong in this time. The Middle Ages would have been a good time for him, all got up in leather armor, a sword, or magic, something like that.

Anyway.

Johann wonders what his own ancestors were like. It'll be the song making him think of it. What they talked about, what sort of clothes they wore when they came to church here in the such-and-such century or whenever. He gets an idea what they looked like from the role-playing.

Johann once read that folk liked to build churches on hills so as to look up at God. Johann likes looking down. Johann doesn't believe in anything. Ma reckons they're all atheists in the Vatican, otherwise how would they be allowed to get so rich?

And then the Great Fire in 1740. One of his ancestors survived that, a miller called Mertens. But otherwise almost everything burned down. The church bore the full brunt of it. How something made of stone can burn Johann's never really understood, but okay. It was soon rebuilt. The chronicle and the old church registers and books and stuff were all gone. A pity, really. Ma has typed out the chronicle for after 1740. You can see it in the Homeland House. (Great for role-playing if you want to work in something about witches or child-murderers or robbers or suchlike.)

The church was renovated in the 1990s. Since then it's been brick. Brick doesn't really look churchy. Not seriously. A brick fireplace, okay. A brick garage, okay. Brick buildings in Hamburg, okay (class outing there last year, still a virgin all the same). But an altar? Ma says the 1990s were a crime against architecture and music, all that stuff ought to be locked away now, except for Nirvana.

And thinking of Nirvana: there's a Grüneberg organ in the church. Johann knows that, because he had to learn about it for his bell-ringing exam. It's great. Not that he can really judge, but if a thing has the name of the person who made it, like Grüneberg who built the organ, then it's better than one without a name. A Ronaldo free kick is always on principle going to be better than a plain old free kick. Even if Ronaldo misses the goal.

Johann hears something crack, like wood, somewhere up by the church. Sounds almost like it comes from the tower. The bells are impatient. . .

Tomorrow's exam isn't entirely official, like the apprentice-ship isn't official, like the profession isn't official, and Johann doesn't get any pay and there certainly "won't be any future in it" (says Ma. That's why she was shouting just now). But that doesn't mean he (and the Master) don't take the exam seriously. Johann liked church bells even before he was born. When they rang, says Ma, he kicked inside her. So there's something in you, she says. In others it could be regional features, or hands (for instance with mass murderers).

He's already passed the theory part (history of the church and of bells, casting of bells, techniques of ringing bells). The practical part is ringing for prayers at twelve and at six. That's no problem, he does it on his own anyway, the Master hardly has the strength these days. And at twelve he must also ring his own little composition. That's not really a custom or suchlike, Master just likes it. He's ninety or more, and he likes to be called Master (though he'd never admit it).

Johann shivers. Cold is really good for you, he read on the Steel Muscles forum. Stimulates the circulation of the blood. He likes Internet forums on abstruse hobbies. Like role-play-ing. Easily the best is the GDR Bunkers forum. Hundreds of guys traveling around the area looking at bunkers and discussing their photos. Right nearby, on the old rocket base in Wegnitz, there's two of them. And one here in Fürstenfelde behind the old folks' home. Its wallpaper is the same as in the old folks' home. Wallpaper in the bunker!

Anyway.

The thunder's coming closer. Goosebumps. Hardly a light on anywhere. In the parsonage, where Hirtentäschel is busy not smoking pot. The roads are empty except for the lady who paints. Going down to the lake. Ma once said she's definitely all right, but something about her is definitely all wrong too.

Johann sets off to collect the bell-ringer. Since the beginning of human history every single one of his ancestors has survived, every single person on his mum and dad's side has successfully passed on life, and now it's autumn and when Johann next rings the bells he will firmly believe that they, his ancestors, can hear his bell-ringing.

WE HAVE THREE CHURCH BELLS. THE TWO SMALLER
ones are twins: Bonifatius and Bruno. Johann calls them "the
Bees." They're still young, two slender, playful lads, ringing
with a bright sound, in C sharp and E sharp. They were cast
in 1926 as replacements for two bronze bells that had been
called up to go to war ten years earlier.

LET HEATHENS ALL WITH FURIOUS IRE
ATTACK ME HERE WITH SWORD AND FLAME

says the inscription on the metal casing of Bonifatius,

I'LL RING THEM DOWN INTO HELLFIRE
AS I CAN WELL DO IN GOD'S NAME

says the wording on Bruno's casing.

Our main bell doesn't have a Christian name. The bell-ringer
just calls her "the Old Lady." A massive, almost black chunk of
metal, with a mighty clapper, year of casting unknown.

The twins sound good with each other. The Old Lady gets
on best with silence. You can tell that from looking at her, the
way she broods in the eternal twilight of the belfry, the lazy
way she begins to swing, the dry, lingering resonance of her
note. We guess that she could sound louder, deeper, somehow
more, but she doesn't have the right audience for that. Or a
good reason. Or the strength.

She has no ornamentation, she doesn't tell us the name of the man who cast her or the donor who gave her to us, as bells sometimes used to do. Only an inconspicuous inscription inside her rim tells us:

BE PATIENT IN TIME OF TROUBLE

The bell-ringer and Johann don't often persuade all three to ring together with a sound like cymbals. The bell-ringer rings the Old Lady, his apprentice rings Bonifatius. If the Old Lady happens to forget herself, all Fürstenfelde down below pricks up its ears. People can hear: there's something up.

Frau Schwermuth tells two stories about the Old Lady. In the first, the black bell is ringing in the middle of the night. This is sometime in the sixteenth century, and as the bell won't stop, more and more people assemble in the church. But there's no bell-ringer there, no one is pulling the bell ropes. The people are feeling afraid of this bell with a mind of its own, when a storm suddenly sweeps over the village, destroying houses, burying men, women and children under trees, injuring dozens. Those who made their way to the church, however, are unhurt.

The second story runs like this: in 1749 the black bell rings again in the middle of the night, and as it won't stop, more and more people assemble in the church, once again there's no one pulling the bell ropes, etc. Then the rural district shepherd tells those present the first story—about the black bell calling the people to take refuge from the storm in the house of God. All of a sudden screams are heard outside; the village is burning! Several people hurry out to rescue those who didn't leave home, most of them stay in the nave of the church, thinking themselves safe from the sea of flames. The fire burns everything down. Many, many people die, including those who stayed in the church. The black bell is left enthroned on the rubble, looking even darker than before.

We like the idea of a shepherd appointed by the rural district council.

We trust the old stories, and we believe in the value of copper.

WE'RE NOT WORRIED. ELECTRIC FLASHLIGHT, RAIN cape, gumboots and her umbrella: Frau Kranz is well equipped. In her little leather case, cracked, on its beam ends, a thousand and one expeditions old, are her watercolor paints, brushes, the old china saucer for mixing paints and some loo paper. For provisions: a cigar, a thermos flask of rum with some fennel tea in it, a sandwich. She carries her easel over her shoulders— Lada has built a little light into it specially for tonight. She has all you could need when you set out to paint on a night when it looks like rain.

"Does rum in fennel tea taste nice?" That's the journalist. He's been visiting Frau Kranz this week to write a column about her ninetieth birthday, for the weekend supplement, under the heading "We People of the Uckermark—the *Nordkurier* Introduces Us," and he's been firing off all sorts of other exciting questions, one H-bomb after another: homeland, hobbies, Hitler, hopes, Hartz IV social welfare benefits, in no specific order. "Yes, I'm afraid I really must have a photo, that's non-negotiable; right, not in front of a tree, no, it wouldn't be so good taken from behind; yes, I'd love some juice."

Frau Kranz is hanging out laundry in the garden. The journalist sniffs at a sheet.

"Let's begin at the beginning. Your homeland and how you left it."

"Good God."

"I'd be interested to know how you felt, young as you were then, going here and there all over Europe in the confusion of wartime."

Frau Kranz smokes a cigar, drinks rum tea with some fennel in it, has a little fit of coughing and takes the journalist round her house. Canvases all over the place. Fürstenfelde everywhere. Small pictures, large pictures, serious, gray, brown, empty, post-war, festive, collective, rebuilding, new buildings, in the past, back at a certain time, a few years ago, today, at every season of the year. Since 1945 Frau Kranz has been painting exclusively Fürstenfelde and its surroundings.

"*Paysage intime,*" the journalist remembers. He spent a year studying the history of art in Greifswald, before he abandoned the course for being "too theoretical." He sips his elderberry juice and makes a face. "Wow. Is it homemade?"

"It's elderberry juice."

"So you are originally a Danube Swabian."

"I know."

"Or to be precise, a Yugoslavian German."

"What are you getting at?"

"Can we talk a little about that?"

"About the accident of birth?"

"We could talk about the Banat area. I've seen photos of it. Flat, rural, like the Uckermark. Did the similarity of the landscape help you to get used to living here?"

"No." Frau Kranz makes very sweet elderberry juice.

"Right, and thinking back now do you sometimes feel homesick?"

Without a word, Frau Kranz leads the journalist into her bedroom, where a huge painting of nothing but rapeseed in flower shines all over one of the walls. The journalist, forgetting his question and also forgetting himself, delivers his verdict: "Like yellow rubber gloves for cleaning the loo, only prettier, of course."

At last something on which he and Frau Kranz can agree. She pours him more elderberry juice; he puts his hand over his glass just too late.

We're worried now. Frau Kranz walks down to the lake with a firm tread. We're not happy about the evening dress she is wearing under her cape tonight. It doesn't suit the night, it doesn't suit her work, although it suits Frau Kranz herself very well indeed.

Last time she wore that dress was in 1977 in Schwerin, when she was given a certificate for artistic services to the Schwerin area in the category of painting, sub-category "The land and its people." Frau Kranz went up on the platform, but she didn't make a speech, she sang a song in bad Croatian. It was called "*Polijma i traktorima*" (In praise of fields and tractors), and one thing soon became clear: Frau Kranz does not sing well, but she does sing at the top of her voice, and what with that and the loudspeakers being turned up, and what with her ignoring the planned program of events, and a few men made more and more aggressive by the crude Croatian language and wanting to escort Frau Kranz off the stage after seven or eight verses when it looked as if the song was going on for ever, but some other men didn't like their attitude and tried to protect Frau Kranz—well, what with all of that, there was a scuffle as background to the music that sounded like the roar of a rutting stag, and thinking it all over you can hardly imagine what a crazily wonderful evening that was for Frau Kranz in Schwerin in 1977. The certificate is hanging in her kitchen, rather yellow now from all the steam.

Why has Frau Kranz dressed up like that tonight, when she usually goes painting in the Fürstenfelde Football First Eleven tracksuit? On arriving at the ferry boathouse, she unloads her stuff and stands at the water's edge. The ash trees breathe in her perfume. They know the smell of her. Frau Kranz unscrews her thermos flask, raises it to the boathouse, drinks and closes her eyes.

IMBODEN WANTED TO TELL A STORY OF THE OLD days, but the garage interrupted him and only then took the piss a bit. Nothing can be taken seriously at the garage unless someone answers back. Things are serious enough at home and at work. So there was some teasing, which is only right, and Imboden let it all wash over him, which is only right too, so that a good feeling of peace could come back sometime, respectfully, which is right as well, when an old man who doesn't usually say much, sitting with a cold beer in his hand, a Sterni, like a jester holding his bauble, says something that begins like this:

"A brawl doesn't make any Feast better unless it saves the day. And it's not true that we had better Feasts in the old days. Times were even worse then. The worse the times, the more important the Feasts are. Hairstyles and shirts were clearly worse, but the dancing was much better."

By "the old days" Imboden, like everyone else, always means the entire time before the Wall came down. In theory, "the old days" could mean the darkest Middle Ages, but definitely not the time when Gerhard Schröder was Chancellor.

In concrete terms, Imboden meant an Anna Feast in the early 1960s. He meant a tombola, singing, a variety show, and then dancing in Blissau's restaurant—when did Blissau's actually close down? The early 1990s, when else? Was it where

Gitty now has the kiosk with the neon ad over it? Well, not really an ad, it just says "Open" when Gitty opens it. Gitty is Blissau's granddaughter. Gitty, Gitty, Gitty, what about her? Four kids, or is it six? Hardly any teeth left, otherwise she's fine, her character too—yes, and now you see how easily the garage goes off at a tangent when someone features in a story and they know everything about that person.

Imboden waited politely until everything there was to say about Blissau and Gitty had been said, and then went on with his story. A day before the Feast he had asked Fräulein Zieschke for a dance. He wanted to give her time. Because if she said yes, then—and Imboden was sure of it—she would never want to dance with anyone else again. Except maybe Ditzsche, but in other respects Ditzsche was no competition.

The garage drank to that. You should give yourself proper credit, no one in the garage objects to that.

"I remember the fabric of her dress perfectly. I'd know it among a hundred fabrics. It scratched like anything." Imboden closed his eyes. Danced a few bars of the music with Fräulein Zieschke. Hummed their song. Scratched his wrist. Imboden's hand on Fräulein Zieschke's waist at the Anna Feast, the flames blazing up, the ruins cleared away at last.

Imboden didn't call it the Anna Feast, but "the Feast of Comrade Anuschka." That was rather amusing today, but in the old days you had to be careful who you said a thing like that to. People were quick to take offense and easily responded to provocation. And you always wanted to give offense and provoke them, because you were always just the same: easily offended and provoked. For instance, over and beyond giving offense to those who had the say then, you'd always have liked to smash in their faces. But he was forgetting to stick to his subject, said Imboden to his now fully attentive audience. They didn't mind. The key phrases "provocation," "those who had the say" and "smash in their faces," arranged in that order, sounded very promising.

The dancing had just begun when several Blueshirts from Prenzlau turned up. They were recruiting for the FDJ, the Free German Youth organization of the GDR, and one of them was on the point of making a speech. You don't make speeches when people want to dance. The ferryman intervened. The bell-ringer was with him, and a couple of other guys. For now, there was going to be more dancing, minus speeches.

"The Blueshirts fancied dancing too. One of them wanted to borrow Fräulein Zieschke, and I swear I'd have let her dance with him, I mean anyone can dance with anyone else, only she didn't want to. Of course she didn't want to because—well, what did I say?" asked Imboden, and the garage loved rhetorical questions. He'd said nothing on the political question, but he wasn't taking this kind of provocation on behalf of himself and Fräulein Zieschke.

The garage drank to him again—that's a habit of theirs, drinking to someone who wasn't taking that kind of provocation.

Imboden, so he said, had only warned the lad for a start, but that didn't help, so what was bound to happen did happen. Imboden invited him to step outside so that fists could fly; there wasn't room for that on the dance floor. And fists did fly.

A few days later what was bound to happen did happen once again. Imboden was summoned to Blissau's, and this time his dancing partners were two comrades from the District Administration: someone had reported him. "They were saying I'd stirred up trouble, denigrating the FDJ and therefore the German Democratic Republic."

The garage drank a toast to that nice long foreign word *denigrating.*

"But they were wrong," said Imboden, and as he also said, he'd told them so. "No one was doing any denigrating." Yes, there'd been a spot of trouble, and he'd take the responsibility for that. But no ideas had been exchanged during the trouble, only blows. It was nothing to do with politics, it was just a normal instinct to defend a young lady from being bothered by a pushy lad carrying on.

However, the comrades from District Admin didn't want to know about that. They said there were witnesses, a group of observant young men from Prenzlau, who stated that Imboden had been the spokesman and had thrown the first punch.

"And then I found out why they were kicking up such a fuss. 'You're a troublemaker and liable to be the ringleader, Imboden. What else can we expect of someone whose father, that Nazi arsehole, is in jail in Waldheim Prison?'"

So at that, said Imboden, he'd jumped up and was about to show them what kind of trouble he could stir up, but then instead of letting his fists speak for him, he heard an apology coming out of his mouth.

The garage was slightly disappointed.

Imboden drained his glass. Imboden bowed his head.

"I'm ashamed. To this day I'm still ashamed of myself for not defending my father. He'd only been in the police, he'd never hurt a soul. But I did right to show restraint. Or the whole thing would have turned out badly for everyone. For those two Party guys there and then, but later for myself, and that would have been for ever. Do you want to know what held me back?"

The garage did want to know.

"If I'd fought those two, then with my family history I'd have had no option but to run for it if I didn't want to end up like my father. And I'd never have seen Fräulein Zieschke again, or not in a hurry anyway. And I didn't want that. I wanted to see my girl again, and I wanted to dance with her again, my hand on her waist, she'd surely have other dresses made of other fabrics.

"So that's how it was. We got married a year later. Yes, we had good times and bad times, but more of the good than the bad. Tomorrow, tomorrow we'd have been. . ." The old man broke off, and the garage didn't interrupt his silence. He looked down at his hands and the wedding ring deeply embedded in his finger.

"Gentlemen," said Imboden, getting to his feet, and no one had to support him. Guessing that the end of the story was coming, Ulli was quick to hand him a nice little Sterni fresh from the fridge. The other jesters added their baubles, one touching another like hands in a quick dance, crossing and coming apart again.

They drank to dancing.

To stirring up trouble.

To Sterni beer.

The garage drank. To one of the old boys, one of us, Burkhardt Imboden, known as Imboden.

THE VIXEN TAKES THE LONG WAY ROUND THROUGH the rough terrain of the fallow field. There's not much land left like this between the old forest and the human houses, land that human beings don't change with their powerful, noisy diggers and cutters. Nature lashes out on the fallow field, untamed. Grasses, tough bushes reach for the vixen, hundreds of aromas swirl in wild confusion in front of her nose, thorns bite into her pelt. She is happy to go that difficult way—no humans are ever there, and the thick undergrowth gives her cover all the way to the first buildings.

From the tallest of those buildings iron strikes against iron—again, again, again, echoing far over the land. The vixen knows that sound, the regular rhythm of it. She also knows the pigeons who sleep up here, and the little old man who sometimes feeds the pigeons and sometimes drives them away.

The iron chimes sound different. Louder, less regular than usual. The iron hesitates, drags. Gets into difficulty. The vixen crouches low to the ground, makes herself inconspicuous. Something that isn't rain or chiming iron is lurking in the clouds above the tower. Lurking like men lying in wait for game in the old forest.

The last iron chime hangs like a cloud over the land, echoing away, away, away. The wind brings nothing to the vixen. She's not used to smelling nothing. Smelling nothing means she must be on her guard. Everything could be hidden in nothing.

She thinks of the hunt, her concern for her cubs is aroused. She wants to stand up—and can't. Can't turn her head or even prick up her ears. The last iron chime lies heavy as iron itself in her paws. A raindrop hovers in front of her nose. Drops don't do that. Don't do nothing. It ought to go on falling, but something stops it.

The vixen knows she ought to run on, but something stops her.

Something stops the world.

—

The long iron chime dies away. All is so still around the vixen that she can taste the silence. When it is so still, the silence tastes of everything all at once. There! Firm and bright and enormously loud, the Up Above discharges an arching light so bright and large that the vixen feels the tingling of its power all the way to the tip of her brush. She whines, the raindrop speeds up, falls.

The vixen runs as fast as the field will let her. Only gradually does her instinct come back—she scents a human. In the building closest to the field, where there haven't been any chickens to be found for a long time, and hardly anything to eat at all, a human female is standing at a lighted opening. The vixen has known the female since it was a cub. She has learned that the human female is no danger. It has a sweetish smell of fear. Maybe it knows of something up above that is hidden from her down below?

The vixen turns and trots under wild, branching shoots toward the human lights.

Anna, at her window, doesn't know there is a fox in the field. Anna stands there composed at the window, as thunder tears the silence like hands tearing paper. In the lightning flash the field opened an eye, but Anna kept calm.

She closes the window. Rain beats wetly against the glass. Tights, windbreaker, cap, headlight, Anna is ready for her last run. She takes a deep breath, closes her eyes. The finely branching lightning is etched into her eyelids.

ON THIS DAY THE NIGHT WEARS THREE LIVERIES:
What Was, What Is, What Is Yet To Be.

THERE'S A STONE ON THE SPORTS FIELD, BETWEEN the clubhouse and the disused bowling alley. Nice and square, nice and practical, two meters high. It could have been made for commemorative plaques. It's what they call an erratic block. An erratic commemorative block. At the moment the erratic block isn't commemorating anyone. The holes from the last commemorative plaque on it are still left. There's a cigarette end stuck in one of them.

The sports field and the erratic block are both in Ernst-Thälmann-Strasse, and the last commemorative plaque on the erratic block in Ernst-Thälmann-Strasse was put up there for Ernst Thälmann.

Ulli's garage is on the other side of the sports field. He threw the men out earlier than usual this evening because of tomorrow. Lada helped him to clear up. Ulli stood him a drink. Now they are sitting on the piles of tires outside the garage smoking, drinking and looking at the clouds. Looking up and down Ernst-Thälmann-Strasse. Ulli shakes his head.

Lada's orange Shell overalls glow. Somehow or other they positively glow. Ulli is in a denim jacket, jeans and a white T-shirt, and he is nervous. Because of tomorrow.

"I'll open early tomorrow," he says.

"Mhm," says Lada.

"The men will fancy a little nip before the Feast gets going."

"Mhm," says Lada.

"I was thinking of asking Krone to let me have one or two platters of cold cuts from his stall. He has good salami-type sausage. A little something for people to nibble."

"They can nibble anywhere tomorrow. Open at eleven or whenever, they'll start nibbling." Lada spits.

"Stop that."

Lada looks at Ulli. Lada rubs the spit away with the sole of his shoe. Drinks to Ulli, who waves the gesture away. They drink.

The bells are ringing. The bells sound strange. Lada and Ulli would look at the church if the new buildings weren't in the way. There's a loud roll of thunder.

"Hey, it's the forest fairy." Ulli looks at the clouds. Lada looks at the clouds. Raindrops begin falling.

Ulli points his bottle at the sports field. "Know it, do you?"

"Know what?"

"The stone."

"The Hitler stone?"

"That was all done away with long ago."

"Yup, you can see it was. Something's left, all the same."

"Know why it lost its little mustache and its parting?"

Lada pushes out his lower lip. Stands up and strolls over to the erratic block. "Because it looked good? Here? It looks like a face anyway." He traces the outlines of a forehead and nose on the block. Tap-tap-tap over the stone.

It's very quiet after the thunder. Only now that Lada is playing percussion with a bottle of Stierbier on a boulder five hundred million years old do we notice how quiet. It's as if, all of a sudden, only one sound would be possible.

Ulli joins Lada. Puts his hand on the cheek of the erratic block.

"It's not that," he says. "Until '95, there was a plaque here in memory of Thälmann. Know him, eh?"

"Not personally, nope."

"Very funny."

"GDR, right?"

"Exactly. And do you know what this place was called until '45? The Adolf Hitler Sports Field. And there was a different name on the plaque, guess whose?"

"Makes sense." Lada spits.

"Right. And whoever painted it on knew that."

"Mhm." Lada nods.

"And before him, before Hitler, we had a plaque on this stone here," says Ulli, tapping the erratic block's forehead, "commemorating the Crown Prince."

"What Crown Prince?"

"What Crown Prince? How would I know? *The* Crown Prince. They were all called Wilhelm. The oak trees at the railway station were planted in his honor too. That was before the First World War."

"My father planted a birch tree in my honor when I was born, but later he couldn't remember where." Lada grins. Lada spits.

Ulli walks round the erratic block. "Back in those days we were well off. People came on purpose to settle here. Can you imagine that? Someone coming here on purpose to open something in this place?"

"That woman came to open the china shop. And there's the guy from Magdeburg wants to open a shop selling old books."

Ulli has stopped listening. "And mind you, there's more. Hans Steffen, know about him? Don't bother to tell me. . . Steffen, he came from round here. He was a geographer. Prevented some war or other, I think it was between Chile and Argentina, because he found out the border and told them, look, this is the border between you, stop quarreling. Think of that! A guy from here! A geographer! Went on real expeditions of discovery in the jungle. He's so famous in Chile, they gave him a Chilean name of his own: Juan Steffen!"

"Juan," says Lada. "Cool!"

"Yup. Suppose you do so much for some country, let's say France, that they call you Roe-Bare Zieschke!" he said, pronouncing Lada's real first name of Robert as if it were French.

"No, La-Da," Lada puts him right. And a moment later, after thinking it over, he adds, "I don't want to do anything for France."

Ulli nods.

"But this guy you were talking about did?"

"Nope, but I wouldn't have minded if he had."

"Mhm." Lada leans against the left-hand side of the erratic block, Ulli leans against its right-hand side. They look at the clouds, they look up and down Thälmann-Strasse, they see a fox, bloody foxes.

The vixen picks up the malty aroma of the two human males, keeps her distance, makes for the water.

"Was it you and your lot did that about Hitler?" asks Ulli.

Lada shakes his head and fishes the cigarette end out of the hole in the erratic block.

"Who was it?"

"No one." Lada spits.

"Yeah, well. . ." Ulli raises his beer bottle enquiringly. "Another?"

"No, I'm okay. Got to get up early tomorrow."

"Since when was that a problem?"

Lada looks the erratic block in the eye. "Suzi and me are clearing out Eddie's place tonight," he says slowly, deep in thought.

"Our Eddie? Wow, oh wow."

Lada is thinking. When Lada thinks, he blinks a lot.

"If you're through by nine," says Ulli, "come to Netto with us."

"Netto is shit. Go to Kaiser's. For the Feast, get it? I have a kind of a feeling." Now Lada is grinning as if he'd been cooking something up. He puts his hand on the place on the stone where the commemorative plaque must have been. "All at once I kind of have a good feeling. And that about cold cuts for the men, yes, do that. I think tomorrow's going to be good."

Lada spits by way of saying goodbye, waves and wanders down Thälmann-Strasse in the rain as it gets heavier. Ulli and the erratic block watch him go.

There's a stone on the sports field between the clubhouse and the bowling alley. We put our names there and pinned our hopes to it. Nothing came of that.

The commemorative erratic block doesn't commemorate anyone any more. But it's still there.

IN THE YEAR OF OUR LORD 1587 IT CAME TO PASS that the Miller's Sow brought forth a Young Pig here, beside the Pillory on the banks of the Deep Lake, and that was a Sign and a Portent, it being in all other points of Form and Feature like a Pig, but having the Head of a Man.

The people came down to the Lake to see this Curiosity and take Counsel concerning what were best to be done. The young Pig lay there for all to see, and even the Sow had join'd the Men and Women, as if she herself did not believe what had befallen her.

So the People examined that monstrous Pig at close Quarters, some even kneeling down to inspect it gravely Eye to Eye. The Conduct of others was such that it might seem as if they knew the little Monster's Face. Perchance it was the way the Pig turn'd up the Corners of its Mouth, as if it were Smiling impudently, or perchance it was the Birthmark that it bore, or the Voice in which it squealed like a Starving Babe for its Mother, but it caus'd the Men to talk Noisily and Wrathfully. Mayhap all would have been well, had not Semmel the Blacksmith foolishly cried out: Good folk, my own Reasoning can make Naught of it, and therefore I make so bold as to ask, does not that Monster remind you of. . .? Whereupon the first Blow was struck, falling on Semmel his own Mouth, and there was much pushing and tugging and a Quantity of Profane Utterances, and old Wennecke landed Head over Heels in the Lake, and what with all this Hurly-burly the Pig was near forgot.

Then up came Miller Mertens in the company of Count Poppo von Blankenburg, Lord over our Town. The Presence of the Nobleman and the Owner of the Sow brought the Men to see Reason again, so that they Left off Brawling. They adjusted their Weskits and took off their Caps, in so far as the said Caps did not already lie upon the Ground. All was still but that the Piglet snorted, like as it were an old Dotard dying of the Pleurisy.

The Men moved closer together to conceal the Monster, or so it seemed. The Noble Lord parted the air with his Hands to right and to left—whereupon the Men left a Path free through their Midst for him.

What followed was not to be forgot, albeit those Present denied it vehemently at a later date, as if there were a Crime or a Sin to be recollected. The noble Count and the Miller looked the Pig fearfully in the Eye, and the Pig looked cheerfully back at them. They cleared their Throats as a man might clear his Throat when something displeases him mightily, and those close to the Pig thought that it also clear'd its Throat.

The Miller and Count von Blankenburg turned White as Whey in the Face, and said not a word.

Then a young Man stepped forward, 'twas the tailor's Journeyman, Anton Kobler of Jakobshagen, and he said:

Gentlefolk and good People, God be my Witness that I do not know that Sow!

The Men looked at Kobler, greatly confus'd, but then in Anger, so that he also cried: Other Folk besides me go in and out of Master Mertens his Mill!

Then a Laborer by the name of Droschler spoke up. Anton, said he, I hope your Idle Talk is not meant to anger me, or God help you! There is no Call for Insinuation, I tell you freely, aye, to be sure I know the Sow, but not in the sinful Manner that you mean, there I have no Knowledge of her at all, albeit the Pig's crooked Nose could not be more Familiar to me, resembling as it does mine own. However, I could never commit so wickedly godless a Sin! I tell you, this is the Devil's Work, so it is—aye, the Devil's Work, I say!

There were those who agreed with Droschler's words, and folk made haste to say: Aye, 'tis Magick and Sorcery!

Old Wennecke was not heard amidst the Tumult. He was Surpriz'd to hear Droschler speak of the Piglet's crooked Nose, since he saw that Nose as Flat and much like his own, Wennecke's, Nose. But the Townsmen heard only that which they wish'd to hear, and said only what show'd them to be in the Right of it, and this was Devilry. So now each spoke up for his Neighbor as they seldom did, for Man often strives only for his own Advantage, and to show his Fellow Men in a bad Light. Great Wrath was stirr'd up against the Pig, that same Pig meanwhile squealing pitifully, but none could say whether 'twere with the voice of a Babe or of a Pure-born Pig.

At last Miller Mertens did seize the Piglet around its neck with both his Hands, and he rais'd the Piglet over his Head and he threw that Piglet high into the Air, to fall into the Lake, where it immediately sank, never to be seen again, or so the People thought. The Men rejoic'd, and the Count laid his Hand on the Miller's Shoulder, and then it so chanc'd that the Pig came to the Surface again and began swimming to the Bank, grunting right merrily.

It was old Wennecke who threw the first Stone.

That same evening the Sow was first blessed and then eaten.

And it was in the little town of Fürstenfelde, in the year of Our Lord 1587, that here by the Pillory, on the banks of the Deep Lake, the Miller's Sow gave Birth to a Pig of monstrous Kind, for in all other respects it was made like a true Pig, but it had a human Head, and a Face like mine, and a Face like thine, and a face like the face of Everyman.

HE DOESN'T WANT TO DO IT TONIGHT; THE BELL-ringer doesn't want to ring the bells any more. He should have been in the church by now, instead he stays lying in his bell-ringing uniform and his bell-ringing boots and his bell-ringing gloves, with his bell-ringing top hat lying beside him. He doesn't want to ring the bells, never wants to smell the church again. The church smells like Great-Aunt Elsbeth's wig, of pomade and dust, and Great-Aunt Elsbeth puts her wig over the little bell-ringer's head, his whole face disappears under it, pomade, dust *and* sweat, and he's supposed to turn round in a circle saying a prayer, his great-aunt hides and he looks for her, what a brutal game, you can only lose, you could lose consciousness too, that must be nearly ninety years ago, his great-aunt choked to death in '44, think of choking to death on your food when there was almost nothing to eat.

The bell-ringer is cold. If he'd listened to Rosa he'd have retired long ago, he'd be a pensioner watching the box in his slippers all day long, and now his knees hurt even when he's lying down. Twenty steps three times a day, every day since '43. He's had enough of it. Johann will have to ring the bells alone, yes, Rosa, you do know him, Johann Schwermuth, son of Herrmann and Johanna of the Homeland House, yes, my apprentice, surprised, aren't you?

Seventy years, and how many days has he missed? Three! No bells ringing for prayers in Fürstenfelde on only three days! Not counting holidays and days when the bells were being maintained.

Once in April '45. At first he ran away like the others, but you easily died on the road, so he and his family came back and he went straight to his bells. The Russians let him ring them.

Again at the end of the 1970s, because of Schramm. Schramm came by, Comrade Lieutenant-Colonel, asked whether the bell-ringer wouldn't like to give it up, that noise reminded people of other times. But those times were over, said Schramm, we weren't living in the Middle Ages any more, thank God, and in these new times the church was needed only as a place for events to be held, was wanted for deeds and not bells. Gustav, watch your step. I'm asking you nicely. Others will order you.

The bell-ringer stayed at home that day and the bells didn't ring, and after a while Rosa said: there are hundreds of reasons not to ring bells but politics isn't one of them, so he went on ringing the bells. Schramm apologized to him last summer, thirty years late, but never mind that.

The third time was when Jakob came into the world, and then he and Rosa were in Prenzlau. He made up for it with a jubilant peal the next day.

When the ferryman was buried recently, he wanted to ring his old friend of so many years into the last darkness with the chiming bells, but his knees failed him. Later, he went to the ferry boathouse and struck the ferryman's bell. The lake was calm. He sat in a small boat. The landing stage was empty, the little boathouse deserted, no one had heard the sound of the bell. That's the real meaning of Nothing, Rosa. When something exists and works, but is no use to anyone. Objects, implements, a whole village. The bells. They are still there, that's all.

Once upon a time, ah, once upon a time bell-ringers marked the beginning and end of important events, warned the people of dangers, of enemies, of the elements. Many bell-ringers were struck by lightning while doing their duty. By night, in a world not over-full of light as it is now, the bells were a lighthouse of sound for all wandering in the darkness. Here, where we chime, living hearts beat. Today? Today bells are the acoustic reminder that the church still stands. A wake-up call that no one has asked for.

The best part was going home to Rosa after ringing the bells for morning prayers, and Rosa would wake up and hold him close. Her hair, still soft from sleep. She would whisper his name, getting the emphasis wrong all those years, beautifully wrong.

The mechanized system will have to take over if Johann doesn't want to ring the bells. Johann is always punctual, what a hypocrite! An atheist. Johann will want to ring the bells. He knows what to do, and he can do it on his own. Johann's hands are not soft and delicate any more.

The bells are ringing.

The bell-ringer opens his eyes. He is lying outside the front door of his house, with his bell-ringer's top hat on the gravel, his head on the gravel, blood on the gravel, the crunchy sound of footsteps on the gravel.

"Rosa?" He smiles. Rosa says something, it isn't his name with the emphasis wrong, the bells lose their rhythm and the sound dies away. Johann, my boy, and you've practiced this so often. Now, quick chimes as the clapper strikes the bell, rhythmically, the steps on the gravel come closer, the first drops of rain fall, Rosa bending over him—"Master?"—Johann crouches down, takes the bell-ringer's arm, tries to help him up. "You're bleeding, Master!"

"Never mind. It's all right." Slowly, the bell-ringer sits up.

The last chime of the bell and its long echo.

"Johann, what's going on?"

We ourselves are confused, too. If the bell-ringer is here, and Johann is with him—then who is ringing our bells?

Gustav drags himself up the steps, unlocks the door, staggers. Johann supports him, helps him over to the sofa. The bell-ringer's head drops back. Abrasions on the palms of his hands, a deeper cut on his temple.

"Johann?"

"Yes, Master."

"My times are in thy hand."

"Master?"

"That was the tune. Well rung, almost perfect. My times are in thy hand." The bell-ringer grimaces. The hair above his temple is sticky with blood. He closes his eyes. Johann cleans his injuries and bandages them. He learned all that from role-playing, who says it's just a waste of time?

"That's good. Thank you, Johann. Please will you—will you go and see to the bells?"

It's raining harder now. The bell-ringer's top hat is still lying on the gravel. Johann picks it up, turns it in his hands. Puts it on. Hurries out into the roads by night.

WE ARE WORRIED. NO ONE KNOWS THE BIBLE AS well as church bells. Psalm 31:15. *My times are in thy hand: deliver me from the hand of mine enemies, and from them that persecute me.*

IN THE YEAR OF OUR LORD 1588, IN THE MERRY month of May, two fine Horses were Spirited Away from Ulrich Ramelow, Inn-Keeper in this Place, and two Starveling Nags left in their Stead. His Groom gave Word to the Inn-Keeper, as had been given to the Groom himself by two Men, one tall as a Tower and t'other round as a Barrel, that since he, mine Host of the Inn, kept good Beer aside for himself but Water'd what he serv'd his Guests, so that it tasted thinner even than Small Beer, the Horses he kept should be such Sorry Nags as those the two Fellows left for him.

ANNA STANDS BESIDE THE FENCE, STRETCHING. The wood feels soapy, it is rotting and splintered. Slats are breaking away from the fence, coming loose, missing. In the beam of her headlight the green of rot shows through the brittle veining of the wood. Anna has never seen the fence in anything but this ramshackle state, nor the field on the other side of it as anything but running wild. The undergrowth rustles in the wind, the branches of wild rose bushes reach out to her. Rain falls slanting down. Anna can smell cadaverine; the field has made a kill again, it gives and it takes away.

Anna has grown up with that field. It was waiting outside the window while she was studying, it watched her playing in the yard, it was never a playground itself. Right next to the garden. On her way to school. Never beautiful. Hard and dirty, even in spite of dew and hoar frost. In the evening it disappears abruptly into night, it won't linger in twilight. Ordinary stinging nettles. Debilitated greenery. No one calls it "mine." Well, Anna does now and then. Untamed, unused, uncleared of vermin. The next world beside this world, beside Geher's Farm that will be inhabited again some day. After Anna. After Anna, her mother and her grandfather. Briefly, there was a father too. Before that, during the war, Polish forced laborers. People called it the Polish farm, the Poles leaned on the fence, quietly reciting poetry to each other, and before that two or three more generations of the Geher family, all farmers except for one innkeeper, and the field was always there. It has listened to them all, has taken an interest in them all as it takes an interest in Anna now: does the field think she looks sexy in those tights? With her leg on the fence, Anna is stretching the back of her thigh.

The seasons are hesitant; if snow didn't lie where it falls now and then, you would think it was always cold spring weather in the fallow field. All the flowers are colorless, you don't notice them. No bumble bee fancies a flower like that. Bramble shoots like hair, the blackberries too black, too dry. Holes in the ground all over the place, with nothing and everything living in them. Stones like scars, grasses like swords. And anything that doesn't have thorns and can't defend itself won't live to see the end of the day.

A solitary oak tree stands in the middle of the field, roughly speaking. Not necessarily the prototype of solitary oak trees standing, roughly speaking, in the middle of fields. In spite of its situation and plenty of light it is pale, its leaves are sparse, its dry trunk stands at a crooked angle, stuck between the field's teeth.

Anna's lower jaw quivers as she jumps up and down on the spot a few times. She reaches cautiously over the fence, tries to break off a sprig of wild rose. The wild rose defends itself vigorously. Anna tugs at it, pulls. The field fights back. Only in mankind does Nature open its eyes and look at itself. The field is mankind in thorns' clothing, you can't believe a word it says.

Anna starts her timer and begins running.

Anna has known the field a long time. We've known it longer.

. . . there was so early and persistent a Frost in Fürstenfelde that all Nature froze, and the Harvest fail'd, and the People were sore anhungered, likewise was there a strange Phenomenon, in that one Day in the Depths of Winter, Apples were seen to lie in great Number under the Oak Tree. . .

Suppose the oak tree were a sight worth seeing? Suppose tourists came to gawp? A bus full of little black-haired men in little beige jackets. They get into position in front of the fence. Someone takes a photo. He crouches down so that the others will look taller. He makes a speech. Anna doesn't understand a word of it. Anna knows he is telling nothing but the truth.

No tourists come. Young men come on the way back from White's in Woldegk, early in the morning they leave a drunk to sleep it off, comatose under the oak tree, while they drive on, it's kind of a tradition of ours.

Anna is breathing with difficulty. She slows down.

The field has killed. It wants to show Anna what.

Anna doesn't want to know.

EVIDENCE OF THE FINDING OF TWO UNUSUAL SETS
of antlers at localities near Fürstenfelde in the Uckermark, first
mentioned in letters from Count Poppo von Blankenburg to Herr
Bruno Bredenkamp on 17th and 19th March 1849.

The skull and horns of the first set of antlers were found in the sand at the bottom of the Great Lake. Dissatisfied with the catch brought in by his fishermen, the Count had been about to lend a hand himself, to show those idle fellows how to do it. His net was caught in the tines of the antlers, whereupon he pulled hard and, not without difficulty, brought the antlers up on land in all their considerable glory. On investigating the antlers, the noble Count scratched himself on a sharp edge of the right-hand horn, and the scratch bled, staining Herr von Blankenburg's linen shirt, not a little to his annoyance.

The Count could not explain the find to himself. Back at his hunting lodge, he wrote to his friend, saying: antlers of that kind are not native to this place! He knew that, he added, as a huntsman himself. He therefore thought, he wrote, that this set of antlers must be a very ancient specimen, thousands of years old, dating from the time of the dense forests and the Great Moor, when bears, crocodiles and God only knows what other creatures still roamed the Mark of Brandenburg. He was now wondering, he added, whether those antlers might not make him a few thalers; they were strangely well preserved.

He would happily keep them for himself, but Lisbeth did not like to have dead eyes staring at her.

In his second letter, Herr von Blankenburg describes, with considerable excitement, as his handwriting and choice of words bear witness, the second extraordinary find. He was employing several despondent and useless day laborers to grub up the vegetation in the fallow field run wild on Geher's Farm, when one of them came upon a remarkably large bone in the ground. That was no bone, the Count realized, but another piece of horn lying there pale in the earth, like something from another world. The laborers, superstitious riff-raff that they were, refused to touch the horn. So the Count undertook the work of salvaging it himself, and a good deal of trouble it gave him, since the earlier injury to his hand had swollen and was very painful. With much difficulty he brought to the light of day the second set of antlers, which was even larger and finer than the first. He wrote to his friend that he would not have liked to encounter a living stag crowned with such antlers had he been unprepared for it.

Four days after making this second find, Poppo von Blankenburg died of the consequences of gangrene in the ball of his hand. His widow had the antlers, which she described as horns of the Devil, removed from the house immediately, and Herr Bruno Bredenkamp accepted the charge of them in Dresden on 2 May 1849, and later generously bequeathed them to us.

FRAU KRANZ HAS FOUND THE RIGHT COLOR FOR everything that grows, stands and dies here. Classics are the church, the old town wall, the ferry boathouse and the lakes. Painted from every imaginable viewpoint. And there are gradations of what Fontane described as the "waste of green" in the Brandenburg Mark, for Nature as a whole is green: meadows, gardens, cultivated fields growing everything from poppies to sugar beet, all sorted by shades of color. Last of all the Kiecker, the ancient forest.

Everyone in the village who is old enough to know names at all knows the name of Frau Kranz. She's already painted so many of them and so much of them. People and buildings in Fürstenfelde, natural scenery near Fürstenfelde, human beings and houses and machinery in Fürstenfelde, in Nature and in time. And she portrays the passing of time: East German industry and today's industrial ruins in Brandenburg. East German agriculture and today's Brandenburg windmills. Unchanging: East German avenues with an East German road surface. Cobblestones and paving stones that make every picture look as if it dates from the nineteenth century.

Frau Kranz has opened more and more doors for the journalist, doors with more and more canvases behind them. On the second floor—or was it the seventh?—a room full of faces. The journalist stands in the doorway and stays put; eyes examine him affectionately, enquiringly, sadly; he sees wrinkles, lips, temples, throats; shirt collars, scars. The only possible question to ask is, "Who?" The journalist opens a window.

"Have you," he asks, "painted me too?" He really doesn't seem to be sure.

"Come along, come along," says Frau Kranz.

None of these portraits are of people sitting for their portrait. They are all busy doing something. Working in the fields, working at handicrafts, working on the black market. Bathing, ironing, visiting Grandpa in the old folks' home.

The one and only neo-Nazi painted by Frau Kranz is asleep. That's the trick of it. In spite of his bald patch, an outsider wouldn't immediately assume that this was a Nazi. But he is. You can read it on the back: *Neo-Nazi Asleep* is the title of the picture. The people of Fürstenfelde would know it was a neo-Nazi asleep anyway, because it's a picture of Rico. We have one and a half Nazis here: Rico and his girlfriend Luise. Luise is a half-Nazi because she goes along with all that shit only for love of Rico.

"I never stopped to think what it looks like when neo-Nazis fall asleep," says the journalist, stroking the air above Rico's cheek.

Frau Kranz's brush has painted entire generations. Including Rico's grandfather, who wasn't a Nazi at all. She has painted people from outside the village. Animals. They'd all have been forgotten sometime, but you can't forget a picture like that. Almost seventy years of a village, a chronicle in oils, watercolors and charcoal. *Savings Bank at Sunset* is the latest title listed.

Of course, in spite of the pictures, many of their subjects will soon be forgotten, but it's the principle that counts.

Even we don't know the full extent of Frau Kranz's work. We know her first picture. Its title is *April, perhaps May.* It shows six young women holding hands on the bank of the Deep Lake. They are standing in a row roughly where Frau Kranz has just put up her easel now and is clearing her throat, as if to ask the lake a question. The six women are looking at the water. Their profiles, chins, cheekbones, skin: clear and youthful.

They could be dancing.

The observer is looking at the ferry boathouse. You can see the landing stage on the left-hand side of the picture; on the right, reeds frame the scene. Some houses are left still standing by the wall, some are not. Some still have a roof, some don't. Their facades are sooty, as if night hadn't been able to take her black dress off.

They could be playing a game.

Morning mist takes the breath of the colors away. The height of the sky, the depth of the lake. It is as if the young women were standing in front of faded wallpaper with a lakeside motif. Frau Kranz gave them clear touches of color: a red scarf here, a blue blouse there, sunny yellow hair.

They could all be friends.

Our memory of that morning is hidden in mist as well, although we have nothing to hide.

"A Madonna?" The journalist points to a drawing showing the front of the bakery. "The windows as her eyes. And look, the door—her blissfully smiling mouth. The bread in the basket as Baby Jesus."

Perhaps it's something to do with the elderberry juice.

Frau Kranz takes his elbow and leads him away from the picture.

We can almost understand him. Like us, he is wondering what Frau Kranz's pictures—how would we put it today? Wondering what they mean? They are sufficient unto themselves as they depict the world. Sometimes the choice of colors is freer, sometimes the proportions are unusual, but that's more to do with the fact that Frau Kranz doesn't bother so much with proportions.

It is hard for us to believe that a woman who knows so much, and there is also much she doesn't know, a woman who has looked four political systems in the eye, and heard their promises, and looked those who made the promises in the eye, as well as those who believed the promises and those who broke them, a woman who had to begin again so often and watch the dreams slumbering in her new beginning turn to nightmares, a woman who has known misery and change and change that brings misery, exile, collectivization, redistribution, bankruptcy, possession, dispossession, the collective, collective stupidity, unjustified redistribution, justified extravagance, the stupidity of individuals, of the group, of many, all, malice, hatred, envy, passivity, ambition, delusion—our lousy, lovely, hypocritical, live-saving, reinvented Europe—it is hard to believe that a woman like that, and with what might be called a fairly well-marked artistic talent, is happy merely painting a savings bank at sunset.

We are upset. It's not for us to make demands.

More people die than are born.

Who will paint us when Frau Kranz isn't painting any longer? Who will paint our tools, and our hands holding them? Who will paint the cooking spoons that we carve?

Who will paint the houses cleared by Lada?

Who will paint the new inhabitants? For instance, sensitive Magdalene von Blankenburg, the agricultural machinery mogul's daughter, whose father renovated the little Baroque hunting lodge by the Deep Lake where she spends her summer holidays learning Russian, because that's considered the language of the future in Brandenburg, but also because she likes Isaak Babel and the soft sound of Russian songs.

Who will paint silent Suzi trying to concentrate on his angling, while Magdalene whispers Russian vocabulary to the sun?

Who will paint Anna's last run through our night?

ANNA HAS LEFT THE FIELD BEHIND, SHE IS RUNning along the edge of the clay-pit. The beam of her headlight briefly brings the black water in the clay-pit to life where it lay as if it were viscous, unmoved by rain and wind, under dead leaves and waterweeds.

Anna runs past the old brick kiln. Every broken windowpane has its own geometrical pattern. The brick kiln stopped working early in the 1990s. Anna's uncle lost his job, and didn't become an alcoholic. Someone from Dortmund or Darmstadt bought the building and the plot of land for peanuts. Nothing's been done to it since then. Maybe that was the plan. The plot is a large one, building land with a view of the lake if you chopped down the birch and ash trees.

Sometimes the mice take over the brick kiln and pilot it on jet flights all over the Federal Republic of Germany, visiting other mice in buildings standing empty; they like historic listed buildings best, and meet in abandoned streets, where they stage illegal races against unused business premises and written-off apartment blocks, having no end of fun.

Anna's breath is coming with difficulty again. It's raining harder now, she needs asphalt underfoot, she doesn't feel well here. She turns onto the former railway embankment, runs past the ruined station and on in the direction of the new buildings. A bat drops from the top of the water tower, empty of water now, and flies low over her head.

WE HAVE A PROBLEM WITH MICE. THEY SPREAD IN inhabited and uninhabited buildings alike. They feed on grain and abandoned ideas. They eat out of the hand of the Treuhand organization. They increase and multiply while we're asleep. They dig. They run about. Tap-tap-tap they go over old floorboards. They scare away investors, they devastate the larders of people who have moved into the area. At last the roof has been mended and the asbestos removed, now they want to be able to look at the lake in peace, and then guess what: mice.

Bad luck for Poppo von Blankenburg. The agricultural machinery mogul had invited his family and friends to a little party at his hunting lodge. The Baroque building beside the Deep Lake has been renovated since last summer, the property has been spruced up and fenced in, silent Suzi has to climb now to get to his favorite place for angling, but Suzi doesn't mind. There's also a maze of hedges, but a very easy one; it didn't take Mustard-Micha ten minutes to find the middle and steal the cushions from the pavilion. In addition there are private game reserves, and there's private access to the lake, and until recently there was a wireless local area network. But now, unfortunately: rodents.

Von Blankenburg had dreamt of a party at the hunting lodge in the country for a long time: food and drink at a long table on the bank under the linden tree, staff in livery, a temperature of 26 degrees, and in his dream the male guests wore hunting garb and the ladies white trousers that fitted tightly, but not too tightly. The white trousers were even specified on the invitations, in small print, and there really was hunting, but no one counted who bagged how many ducks. In the dream a Scandinavian string quartet played chamber music under the linden tree.

Mice did not feature in Blankenburg's dream. They did in real life. Their hunt began while the party guests were hunting too. They scurried across the meadow, tap-tap-tap they went over the recently relaid floorboards, hundreds upon hundreds of mice, they ate the food, they drank the wine. The staff screamed, the braver ones stamped as if dancing to that gray music. But what can you do against such an army when it's well co-ordinated?

Silent Suzi watched the chaos from his favorite place for angling, which also had a view of Fräulein von Blankenburg's favorite place for bathing. Before the mice gave battle, Suzi had whistled a little tune, and after it had died away they went back into the chinks and cracks provided by Nature.

The mice didn't spare Magdalene either. Fräulein von Blankenburg (aged seventeen) likes poetry more than agriculture. Hardly ever uses her posh "von" particle. Likes to go barefoot: Magdalene. Moves with a sleepwalker's certainty: Magdalene. Likes Hugo von Hofmannsthal, the Russians and their language: Magdalene. Highly strung. Well brought up. She'd rather have spent her summer holidays on the Mediterranean, all the same.

Magdalene did not take part in the festivities. Once the hunting party had broken up she went swimming, carefully, so as not to disturb the bittern. And then the mice struck, stealing her tiara, an heirloom left to her by her great-grandmother Magdalene. A tiara set with jewels, full of sparkling memories.

"CRAZY SHIT!" CRIES THE JOURNALIST, WHEN FRAU Kranz opens the attic, another torrent of canvases flows out, and Frau Kranz would probably like to lock him in up there so that she can have some peace at last, but she doesn't do that out of consideration for her work stored up here and her cat who goes hunting in the attic.

"Is that Jesus?" The journalist has gone up to a large portrait.

"No, that's Manu from the ice cream parlor."

A Kranz hangs in Manu's ice cream parlor (a still life entitled *Ice Cream Sundae*). A Kranz hangs in Krone's butcher shop. A Kranz in the Prenzlau school dining room smells of Healthier-School-Dinners-in-Today's-New-Federal-German-States.

The picture of Ulli's garage hung in Ulli's garage for some time, but without the calendar showing erotic pictures of Polish girls, which Frau Kranz had replaced by a sunflower, but then Ulli pasted a tiny cut-out naked Polish girl over it again.

This season there has been a Kranz hanging in the clubhouse changing room of Fürstenfelde FC. First XI, as a talisman. The footballers touch the sports field in the picture for luck, before running out on the real sports field. The team did lose the first two matches 0–5 and 1–4, but none of the players were injured.

The journalist looks at an unusual sequence of pictures: the colors are stronger, the heads and bodies more angular. *Threshing Machine with Transmission Drive in the Fields* is the title of one of the paintings. On another, one showing children and Colorado beetles, there is even a text: *Everyone Must Help Fight Off the Yankee Beetles!* The journalist asks about the background to it. Frau Kranz tells him not to be so dim.

"Did you ever paint the Banat district?"

"I was too young."

"But you must surely have some memories of it."

"Memories aren't always a lot of use when you're painting."

Countless, countless pictures, but none of Fürstenfelde by night. There had been attempts. Failing perhaps because of the demands they made on Frau Kranz, or her poor night vision. Failing perhaps because of the night. This time she has promised to paint a night picture for the auction sale. But also for herself.

"Do you have a favorite picture?"

"Oh, well, I've painted so many. Do you see this one? Do you know where it is? It's the dance floor in Blissau's restaurant. End of the 1960s, that was. My goodness, no, I suppose you don't know it, you wouldn't have been born yet. How old are you, twenty?"

"Forty-four."

"And still on a local paper, are you?"

"Depends what you mean by local—the Uckermark. . . I mean, I. . ."

"But I think that's good! You know your way around here, don't you? I think it's good to know your way around. All I wanted was to know my way around. German castles, the Rhine, the Pyramids. It's all right, in fact it's good there are things like that. For whoever lives there, for whoever wants to travel and can. I went on a long journey. Or rather I had to. I'm happy with that. The Banat area, yes. Birth is our first lottery ticket in life. Mine was a dead loss, but there's no need to make a great fuss about it."

Frau Kranz only talks about things that she wants to talk about; she doesn't have time for anything else. She doesn't show her self-portraits to anyone.

"Blissau closed in the early 1990s. Do you realize, Mr Journalist, that they used to brew beer here, there were seven restaurants, and now people meet in a garage to drink? And the likes of you write about the falling birth rate and schools closing. Good heavens above! Suppose gastronomy does die out? Fewer restaurants, fewer children, it's as simple as that. Having a drink together in a place that's right for it counts for more in life than where you come from."

Frau Kranz has dressed up for such a night as this. But there is so much dried mud left on her gumboots from previous expeditions that they look as if they were made of fired clay. She is conducting a conversation with herself. The ash trees drink it in, they drink in the scent of the old woman. She shoulders her easel once again; something about this spot doesn't suit her, she walks down to the water's edge, and it seems as if she might go on walking, simply walk into the lake, just like that.

"All my life I've been painting what I know, nothing but that," Frau Kranz has told the journalist. He has already said goodbye, but he is still fidgeting in the doorway because he doesn't know a polite way to get out of finishing his elder-berry juice.

"If you could travel back in time and into one of your pictures, to experience that moment once again, what moment would it be?"

We admit that wasn't such a bad question.

And Frau Kranz really does walk into the water, just where her first picture shows the six women. If you look closely, you can see something of Frau Kranz in each of them. The scar over her eyebrow, her pointed chin, even her hair was blonde once.

Traveling in time. Such nonsense.

The street lights cast pale patches on the town wall. The church tower is floodlit. The colorless alternation between rooftops and the silhouetted ash trees. Frau Kranz knows it all very well. Once she painted the Berlin Gate from memory, getting every crack in the stones of its arch almost perfectly accurate.

She closes her eyes, and the six women take their first step as if they had practiced doing it at the same time.

Frau Kranz doesn't see her village, she knows her village.

Her mother called her Ana, so that she wouldn't have one more "n" than all the other Anas thereabouts.

Omne solum forti patria est. Everywhere is home to the strong.

She would have liked to paint not reality sometime, but something that became real later. But how do you do that?

Frau Kranz would like to paint what no one knows.

Frau Kranz would like to paint the evil in us, but how do you do that?

Frau Kranz would like to paint staying the course, but how do you do that?

And prevention, but how?

Frau Kranz wades through the lake. A duck is startled out of its sleep and scolds helplessly. Its quacking slops over the wall and into the streets. Frau Kranz's evening dress gets wet.

THE SETTLERS WHO FIRST CAME TO LIVE BESIDE our lakes, hundreds of years ago, found sandy soil that could be worked reasonably well, dense forests in which they killed game and were killed, as well as waters poor in fish but with plenty of fine crayfish in them. The crayfish were considered a specialty in aristocratic circles, although they tasted horrible, until one day someone ventured to say that they did taste horrible, and the fashion for eating them died out at once.

The settlers considered the larger of our two lakes uncanny. Yes, its waters were shallow and a healthy brown color near the banks, but farther out the bed of the lake fell steeply to such black depths that folk said: this is where the Devil washes himself once every thirteen years, this is the Devil's Bath.

The forest was grubbed up, the cultivated fields grew larger, and where there had once been isolated houses and farms there was now a village. Later it was granted a town charter, and a strong wall to mark it off from the land belonging to the town of Stargard. At first people said that they lived in the *vörste velden*, the first fields beside the Devil's Bath—today the name has become Fürstenfelde.

At first, when people wanted to get to the new settlement, the ferryman rowed them across the lake. He capably took them and their belongings on board, and instead of money he often asked strangers to the place for stories as his fee, passing the stories on to the locals at the village inn.

One chilly evening—autumn had set in some time before—the frogs fell silent, the water was calm and the wind died down as if it were holding its breath. Then the bell on the landing stage was rung vigorously, and there stood a weedy little fellow in the twilight, gazing grimly over the lake.

"Tell me, old man," said the little fellow hoarsely to the ferryman, with his bony finger pointing over the water, "what's all that nonsense going on over there?"

The ferryman couldn't see any nonsense, only the farmers busy in their fields with the last of the day's work. Nor did the little fellow seem to expect an answer; he had already jumped into the boat and said he wanted to be taken across the lake. The ferryman hesitated for only a moment. He felt that there was something uncanny about his passenger, but the man was a passenger and the ferryman would treat him accordingly, so he made the boat ready and rowed away.

On the way, he felt that the ferryboat was getting heavier and heavier. Then the manikin asked whether the ferryman wasn't finding it hard work to row. But the ferryman was proud, so he shook his head and didn't show how hard it was. Soon, however, he found that rowing was not just hard work but downright impossible. It was as if his oars were dipping not into water but into thick porridge. The little man asked his question again, and this time the ferryman, gasping for breath, said that he'd never yet failed to row anyone over the lake.

The passenger seemed pleased with his reply. "Then I'll help you," he cried, and he tore off one of his legs and threw it overboard. Now the rowing was easier, but soon they were making even slower progress. However hard the ferryman tried, the oars stuck fast in the black water—or was it still water?—and the boat wouldn't move.

Then the manikin took off his hat, which was adorned with a long, red feather, bent his knee and jumped into the lake. Under the water already, he called back to the ferryman, "Wait for me and you won't regret it."

The red feather in the hat cast a flickering light all the way to land. Where the manikin had jumped into the water, horrible tangles of waterweeds wound their way, and gigantic pike swam around. But whenever the manikin came close to one of them, the plants ducked aside and the fish swam off. Only the nasty crayfish felt no fear. The one leg with which the little fellow struck out like a whip as he went diving down did not end in a human foot. Instead of a heel, it had a hoof.

The ferryman's heart sank. He would happily have gone without his fee, only he was a man who didn't lightly fail to do his duty, and it was his duty to take passengers safely across the lake. At midnight the little man rose to the surface again, holding the leg he had torn off in his teeth like a valuable catch. He nodded to the ferryman as a sign that their crossing could continue.

After a single stroke of the oars the boat came to land—day was already beginning to dawn. His passenger paid the ferryman a princely sum of money. "And since you did not give up, did not complain, and kept faith with me," he said, "I will give you a special reward." So he said, and then he promised to spare the ferryman's life, but the others who had dared to settle beside his lake, he said, would not live to see harvest. "Unless," said the little man, winking, "you can persuade them to move away from here."

The ferryman woke the Mayor to tell him to warn the village. But the Mayor did not care for the ferryman's stories anyway, so he sent him off without hearing what he had to say.

The innkeeper listened spellbound, but he thought the passenger's hoof could be true only in a fairy tale, and gave the ferryman a drink for telling such a good story.

And so it went on: the blacksmith advised the ferryman, who had been awake all night, to sleep off his hangover, the farmers in the fields had not noticed any red light out on the lake, and they even swore that the ferryman had come ashore alone in his boat. Some may have believed him, but said defiantly that they were well off here, and no one could drive them away.

While the ferryman was going desperately from one to another, two fellows came to the inn. They wore hoods far down over their faces, and spoke like men in a fever. In the evening the landlord found them dead, their skin disfigured by terrible marks. Soon the landlord himself was feeling unwell, and so were others who had gone to the inn to drink.

The prophecy of the ferryman's passenger came true. The plague carried people away as fast as the wind. In the daytime the ferryman dug graves and wandered among the empty houses as though he thought that the story might have a different ending if he only looked for it. In the evening he bewailed his fate. But at night he put out on the lake and called his warning again, as if the water and the stars themselves might be persuaded to leave this place.

Much time has passed since then. No Devil carries the plague to our village now. But every thirteen years, on an autumn evening, the frogs fall silent, the wind dies down, the water is still, and you can hear gasping and the sound of heavy oar strokes, and a hoarse voice calling, "Tell me, old man, are you finding it hard to row?"

This year the ferryman said yes, because it was the truth.

FRAU KRANZ IS STANDING KNEE-DEEP IN WATER. She props her easel up so that it is at a slanting angle, switches on the light, moves its feet until it is standing firmly on the muddy bed of the lake. Eddie fitted an umbrella to the front of the easel years ago to protect it from all weathers. Frau Kranz is well equipped. We know that the water is cold.

Roughly here one of the six young women could have turned. Turned to the bank, to the ash trees, to the village. Perhaps she also looked at the ferry boathouse. Ana Kranz, at the boathouse window, did not move.

On that or on some other day, a Red Army soldier, an infantryman from Belorussia, is trying to throttle a piglet under the ash trees. His comrades, shaving each other in the sunlight, egg him on. He's not the most drunk of them, he's the youngest, his skin still spotty, his beard still downy. The piglet is squealing. The soldier stands there upright. His cap has fallen off his head. His pale hair, his red cheeks, the piglet in his hands. Its snout is level with the soldier's face. It all takes some time. The men shouting encouragement get tired. Only the infantryman can still be heard, gasping. His legs look like slender young trees taking root in his boots. He groans as if he were the one being throttled. The louder he groans the less noise the piglet makes, quietly putting up with this human joke.

Ana Kranz, under the boat, didn't move. She heard the squealing piglet, looking through a crack she saw the soldier's legs. She stayed hidden under the boat for a day and a night. The people had run away from the fear that was advancing with the Russians, or had hanged themselves, or had been found. Ana hadn't wanted to run away again. She spent another two days under the boat. She drank from the lake. Was found. By the ferryman, who came back. He took her in, hid her in the space under the floorboards, behind the paddles, ropes and other gear. Gave her food. Told her, from the boathouse above, about low-flying aircraft and marauding soldiers, corpses by the roadside. Down below, she heard him through the floorboards. He warned her: don't show yourself, girl. And once she heard Russian voices. The ferryman didn't understand them. Ana understood the boots on the floorboards. They searched the cupboard, the chest. There was nothing to be found in the sparse furnishings. They opened the hatch. The space inside was dark and full of things. Ana held her breath. They took the ferryman away with them. Only after days did she venture up from below the floorboards. Stood at the window, peering out, didn't move. If people came to fish from the landing stage she climbed down under the boards again. The ferryman was gone for days, they had locked him up, or worse. Bells rang. Shots were fired. And then he came back after all, his face bruised and swollen. He had brought some bread, and charcoal for Ana to draw with. Ana looked out at the lake. At the promenade beside it. At spring. She drew,

Ana Kranz drew all over the walls, the ferryman didn't mind. She drew the people coming back, almost all of them old men and children, they washed in the lake. She drew the soldiers going for walks along the lakeside like lovers. She spent a lot of time alone. She ate the bread slowly, she drank from the lake, she drew. A small sketch beside the window, six figures hand in hand, on the banks of the lake. It was April, perhaps May. The soldiers were turning up less frequently. Ana stayed in the boathouse of the ferry for a month and a half. Six years later she would transfer the six women to canvas, clothe them and comb their hair, give them morning colors, and now, on such a night as this, the six take their first step, and one of them looks round.

Frau Kranz is plagued by an almost physical desire for old stories. It comes of this place, the boathouse of the ferry, it comes of the night. It's a thirst for the answer to her question: what could she have prevented. . . could I have prevented them from doing it?

The rain is falling harder. The bank, the ash trees, home. Frau Kranz makes her first brush stroke. The paper is wet. She tears it off, places it on the water. Begins again. The paper drifts slowly away.

A CARTER EXCHANGES A FEW WORDS WITH THE ferryman, the ferryman asks about his journey here. The carter describes the street fighting in Dresden. Then the ferryman gives him some of his home-distilled spirits. They look at the water, at the sky.

Well, here we go, says the ferryman.

The landing stage, the moorings, the ferryman's bell.

Rubber tires, ferry, boat.

Boots, doormat, plant pot without any plant in it.

Wood, woodworm, better days.

A low bed, one window looking out on the bank, one looking out on the water, the ferryman saw the lakes even in his dreams.

A table on which he ate from a plate with a fork, a knife and a spoon.

A cupboard, a towel, a razor blade.

A chest, massive, with a lock to it and a domed lid.

Damp, mold, mice.

Hatch, space under it, stuff in the space.

A ticket window for selling ferry tickets, a pencil fixed to the wall with a little chain, a visitors' book. The ferryman lets only passengers who have deserved it during the trip write their names in the book. Just seven in seventy years. Angela Merkel is among them.

There are no drawings left on the walls now.

Even after the ferryman's death a light burns, an electric bulb outside above the door, forgotten or left to burn for ever. A sheet of paper floats in its reflection on the water.

ANNA WALKS PAST THE NEW BUILDINGS AND THE Gölow property, down to the promenade. Or rather drags herself, bending over, finding it hard to breathe out. She stops when she comes to the ferry boathouse, with her hands on her knees. It's not the strain, it's stupidity. She forgot to bring her asthma spray.

Someone is standing in the water not far from the bank, faintly visible in some source of light. Rain is falling on the lake.

"Hello? Who's there?"

It is Ana Kranz. Anna tries to breathe calmly, but the air wheezes in her throat.

"Are you a ghost? That's funny. I don't believe in ghosts."

"Frau Kranz, it's me, Anna." Anna gasps for air, coughs, crouches down. "Are you all right?"

"Are *you* all right?"

"Come along, I'll help. . . help you out."

"Keep away. Can't a person even paint here in peace?"

Somewhere a car engine roars. After a pause it roars again. The wind is rising. Raindrops flash in the beam of Anna's headlight. "It's raining," says Anna, and would like to go on, but she doesn't have the breath for it.

"Excellent!" cries Frau Kranz. Anna straightens up, turns away. She can't help the old woman now, she must help herself.

Rain beats on the umbrella above the easel, on the lake, the drops sound like the chiming of small bells, and the lake rumbles, the lake moves.

IN THE YEAR OF OUR LORD 1589, IN THE MONTH of July, Kuene Gantzkow, Maidservant to our good Mayor, bore an infant Child, a Girl, which said Infant the Mayor's Wife took from her, giving it instant Baptism for the Sake of its Immortal Soul, thereafter strangling the Babe and casting it over the Fence and into the Ditch, where we found the Carcase several Weeks later. The Mayor's Wife told her Son, which Same had had carnal Knowledge of the Maidservant, to strike the young Woman dead, as he duly did. For her Crime, the Babe's Grandmother was drown'd in the Deep Lake.

HOME. SHE JUST HAS TO GET HOME. ANNA TAKES the longer way through the village; she would rather not be visible in the light of the streetlamps any more. Her coughing wakes German Shepherd dogs. When she reaches the Homeland House she can't go any farther. She crouches down. Around Anna: dreams among buildings made of sprayed concrete. She presses her lips together and breathes against them, but it doesn't help. She gasps, and can't breathe any air out.

The heart of the night is beating in the streets. Marx-Strasse rises up to the church, brightly lit, and behind the church goes on in the dark, climbing steeply to the clouds. Now headlights glide down through the clouds to the world below, where Anna is fighting for breath, and on window sills cacti stand nearby. The wind hums to the revs of the car engine, drumming out a hollow beat, carrying an aroma on it, the sweet fragrance of grapes.

Anna presses into the gateway, and turns off her headlight as if in flight.

The beat: reggae. The music and the car engine echo between the cloudy sky and the savings bank branch. Frau Rombach hasn't brought her flower containers in for the night; the cats will piss in them, and she'll have to go round with the room spray in the morning, or her customers will be in a worse mood than ever.

Leaves sweep over the porous asphalt, and a metallic blue van makes its entrance at walking pace, bodywork clattering tinnily in the bass. Anna, caught in the headlights, freezes guiltily. Pebbles crunch under the tires and the van stops.

Some thinking goes on, both inside and outside the van.

Anna can't manage to stand upright. The raindrops shimmer in the light, the calm beat makes the night no calmer. The van windows are tinted, the tires muddy, there are splashes of mud on the sides of the van.

The number plate is UM, for the Uckermark. Well, that's something.

The engine stops, the bass goes on playing. The windshield wipers click softly. Nothing has been going on in the van for much too long now. Only when the song is over do the doors swing open. A new beat, a wave of German hip-hop, washes over Anna and—

—TWO MEN GET OUT, OR RATHER BOYS, STILL growing into their limbs, but at night on the road, for all Anna knew, they could be an army of two. The taller: intriguingly good-looking. The hair of the smaller is nicely blow-dried, his glance stern, his eyebrows plucked, his skin treated with a male grooming product. Fur coats over loose trousers, bright red football shirts, on one a lightning flash and the words

FC ENERGIE

for Energie Kottbus Football Club, and on the other, equally unsubtle, a skull and crossbones and under it, in large letters:

STIL

As for Anna, she is white as a sheet. Inquisitive, helpful, low-life—they could be anything in the night she has conjured up: angels' wings folded, hooves in their shoes? She can't tell, she doesn't feel well, or not well enough to judge. She wants to face her illness, not strangers. Only her voice fails her, only a hoarse croak comes out. The tall, good-looking one smiles, his speech sings, soft like a man with plenty of time.

"Mademoiselle," he asks, "are you okay? We saw you in trouble from far away."

Anna whispers, "It's asthma."

"Ah, civilization making a fuss."

"It's nothing at all to do with us," the smaller youth with the glum look says.

"Like a lift to A&E?"

"That's going too far, Q, if you ask me."

"But what if it's an emergency?"

Anna looks from one to the other of them.

"Hey, do you always talk in rhyme?"

In chorus: "Us? Where would we get the time?"

"You—" Anna's voice gives way, she slumps to the ground. Undaunted, the two hurry over, help her up and get her into their van.

"Mademoiselle, we'll take you home."

"You're not fit to be out on your own."

Anna nods; she can hardly speak. "Geher's Farm. Do you know it?"

The two exchange meaning glances that Anna can't interpret. Anna looks at the van door. It's not locked: good.

"We don't know our way well in this town."

"The satnav went and let us down."

"Great." Anna tries breathing deeply. "Down Thälmann-Strasse here, along the main road, I'll tell you when."

The one called Q turns the van.

"Where—where have you come from?" Anna wants to keep the conversation going, however difficult her voice finds it.

"From here, from there, from up and down. Nothing to interest you tonight."

"Henry, you're not being very polite." And turning to Anna, "Take no notice of this clown. On such a night things get him down. Usually he's so good with words he can make counts nervous and countesses amorous, or do I mean it the other way? Never mind, be that as it may, it isn't easy with names of places, they can't be trusted in such cases."

"You. . . okay. . ." Anna's eyes are streaming, her breath is wheezing the whole time. The van speeds up on its way out of the village—

—and at the same time Herr Schramm is stepping on the gas of his Golf. When he is doing 130 k.p.h. he switches off the headlights.

HERR SCHRAMM IS DIVORCED, NO CHILDREN. HERR Schramm is not afraid of death, you don't know what's going on when you die. In summer he hadn't been thinking of death, in summer Herr Schramm still wanted another go at life, maybe he'd fall in love.

Frau Mahlke, manageress of the dating agency, set off on a little tour of Brandenburg to visit six men in search of a partner at home, taking stock of them on their home ground. Herr Schramm's appointment was the last. She arrived in Fürstenfelde at five, rather tired and in a worse temper than when she left the late-summer atmosphere of Pankow behind to drive out into the country.

Herr Schramm was waiting outside the Homeland House with a mug of coffee. His first words were, "Schramm, pleased to meet you," followed by a calm, "Watch out, wasps," as one of them tried to settle on Elisabeth Mahlke's well-upholstered shoulder. Herr Schramm is a punctilious man.

Frau Mahlke has thrown a silk scarf, golden-yellow and pale lilac, over her slightly pudgy figure and is wearing a pair of trousers that are rather tight for her age of fifty-nine. Herr Schramm looked at the trousers in a way that clearly showed he wasn't sure whether such tight trousers were right for this occasion, but never mind.

Frau Mahlke found herself taken out for a trip on the Deep Lake in the oldest rowing boat, which creaks romantically. She was not prepared for that. The cool breeze blowing over the lake did her hot face good, she took off her shoes and dunked her feet in the water. The ferryman owed Schramm a favor, so he rowed them out to the islands. "Come along, Elisabeth, I'll show you the lakes and the deserted farms"—"Why don't we just stay at your place to talk, Herr Schramm?"

Herr Schramm wanted to show the lady from the dating agency both the good sides and the not-so-good sides of Fürstenfelde. To be honest, he wanted to do the same with himself. The ferryman had recommended it. Because if you promise a woman a lie, you'll be bound to disappoint her sometime. "You're not such a splendid fellow, Schramm," the ferryman had said, "but telling lies would make you really terrible."

Frau Mahlke asked Herr Schramm whether midges were a problem in the area, and Herr Schramm said, "Yes, of course." And he added, "On average a hundred thousand midges' eggs are laid per square meter of the marshy land." And, "It would be even worse without the bats." And, "All the same, I've always wanted to go to Finland. They have lakes there that I've never seen. For instance, it would be good if you find me someone who'd like to go to Finland with me. I've got a bit of money put aside."

"Well, let's begin, shall we, Herr Schramm?" asked Frau Mahlke, picking up her questionnaire.

The questions about the lady's appearance were soon dealt with: he liked brunettes. Yes, shorter than him, but not too short. No, he had no objection in principle to makeup. Yes, she should be well groomed but not to excess, you could see plenty of that on TV.

The following came next:

Frau Mahlke: "Should the lady of your heart be the domestic type?"

Herr Schramm: "What does that mean?"

Frau Mahlke: "Would you prefer someone who likes to stay at home, or someone who can join in outdoor activities with you?"

Herr Schramm: "I was an army officer, but I don't get an officer's pension."

Frau Mahlke: "Meaning?"

Herr Schramm: "Meaning I have to work on the black market in the daytime. But don't write it down just like that. Say I don't mind what she does during the day, but I'd like her to be at home in the evening."

Frau Mahlke: "Speaking of work, would you like the lady to have a career?"

Herr Schramm: "I don't mind."

Frau Mahlke: "Do you have any hobbies, Herr Schramm?"

Herr Schramm: "I've thought of something else to do with the last question."

Frau Mahlke: "Yes?"

Herr Schramm: "Well, if she does have a job then I'd like that, if she's happy with it too. Do you see what I mean?"

Frau Mahlke: "I think so."

Herr Schramm: "It's very important. Are you happy with your own work, Frau Mahlke?"

Frau Mahlke: "I meet a great many interesting people."

Herr Schramm: "There you are, then. Ski-jumping and bats."

Frau Mahlke: "What?"

Herr Schramm: "My hobbies. But I don't do any ski-jumping myself. Do you know Jens Weissflog?"

Frau Mahlke: "He was that ski-jumper, wasn't he?"

Herr Schramm: "Not just that ski-jumper, he was *the* ski-jumper. If there's a category for it, please put: 'Would like one who has no objection to ski-jumping.'"

Frau Mahlke: "All right. Under Miscellaneous, maybe. Let's move on to something else. Do you wish for physical closeness?"

Herr Schramm: "Er. If it happens, if we like each other, I wouldn't say no."

Frau Mahlke: "Do you drink alcohol?"

Herr Schramm: "I do drink alcohol, yes."

Frau Mahlke: "Do you drink more than two glasses a day?"

Herr Schramm: "Two glasses of what?"

Frau Mahlke laughs: "You see, I recently had a gentleman who, well, who liked to drink alcohol very much."

Herr Schramm: "I like it very much too."

Frau Mahlke: "Right."

Herr Schramm: "Yes."

Frau Mahlke: "Should she drink alcohol as well?"

Herr Schramm: "With me, yes."

Frau Mahlke: "That's fine too."

Herr Schramm: "Yes."

Frau Mahlke: "There was that Four Skills ski-jumping tournament, I watched that with my son when he was still small, he liked it."

Herr Schramm: "Four *Hills* tournament."

Frau Mahlke: "What?"

Herr Schramm: "Are you married, Frau Mahlke?"

Frau Mahlke: "Not now—how about housework?"

Herr Schramm: "I've been doing it myself for ages. That's no problem."

Frau Mahlke: "I believe you. But it all depends on your expectations. What do you expect of a woman, and what can she expect of you?"

Herr Schramm: "Could I perhaps mention that I don't like ironing?"

Frau Mahlke: "We could say: shared work around the house ideal."

Herr Schramm: "Shared? Good. Shared sounds good."

Frau Mahlke: "A foreign lady?"

Herr Schramm: "No."

Frau Mahlke: "Right. Should we concentrate on candidates from this part of the country?"

Herr Schramm: "Well, if there was anyone here I'd know. I can show her everything. And please write that it's lovely here but not as lovely as some other places."

Frau Mahlke: "I really like ironing myself."

Herr Schramm: "I see."

Frau Mahlke: "How about children? Should the lady have children?"

Herr Schramm: "If they've left home then I don't mind."

Frau Mahlke: "Right. How would you define yourself politically, Herr Schramm?"

Herr Schramm: "Protest voter."

Frau Mahlke: "And what kind of political attitude should the lady have?"

Herr Schramm: "FDP."

Frau Mahlke: "The Free Democratic Party? Ah.—Driving license?"

Herr Schramm: "You can't manage without one here."

Frau Mahlke: "Right."

Herr Schramm: "That bit about the FDP was a joke. And about the lady—you keep saying: the lady. She doesn't have to be a lady, that's really not necessary."

Later, Frau Mahlke and Herr Schramm were sitting outside the butcher's shop in the sunset, but Frau Mahlke didn't want anything to eat; she was wearing her sunglasses propped in her hair in spite of the sunlight, and Herr Schramm thought: maybe that's because her eyes look all right, they're well worth showing without sunglasses, and he told her so, he put his meatballs on his plate and said, "Frau Mahlke, it's quite all right that you're not wearing your sunglasses. Because of your eyes. Because they really look good the way they are."

And then Frau Mahlke decided to try the meatballs after all, just a little bit of one, and later Herr Schramm signed the agreement, and Frau Mahlke shook hands with him and drove back to Berlin with the sunset in her rearview mirror.

Herr Schramm got into the rowing boat and went out on the lake, alone this time. An edgy character, Herr Schramm. Face like the sole of a boot. Firm and leathery and scarred. Bright white hair, the kind of white ex-soldiers get from stress, thin and sparse. He was smoking. He had smoked a lot that day—it's two months ago now. We're not surprised that the representative from the dating agency didn't ask any questions about smoking. Herr Schramm smoked, and made up his mind to stop, let himself drift until the light was only an idea of the gleam in Frau Mahlke's eyes as she ate the meatball.

KRONE, BUTCHER'S SHOP AND CAFÉ—LUNCH

   Monday: roast meat and gravy (€4.40)

   Tuesday: loin of pork with sauerkraut (€4.40)

   Wednesday: meatballs (€3.90)

   Thursday: sausages wrapped in bacon (€4.40)

   Friday: roast meat and gravy (€4.40)

   Saturday (Feast Special): grill behind the shop

IN THE YEAR OF OUR LORD 1589, AT THE TIME OF the Anna Feast, it so happened that the Inn-Keeper here, Ulrich Ramelow, lost his Wife, and got Another in her Stead, a Woman that he did not desire to keep. Folk said that Mine Host had not entirely understood the Warning given him, not to serve his Guests bad Beer, for he had brew'd another Draft at the Anna Feast such as caus'd those who partook of it Grave Incommodity, and it was of a Vile Flavor into the Bargain.

So now the Inn-Keeper had that strange Female in his House, and could not find his own Wife any Where. The Woman told him roundly that he must endure her to keep Company with him, nor think of making any Complaint to the Mayor, for if he did so he would put her Person and his Own, and above all the Person of his dear Wife, in even greater Danger than was the Present Case. His Horses, she also informed him, were Well and throve exceedingly.

Our Inn-Keeper knew not What to do, but the Reason for his Plight was, that until he brewed Decent Beer he should not have a Decent Woman. For the Newcomer was a Sloven who thought Nothing of God and His Word, or of the Holy Sacrament, and she was much given to Cursing and Blaspheming, and moreover had a Vile Stench about her.

The Inn-Keeper resign'd himself to his Lot, so that his Wife and his Horses should come to No Harm, and he also swore to brew bad Beer no more. Before he next brewed Beer, none the less, the Sloven had done great Harm to his Name and his Inn. She plagu'd Ramelow mightily with her Desires and her Commands, and all but impoverish'd him. Furthermore she caus'd all Manner of Riffraff, Foreigners and Scoundrels to frequent the Inn, for hardly an Honest Man would show his Face there. There was much Wrangling and Strife among the Guests, who oft came to Fisticuffs for the Favors of that Woman, who made very free with her Charms.

But on the Night when the Inn-Keeper broached his new, good Brew, the Woman was gone, leaving a Besom Broom in the Bed where she had lain. Soon Ramelow his true Wife came home, and right glad she was of it. She said, that two Men had taken her away by Force to a Cavern in the Kiecker Forest, and oblig'd her to stay there with them. The Aforesaid Men were wicked Scoundrels, Thieves and Sorry Deceivers, yet they did not molest her. They had given her good Nourishment, and she had both grave and amusing Talk with them. Many a time the Couple were Away, leaving her with a Fox to bear her company. This Fox was a very tame Beast, and they lov'd it greatly. When they return'd they brought all Manner of Fine Wares, good Cloth, fine Gowns of Damask, Atlas and even Silk with them, together with Jewelery and such Stuff.

She once tried to run Away, but the Fox had followed like a Dog, and being afeared that the Animal might betray her, she gave up the Attempt.

The Wife of the Inn-Keeper could describe those Men and tell their Names. One was tall of Stature, t'other short and round as a Carp. The first was called Kuno, his Companion's Name was Hinnerk. They were Native to Fürstenfelde, which Disclosure serv'd to account for many a Robbery and grievous Assault. The noble Lord Poppo von Blankenburg led ten Horsemen into the Kiecker Forest to bring the Rogues to Justice. The Cavern was found, but there was Nought therein.

One Day the Congregation did see the Inn-Keeper's Wife in the House of God, adorn'd with a very fine Girdle, stitch'd as it seem'd with Pearls. There was some Gossip concerning that Girdle, which she never again wore thereafter.

ANNA IS BREATHING MORE EASILY. THE PRESSURE in her chest hasn't been so bad since she got into the van. The driver is keeping to 50 k.p.h., no faster. A small, stylized fox's brush hangs from the rearview mirror, along with a pennant with a lightning flash on it, like the one on the driver's football shirt. Something like German rap is coming from the loudspeakers. "We Are Legends."

Anna points to the pennant. "What's that for?"

"All for the best. We just like lightning," says the smaller youth.

"It's our team's crest, not really frightening," adds Q, shaking his head.

There they go again. Anna tries to find some indication that the whole thing is a game, maybe a bet: who will fail to find a rhyme first?

Q hoots his horn. Right in the middle of the carriageway, no lights on, a car is racing toward them. In films you often see a duel like that. Usually one vehicle ends up in the ditch or against a wall. Q simply brakes and steers to the side of the road. The other car slides off the road, scraping past a birch tree, and drives on into the meadow.

Anna says, "He must be really tight."

"Soon be out like a light," Q agrees.

The car is a white Golf, and it makes straight for a tree. Anna gets out. The Golf slithers over an uneven spot on the ground, but hardly seems to slacken speed. Anna runs.

When she looks back, once, she sees no van on the road.

The car stops not five meters from the tree. Anna must go more slowly; the ground is uneven and wet, her breathing isn't steady yet. She is maybe fifty meters away. Someone is sitting motionless inside the car with his head on the steering wheel.

II

IT'S IN OUR NATURE TO TAKE A HISTORICAL INTEREST. And anyone who takes a historical interest in us can go to the Homeland House. Exhibitions take place there, Leitz file folders full of potential research materials wait for researchers on a chest of drawers adorned with decorative film bearing a pattern of grapes, and there's a copying machine that also works as a fax. A senior citizen from California has said he is coming for the Feast, and he wants to explore his family tree a bit. On the phone he told Frau Schwermuth that he's heard this place is at its best in late summer. Visitors can use the telephone, the coffee machine and the visitors' toilet, and can also admire Frau Kranz's charcoal drawing *Mayor Heinz Durden after Shooting Duck*, which shows a duck flying through the air. Frau Schwermuth asked the senior citizen what place *isn't* at its best in late summer.

Opening Times: strictly observed.

The Leitz file folders contain documents on:

People and personalities

History I (1740–1939) and History II (1945–1989)

Present events I (1990–onward, in progress)

Trade, arts and crafts over the ages

Festivals, customs, clubs

Faith, the church (bells), war

Tales and legends (I, II, III)

We don't take any historical interest in the contents of the Leitz file folders.

Above the folders hangs a cork pinboard. Pinned to it are index cards with accounts of milestones in local history. The first is about a giant:

It was not men who divided the waters at Fürstenfelde in such a way that we have two lakes; a giant did it. Long, long ago he broke the peak off a mountain in the Dinaric Alps in Dalmatia, and threw it so that it landed here and divided the waters for ever. History does not relate whether the giant threw the mountain peak on purpose.

They tell this story in the Dinaric Alps too. A mountain peak, as they tell it there, was blocking a giant's view of the Adriatic Sea, so he got rid of it. That version doesn't say that the rock traveled all the way to the Uckermark. Anyway, there are huge fingerprints to be seen on it, and a worn inscription in Old Church Slavonic which could mean, "The love of God is our salvation," or alternatively it may say, "Bogoljub (= Theophilus) is a stalk of asparagus."

We don't take any historical interest in giants.

We don't take any interest in milestones of local history.

Anyone who takes a historical interest in us had better talk to Frau Schwermuth. Frau Schwermuth knows things. She knows where to find the dramatic story of our Singing Club in the Leitz file folders, with the tale of its rise and fall at the beginning of the war, and she knows where to find the equally dramatic story of our Marksmen's Association and its rise and fall after the end of the war.

Farewell, brother marksmen, think of your old comrades sometimes, and we send you greetings: shoot well, and good luck!

Those are the words of Paul Wiese. Wiese was our chronicler until the 1950s. Frau Schwermuth has been his successor since the fall of the Berlin Wall. In between those years, the office of chronicler was neglected. Historically and in relation to Fürstenfelde, Frau Schwermuth knows everything, or she knows how to find it out.

We don't take any historical interest in the Marksmen's Association.

We don't take any historical interest in knowledge.

The Homeland House sells secondhand books out of banana crates. We take no historical interest in them, but they're El Dorado for dust mites. They cost between fifty cents and four euros. The journal *Our Fürstenfelde*, published by the Fürstenfelde Historical Society, costs five euros to local people and eight to tourists on cycling trips. The poster *Fürstenfelde, Seen from a Helicopter* (1996) cost fourteen D-Marks when it was published. The latest CD made by our Firefighters' Choral Society, Sound and Smoke, *We Didn't Start the Fire*, costs 7.89 euros. They were rehearsing Beethoven's "Hymn to the Night" in the evening, for the Feast. It sounded good, very good. And assorted maps of the area can be bought at the Homeland House: walking and cycling maps, maps of the lakes, and four different picture postcards.

At the moment there's an exhibition about tiled stoves in the Homeland House. Tiled stoves used to be our most important and beautiful exports. Another exhibition is also on, showing everyday items from the time of the German Democratic Republic: hair dryers, sewing machines, can-openers, what a People's Police officer looked like, canned food, etc.

We don't take any historical interest in tiles or everyday life in the GDR.

But we do take an interest in the massive wooden door in the cellar. There's something about doors and cellars. Still intact, despite their age and the damp. We're interested to know why so much fuss is made about that door. About the lock on that door. We take an interest in the room behind it. About six by six meters, asymmetrical walls of unhewn rock, more of a cave than a room. And during which war did old Lutz hide people in there?

We don't take any interest in historical accuracy.

And we don't know much about the room in the cellar. It's some kind of local history archive. But our History Society keeps a low profile about what exactly is in that archive. Now that *is* interesting. It's as if you were collecting something but not telling anyone what. So either you're ashamed of it, because you're a fifty-year-old engineer nicking and hoarding, let's say, used tubes of lip gloss, or it's forbidden to collect what you're collecting, for instance because it's threatened with extinction, like some species of monkeys and so on.

Members of the History Society, that's to say the Committee of Friends of the Homeland House, are: Frau Kranz, Frau Schwermuth, Imboden, Zieschke the baker, the bell-ringer and, until recently, the ferryman. We'd know even less about the archive if Frau Schwermuth didn't sometimes talk proudly about it, and if something wasn't exhibited upstairs from time to time.

We first heard about it in 2011. Frau Schwermuth applied to the community, as represented by the Mayor Frau Zink, to authorize the purchase of an electronic lock for the massive wooden door and a device to regulate humidity in the cellar. There was talk of a "sensational historical find" that the History Society wanted to keep suitably safe and sound. Part of it was documents that wouldn't even be regarded as lost because no one had known that they existed. Examination of them had apparently already begun, and it was hoped that the papers could soon be made accessible to the public and to scientific research. Frau Schwermuth called the archive then being set up the Archivarium.

The Mayor wasn't the right person to apply to, but of course she turned up at once wanting to see the "sensational find." Frau Schwermuth wouldn't let her. Frau Zink was first amused and then upset to discover that it wasn't a joke. Frau Schwermuth said she was sorry, but she couldn't let just anyone in to see it. What did she mean, just anyone—and so on; Frau Zink was on the point of forgetting the dignity of her office, but then she asked to speak to the chairman of the committee, who was the ferryman at that time. They went into a room and talked privately for quite a long while. After that the community agreed to finance those two purchases.

The fact is that no catalog of the Archivarium exists, and to this day no public use for it has been found. Does the Museum of Brandenburg History know about the archive and the "sensational find," and what does it think of them? From time to time Frau Schwermuth puts something on display in the glass case on the upper floor: an old lease, a marriage certificate. Or statistics: the quantities of fish caught in the year 1744, those from Fürstenfelde who died in this or that war.

In 1514 the feudal lord of the time, Poppo von Blankenburg, required four wethers a year from the shepherd appointed by the rural district council in consideration of his use of the meadows in Blankenburg's possession.

We do take a little interest in the shepherd, but only because we like the idea of a shepherd appointed by the rural district council.

The Blankenburgs in general appeal to Frau Schwermuth as archivist: a document of a hundred years later records the purchase of an ox by the former feudal lord's descendant, also Poppo von Blankenburg by name. Frau Schwermuth connected the record of the purchase with a letter of complaint about the *sadly unedifying character* of the said ox, rounding its story off with Blankenburg's account of the truly remarkable end of the ox, which was driven to the Baltic and there fell from a cliff into the sea, history does not relate whether of its own accord or not.

We do feel a little historical surprise about that ox.

We take an interest in the fact that both documents are dated from the time before 1740 and the Great Fire. So they were preserved from the flames by a small miracle, and remained undiscovered until recently by a larger miracle.

We take an interest in the tooth of time. The tooth of time is not sharp in the cellar of the Homeland House. The document about the shepherd appointed by the rural district council shows no signs whatsoever of age; it is immaculate. Like all the other documents exhibited to date.

Now that, too, is interesting.

We are more inclined to believe our reason, which tells us that those documents are remarkably clumsy forgeries, than to believe Frau Schwermuth, who says that the device for regulating humidity in the atmosphere is super and top-notch. The archivist says nothing to explain how the documents managed to stay in such good condition before the acquisition of the device.

Johanna Schwermuth interests us enormously in terms of human and criminal history.

EARLY IN THE YEAR OF OUR LORD 1607, THE remarkable Discovery of a great Quantity of Pippins in the fallow Field on Geher's Farm led to a Disputation concerning the rightful Owner of the said Fruits, and in Consequence the Ownership of the entire Field. Four Men had stated their Entitlement, three of them submitting documentary Evidence, to wit a signed Agreement, in proof of their rightful Claim to have leased that same Field. The fourth, his Honor the high-born Poppo von Blankenburg, had no Document to show, notwithstanding which he challeng'd the others in a loud, insistent Manner to a Bout of Fisticuffs, in order to decide upon the Matter—namely, to the Effect that he who was the Last left standing be declar'd Owner of the Apples.

Not three Days after that Challenge, the Mayor, a bankrupt Schoolmaster, determin'd, albeit amidst great Indignation and Protestations, that the Fist-Fight be deem'd a proper Method of reaching a Verdict.

Poppo von Blankenburg struck down All concern'd, including the Mayor, and was ajudged to have Carried the Day. That same Evening he wax'd roaring Drunk, ran out into the Field intending to Embrace the same, fell, struck his Head upon a Rock, and expire'd of that Injury.

Therefore the fallow Field laps'd into the Wilderness of its unknown Origin again, in which Condition it bringeth forth

Wasps, and Coneys, and wild Roses Year after Year, only to engulf and consume them once again.

MY MA WEIGHS TWICE AS MUCH AS MY PA. SHE weighs 130 kilos. In spring she puts on another 30 kilos of weighty thoughts (worries, fears, shame and general listlessness). Then my 160-kilo Ma lies down among the daffodils in the garden, because when she is lying down the dark clouds are about 160 centimeters farther away. Her eyes are closed, and we're supposed to leave her alone. There's nothing any of us can do about that, as a husband or a son or a daffodil. It's impossible to get my 160-kilo Ma back on her feet if she doesn't want to stand on them, it's impossible to get her to cheer up if she doesn't feel like it.

If it gets colder in the evening we cover her up. We sit with her. In fact it's almost nice for all the family to be doing something together. Pa is busy with DIY of some kind, I'm preparing for our next role-play meeting (I'm going to be a thieving half-elf, good at fencing and flight). Demographically, my hobbies ought to be first-person shooter games and right-minded ideas, but neither of those is as cool as the role-playing.

Sometimes I lie down beside Ma and read her old stories from hereabouts. She likes those. The one she likes best is the story of Jochim the invisible tinker. Ma's mouth twists. Maybe she's smiling. Or maybe she'd like to be invisible.

I've never known Ma to be any different in spring. My 65-kilo Pa and I and Dr Röhner in Prenzlau don't kid ourselves.

Ma is not okay. She knows it herself. It's in her nature, she says, and there's nothing you can do about your nature.

There's a lot of gossip about Ma, but people will gossip about everyone. They praise Ma a lot too. Most of all they praise her for working so hard at everything to do with the Homeland House. Ma runs the Homeland House because she has real ideas about it. Ma has a better idea of the village than anyone else. She's not interested in the country round the village. If the tourists ask her about it she just points to the brochures on display in the Homeland House, or to Frau Schober who sits around there and has family in the area, but Frau Schober is usually sitting around in the Homeland House because she's old, and her family never come to visit, and she'd be bored to death on her own, so it's teamwork between Ma and Frau Schober.

Ma also belongs to the History Society. They meet twice a week, sometimes Ma doesn't come home until the morning after a meeting. I haven't the faintest what goes on. A few old folk who like each other and like history too, sitting together jabbering away, that's how I imagine it. After a while someone says, "Right, let's talk about witch-burnings today. How do we feel about that? Anyone like to say something? Johanna? Yes, go ahead."

They're responsible for *Our Fürstenfelde*, too. That's kind of a magazine full of old folks' memories. The old folk are always complaining that no one's interested in their memories. *Our Fürstenfelde* shows you how wrong they are.

Ma always writes something for it. The latest edition is subtitled "The Fire Brigade and Other Associations." Ma has two pieces in it, one about the church choir, she didn't sing well enough to join it herself but Ma's not one to bear a grudge, and one about our fires. It starts like this: "Fürstenfelde isn't a bad place for fires." Great opening, Ma. It's a fact that there have always been fires in Fürstenfelde. That's a tragedy for Ma. Not because of the victims but because so many books and stuff like that get burnt. Old books mean to Ma what the bells mean to me. Her fingers sometimes smell like the last century when she comes back from the Homeland House (it's all that yellowed paper).

For instance, Ma found out that Fürstenfelde was once a town, only the right to a town charter got drunk away so now Fürstenfelde is only a village. And she knows all the old folk tales about this place. Better not ask her to tell them: she tells them so as they're really frightening, does different voices, body language, all that. The kids either love it or run away.

This is what I think: I think Ma uses the past to take her mind off the present. I mean off her body and her worries. Including in spring. In spring she lies there whispering stuff from the folk tales to herself. Sometimes it sounds like there's someone answering her. I like that. I like anything that cheers Ma up a bit in spring.

Ma swallows vitamin pills, avoids eating fatty food, goes for a bike ride every day, but it makes no difference, she's very fat and she sweats and gasps for breath. I can see how difficult going to the loo is for her. And how badly she suffers from the heat of summer and her own body. She complains of it, naturally she complains of it. And I think it's disgusting too, of course, but I'd flip my lid if anyone said anything nasty about Ma.

Ma is organizing an anti-Fascist bike ride for the Feast. People wanted a long route going right out of the village: Fürstenfelde—Wrechen—Parmen—back to Fürstenfelde. Ma said: "Thälmann-Strasse—Berlinerstrasse—Mühlenstrasse—the barn by the wall—Thälmann-Strasse. I'm organizing it, so I say where the route goes."

Ma doesn't much like going away from here. I guess that's because she feels okay in Fürstenfelde. Everything's always the same, or if it changes, it changes very slowly. The lake is shallow close to the banks, the depths lie in wait farther out. Ma gets nervous when things aren't just as she expects. At home she always chooses the same route. She could go straight into the kitchen from the living room, but she takes the long way round down the corridor. She has *her* sofa and *her* chair. Visitors have to say in advance that they're coming. You might think all those new tourists turning up in the Homeland House would bother her, but the differences between them are too small for that: some wear North Face jackets, some wear Jack Wolfskin jackets. Some want to know if there really isn't a restaurant around here open on a Monday (yes, there is, but you have to go to Feldberg), others want to use the toilet (down the corridor, door to the right of the TV set). That's all the difference there is to it.

Sometimes she calls from the Homeland House at night. "I *mustn't* come home tonight." Right. I fetch Pa, and all three of us spend the night in the Homeland House.

I think that if for some reason or other the rapeseed wasn't to come into flower, Ma would run amok in the fields with her gun. Yup, her gun, that's another thing.

I once asked whether she was a good shot.

Yes, she said, just not very quick off the mark.

Ma is funny, that's for sure. She doesn't function like anyone else I know, but then again she does really: she wants to get through the day somehow. She's never nasty. Likes everyone except for people she's right not to like. Reads a lot. Votes for the Left. But then she goes and cooks nothing but stuff with beetroot in it for two weeks, which is great because beetroot is great, but eating beetroot every day for two weeks on end, well, that's different.

All the same, Ma is no crazier than the rest of us. You don't have to take it seriously when she does something wild like getting a gun (it was for security). Pa says, even if what she does seems strange, take it seriously. Yes, strange, but suppose it's also true and not so harmless?

That about levitating is harmless. Ma says she can make small objects levitate. I'm not arguing. Maybe it's her weight that does it. Everything else around my 130-kilo Ma loses mass by comparison, I feel lighter myself. She sits on her sofa, practicing on mini-carrots. She holds a mini-carrot between her fingers and concentrates on it.

I ask why she's doing that. Why does she want things to levitate?

To make people happy.

That's my Ma for you: wants to make people happy.

Ma's reached her limit. I get that much. Could be she thinks up stuff like levitation to move back from the limit a bit. Maybe she thinks that as long as she *can't* do it, *can't* make things levitate, everything's okay with her. And if she really has a gun so as to feel more secure, then that's okay too. If she only thought that up about the gun and feels better all the same, so much the better. I'm her son. Ma could never shoot anyone. (Where and when it's okay by you, don't change anything about that where and when.)

This year her springtime blues went on until the first of May, which was a really warm day. Ma got up and made beetroot with fried eggs for breakfast, so we knew she was feeling better. Then she lay down on her stomach in the garden and rowed in the air with her hands, sweating like an iceberg, all over bits of grass from head to toe.

Me: "Ma, what are you doing?"

Ma: "Learning to swim."

After an hour of that she runs out into the road, turns off toward the promenade, going faster and faster, an outsize version of Sebastian Vettel, runs to the landing stage by the ferry boathouse, cuts in past the ferryman and jumps into the lake like a bomb, throwing up water to form new landscapes.

Pa and I go after her, worried. Well, of course we're worried. But Ma was happy. Ma was swimming. It's not cold, come on in, you cowards! The ferryman is in already. Ma and the ferryman swimming a race. Ma lets him win.

Maybe she could always swim, and Pa didn't know. Maybe she learned to swim that day in the garden. At least my Ma didn't sink. "Yoo-hoo!" cried my Ma.

IN THE YEAR OF OUR LORD 1590, AT THE ANNA Feast, there was a tightrope-walker present who fasten'd his rope above the Church Gable, fixing the other End to the Berlin Gate, so that he flew down from the Gable to the Gate uninjur'd, all the While pushing a Handcart!

On that same Day, however, there was a Cutpurse at large in the Crowd, the latter being distracted by the Tightrope Dancer, so that there was great Suspicion of the Dancer as being one of a Pair of Rogues!

Thus was it confirm'd again that 'tis not Opportunity maketh Thieves, but Opportunity is the greatest Thief itself.

THE NIGHT BEFORE THE FEAST, ON THE FIELD, with his forehead on the steering wheel: Wilfried Schramm, former Lieutenant-Colonel, then a forester, now retired and also moonlighting for Von Blankenburg Agricultural Machinery. On average, more dead drivers lie with their heads on their steering wheels in the German TV series *Crime Scene* in any one year than in six selected American crime series in the same space of time.

Herr Schramm is a critical man. Herr Schramm thinks it's silly to have so many dead drivers in *Crime Scene* lying with their heads on their steering wheels. Sometimes it's their cheeks on the steering wheel, and the face is all crumpled up, but usually it's the forehead. Herr Schramm is sure of it; when yet another body lies like that, Herr Schramm switches channels.

So Herr Schramm is lying with his head on the steering wheel, whistling the theme tune of *Crime Scene*. Herr Schramm imagines what it would be like if an episode of *Crime Scene* were set in Fürstenfelde. Which death would be most suitable for the episode? Not counting his own. Among the top three would probably be: the Chinese man, the tractor and Frau Rebe. By the tractor he means Rüdiger under the tractor.

The Chinese would be good, because it probably wasn't self-defense as everyone claimed. But the Chinese was, well, Chinese, and the murderer was someone from here. However, that was almost a century ago, the first episode of *Crime Scene* set in Fürstenfelde doesn't have to be that far back in history.

The tractor would be better. Rüdiger lay dead under it all night. And Rüdiger's dog brought him a dead pigeon all the same. Put it down beside his head, terrible. Drunk as a skunk, people said, an accident. The tractor under which Rüdiger was lying was Rüdiger's tractor and it stood on Rüdiger's farm. Rolled backward. And the dead pigeon was lying there in the morning. Terrible.

"I don't know." Herr Schramm has stopped whistling. His voice inside the car sounds like some other person's voice, any voice, not his. Because it's like this, thinks Herr Schramm: first, Rüdiger had a good head for liquor. Herr Schramm found that out by comparison with his own headache on several occasions. And second, he knew his tractors better than Herr Schramm knew the *Crime Scene* theme tune, and a tune like that is a lot simpler than a tractor. Although he has just this minute noticed how tiring the tune is to whistle. Yes, and third, a few months after Rüdiger's death von Blankenburg finally managed to buy Rüdiger's agricultural machinery business. The heirs weren't objecting, unlike Rüdiger.

Herr Schramm goes on whistling.

But Frau Rebe's would be the best case all the same. On 3 October, it had been, in 1990. Who'd have thought it? Eleven stab wounds. Anyone who knew Frau Rebe, and that was a lot of people, couldn't really celebrate 3 October after that, not that many really do celebrate it, and there you go, that shows how little some in Fürstenfelde, the murderer included, thought of German Reunification.

Anyway, the murderer had been an apprentice of her husband's. He always looked at Frau Rebe when she came into the works, and he imagined her naked, he wanted her to undress for him. But unfortunately she didn't want to do that, and we have to say she really was very good-looking, and then he helped himself, eleven times.

Someone called Sigrun, a psychiatrist, with a name like that Herr Schramm isn't quite sure whether a man or a woman, has found out that on average women are more creative killers than men. And in crimes where a knife is used, women are stabbed more times than men.

However, sometimes Herr Schramm wonders: who actually thinks up the questions to ask about these statistics? And then he's glad that the people who think them up exist. Herr Schramm believes in talent, Herr Schramm thinks that he himself would have been talented in thinking up such questions, always thinking of questions to ask himself and hundreds of other people wouldn't have been a bad career for him back then.

Of course the fact that Frau Rebe was good-looking is no excuse for murder.

Herr Schramm had liked Rüdiger. He was Herr Schramm's first boss after the fall of the Wall. Rüdiger had taught him a few things about tractors, or he surely wouldn't have been taken on later by Von Blankenburg Agricultural Machinery.

Herr Schramm whistles the *Crime Scene* tune; well, so it didn't work with the car, he'll have to use his pistol after all.

The Rebe case would have been a good one, because a few days after the murder her husband was taken in by the police. To this day no one knows why. Jealous husband, wife generous with her favors. People will always talk. Then the apprentice was arrested, and Herr Rebe was a free man again.

The boy never admitted it. He did admit that he'd have liked to take a look under Frau Rebe's coat, yes. And that on the night of the crime, it was the night before the Feast back then, too, he'd asked if he could look. He'd really just wanted to look, not touch. Under her beautiful coat. But she wouldn't let him. In the end they both went their separate ways. There wasn't any more to admit, he said.

Herr Schramm whistles, and Herr Schramm puts the pistol to his temple, but he raises his head from the steering wheel, so that when he's dead he won't look like one of those dead drivers at the wheel in *Crime Scene*. He even tries to slip down between the seats, so as to make quite sure, but there is a knocking on the pane. A young woman is standing there, making the gesture that means: wind down the window, although even Schramm's old Golf has windows that go down automatically.

18 MARCH 1927. INCIDENT HAS FATAL OUTCOME.

A Chinaman peddling his wares from door to door without an official permit was stopped by Police Sergeant Polster. The Chinaman spoke angrily to Polster and attacked him violently, so that the Sergeant was obliged to make use of his sword. When the Chinaman wrenched the sword from his grasp and attacked the officer with it himself, Polster fired his pistol and struck his opponent down. The Chinaman, severely injured, was taken to hospital in Prenzlau, where he passed away soon afterward.

No one could understand his last words.

WE TAKE AN INTEREST IN THE ELECTRONIC LOCK
on the massive oak door to the Archivarium. The Homeland
House was renovated in 2011, and the old padlock was replaced
by a lock with a code that you have to tap in. 2011 was 700
years after the first mention of Fürstenfelde in the records,
and between January and July three young drivers collided
with the plane trees. One of them did not survive: Thorsten
Brandt, a passionate computer-game player, placed third at
the German Counter-Strike Championship in the team event.

Only the History Society knows the code.

We take an interest in all that secrecy.

The Homeland House celebrated the 700th anniversary
of Fürstenfelde with an Open Day. Even the Archivarium
was to be opened. Frau Schwermuth wore local costume,
although it wasn't 100 percent certain what locality the costume came from. The Mayor made a speech, mentioning
the new lock among other things. She called Fürstenfelde
a site, because that always sounds like new jobs. She waved
her arms about as if showing the size of a very large fish.
Then Frau Schwermuth tapped the code into the lock, and
the massive wooden door swung open, buzzing.

Ooh, aah, applause.

The walls were covered with sheets, but the room was
empty except for a Perspex podium with a stack of papers

on it, and about eight members of the Sound and Smoke Firefighters' choir. They had had to wait in that little room behind the locked door for an hour because of delays to the planned course of events. They looked annoyed and heated.

The papers were the original manuscripts of the chronicle of the village by Paul Wiese, which is famous all over the village. Frau Schwermuth had "acquired" the chronicle from the Museum of Brandenburg History for the anniversary celebrations.

We were disappointed. We had hoped for better from the Archivarium. Frau Schwermuth explained that for want of suitable means of displaying them, and in the expectation of large crowds, she had been obliged to take the items in the Archivarium, which after all were valuable, to be kept in a place of safety. Not everyone went along with that, but fair enough.

Sound and Smoke gave it all they had. The acoustics of the cellar were sensational. Senior citizens went red in the face, junior citizens took their hands out of their pockets. The vaulted room was very full. The unhewn rock of the walls was sweating. The air almost ran out with all those people in the cellar, just ask Frau Kranz.

Our historical interest in Paul Wiese is confined, at the most, to Paul Wiese's melancholy. In his day, Wiese tried to compile records of all the houses in the village and their inhabitants. Such-and-such a house built at this or that time by such-and-such a person, passed into the possession of whatsisname, fell into ruin at such-and-such a time or was still standing. A joke here, an anecdote there. Sentences beginning "Ah!" and charmingly excited, as melancholics tend to be when they have a good story to tell. Paul Wiese liked Fürstenfelde. A man who longed for steadiness in unsteady times.

The old windmill was demolished in 1930. I was there to see it come down. The demolition was necessary; it was extremely dilapidated. In 1945 the miller's house burned down and was destroyed. I saw the flames. No one had to light a fire. What will happen now we cannot tell. Everything is transitory. . .

There's a portrait of Paul Wiese, a charcoal sketch done by Frau Kranz from a photograph. A man with a round head and a small moustache. His eyes are full of regret. We take a historical interest in whatever Wiese's eyes are regretting.

We are even more interested to know why, on the Open Day at the Homeland House, all the other doors had to be locked while the door of the Archivarium was open. Even the doors on the ground floor, and even after Frau Kranz was left gasping for air when the Firefighters' choir sang the folk song "Cling-clang," and Imboden only just managed to catch her before she fell down in a faint as the singers reached "the tolling bell."

Cling-clang, drink up and sing! / Tomorrow may yet bring / The ringing of a knell. / The world may fall apart / but sing with all your heart / above the tolling bell.

For the curious, copies of Wiese's melancholy writing were available next day, ready for anyone on a little table between the tiled stoves.

To this day, however, no one has had a sight of the archives. Aren't archives there to be consulted? Ah, but there is so much material, says Frau Schwermuth, and it hasn't all been properly assessed yet. In addition, some of the documents are so fragile that they seem to tremble when you look at them for any length of time. So fragile and so valuable.

Well, let's hope they're valuable! If not, the parish would hardly have paid good money for the new lock and the humidity-regulating thingummy, while the *Nordkurier* complains that the long-distance cycle path is in a "shocking" condition where it reaches Fürstenfelde; the last time it was cleared was when Rudolf Scharping, the cycling politician, rode from Berlin to Usedom when he was standing for Chancellor.

Okay, so it's not quite true that we don't get a sight of the archives. Frau Schwermuth provides it. She notes down what we want to know, and makes copies if she finds anything. Or doesn't make copies, but says, "Come back the day after tomorrow," and we do go back the day after tomorrow. And if it takes longer than that, she says, "Things don't move as quickly as all that in the past," or something similar, and her heavy head sways on the neck under it, which is much too thin, like those long rocking horses you see in kids' playgrounds going up and down on their metal springs.

We are surprised that no stories are growing and proliferating around the room in the cellar. That sort of thing usually happens when we come across cellars, locked rooms and open questions. We take a historical interest in the non-proliferation of stories. For instance, why Paul Wiese's entry on House Number 11, today the Homeland House, ends with an incomplete sentence: *In the cellar of the house I found, in a small room. . .*

We take an interest in incomplete sentences.

We take an enormous interest in when the window of the Homeland House was broken into, and who it was that Uwe Hirtentäschel saw from his studio moving around: the shape of someone, and a beam of light traveling over the wall.

Now that, yes, that is really interesting.

IN THE YEAR OF OUR LORD 1592 THERE WAS A VERY
wet summer, during which Season the Rain fell in Cloudbursts,
and the Fields and Meadows were flooded, Gardens laid Waste,
and the Great Lake rose so high that the Carp in the Pond
swam out of that Same. Cattle and Sheep also contracted the
Rot, of which many did die, and whole Flocks and Herds
perish'd, and the same was noted of Hares. Then there was in
the Autumn a terrible Drought, making the Land intractable
to work and Harvest very poor. The People, being in great
Want, fear'd the Winter, and Famine threaten'd.

On the Morning of the second Day of November, however,
there appear'd under the Oak Tree hard by the Church five
Wagons full of Grain, Butter, dried Meat and Beer, the Origin
whereof None could explain. The Church expected Prayers
of Thanksgiving, yet it remained empty. However, a Quarrel
had broken out concerning the rightful Owner of the Food,
in uncouth and unChristian Fashion, like the Brute Beasts,
and a Fox was even to be seen watching, Every Man took
what he could carry, and tried to trip up his Neighbor who
was carrying more.

But Joy in the Booty did not last long; that Miracle fail'd
as quickly as it Came. The Foodstuffs vanished once more
from Cellars, Storehouses, Chambers and Halls, sometimes
even from Tables.

Where did it go? None could say.

And why? Some guess'd, and came to Church in a penitent Condition.

UWE HIRTENTÄSCHEL LEAVES THE PARSONAGE AND steps out into the night, only for a moment, but long enough to be drawn into our round dance. The ferryman takes his left hand, we take his right hand. Let's just give him a moment to update his placard on the oak in front of the church.

> *On 21st September, at 5.30 p.m., the new basic course on the Christian faith begins at Fürstenfelde parsonage. We will devote ourselves to the subject of "Rapture" on the occasion of the Anna Feast. More information available from: heilands@freenet.de*

Above the date he wrote in red marker: TODAY!!! and added a * before the T.

Uwe Hirtentäschel looks after the church, keeps it clean, encourages other people to visit it, talks to them benevolently about the faith. He provides them with candles and incense sticks, plays the saxophone in front of the altar, and after the service he leaves the radio playing, so that silence won't seem to descend so suddenly. He takes care of the place, and that's good; taking care of things is always good.

Hirtentäschel's business card shows Jesus as the Good Shepherd, surrounded by sheep, holding a little lamb in his arms. If you tilt the card Jesus raises his arm and the lamb raises its head. On the back is the bit from the Gospel of St John about Jesus being the light of the world, so we must follow him and not walk in darkness.

Uwe Hirtentäschel has been saved. Either the ferryman or an angel saved him. Hirtentäschel is grateful for that every day. Every day, except when the weather is bad, Hirtentäschel puts up a folding table under the oak by the parsonage well, and serves tea and biscuits. All are welcome. Frau Schober made him a crochet tablecloth. She and Frau Steiner usually sit at his table, because they just happen to be in the area. They are both on the point of retiring, but Frau Steiner is very well preserved. She still does some newspaper delivery rounds to make ends meet, and Frau Schober sews and crochets. And then they sit at Uwe's table in the middle of the day. There's not much else going on at that time, the house is empty anyway, the Ossis on the midday TV program are always a bad lot and incorrigible. Only in the evening are there normal Ossis like you and us on TV, in *Police Call* and athletics and *Wife Swap*. The church oak tree provides shade in summer, and the optimism of the reformed Hirtentäschel provides warmth in winter.

Hirtentäschel puts the marker away and sets off for the parsonage. It is in Karl-Marx-Strasse, of all places, on the corner of Thälmann-Strasse. He has a small apartment and his studio on the top floor. Hirtentäschel's latest work of art, done for the Feast, is stretched between the branches of the oak. It consists of white scarves. Frau Schober likes the scarves but doesn't know what they are meant to be. It would be embarrassing to ask the artist in case she looked stupid. She would far rather have been able to say, "What lovely, lovely angels' wings!" than be guessing, "Are those half-moons?" Or, "Is the white something to do with heroin?" To be honest, we don't know the answer either, but they make a nice noise fluttering in the wind.

Uwe Hirtentäschel speaks softly and hardly ever asks questions. He wears only white or black clothes, to reflect the light and shade of his life story. He doesn't mind showing his bald patch, and his glasses have thick lenses because he's almost blind. That comes of the heroin. It was blinding him for years, he says, both spiritually and literally. Remarks like that show how serious his conversion is. It's easy and pleasant to listen to someone who hardly ever tries to be funny.

Up on the top floor of the parsonage, Hirtentäschel goes on making his little figures of angels. He's tired, but he will carve one or two more, one or two more tonight.

The village knows and likes the story of his enlightenment. He also tells it, unasked, to tourists when they stay to drink tea after looking round the church. He likes telling the story, because it was more important than anything else in his life, and because all of us—if we're honest—are waiting for a miracle, so we like to hear about one.

Uwe Hirtentäschel was born in Fürstenfelde, and at the age of fifteen he ran away from Fürstenfelde. He describes the next fifteen years as a single moment and a never-ending trip.

It had been a time full of small flashes of enlightenment in his drugged intoxication. He calls them "disorientations": false, uncertain joys, siren songs. Sins. But then he had his great epiphany, when he was "found." It happened in Fürstenfelde.

After years of taking drugs and addiction, Hirtentäschel passed the Woldegk Gate on his way to the Baltic early one morning, and there was the old wall, there were the lakes, there was the promenade, there was the ferry boathouse, all the same as ever, and he got out, *had* to get out, sat down beside the lake and drank perhaps his sixth beer of the day, and then the ferryman came by. He recognized Hirtentäschel. He recognized the boy who had just disappeared one day, leaving his parents with a thousand questions. The ferryman didn't know about the disorientations, says Hirtentäschel, but he surely recognized his, Hirtentäschel's, demons.

He took Hirtentäschel out on a boat trip with him and insisted on his lending a hand. As soon as someone comes back, Hirtentäschel cried, you want them doing your work for you, but the ferryman thought that was funny. Hirtentäschel rowing, all skin and bones. He found it terribly difficult. In the middle of the lake he couldn't row any more. Then the ferryman made him promise something. He wanted Hirtentäschel to listen to him, he wanted to tell him a story. Hirtentäschel agreed, and listened, but he couldn't concentrate, and to this day he doesn't know what the story was about. They had reached the little island with the barn on it. Hirtentäschel got out, and as soon as he turned round he saw that he was alone, surrounded by tall grass and insects. "I called to the ferryman, but only a jay answered. I wanted to get back to the water, but the water had disappeared too, I couldn't find the water any more, imagine that, and you'll know what a bad state I was in."

At this point Uwe Hirtentäschel liked to pause. Frau Steiner and Frau Schober have heard the story so often before that, at the mention of the jay, their lips form the word "jay" soundlessly, and they nod to one another, just as they did today when he was telling his story to a man who had come to dive in the lake, and they do the same with the words "gloomy" and "brittle" in the next sentence: "All was dark and gloomy inside my head," says Hirtentäschel, "and my mind was brittle, and I saw a weeping willow with moss growing over it, soft, thick moss, so I was going to lie down on the moss, smoke a joint, ease myself out of it, but then something hit the nape of my neck, and I fell over, then something hit my back once, twice, it hurt like hell, it was doing me in, finishing me off, and there was absolutely nothing I could do about it. The ferryman was thrashing me! He hit me with an oar, he hit my head, my arm. I couldn't let myself lose consciousness, I wanted to see the ferryman above me with his beard full of grass. The blows came raining down on me, my light, I thought, my protector, I thought—then it all went black.

"When I came back to my senses, I was lying naked as a blade of grass on the moss. It was dark. The half-moon hung above me, and it would have been better if it had been a full moon, but never mind that. A wind was blowing over the lake, over there was the village and the kindly church spire. The ferryman was standing in the water, in the light cast by a strange stone. He was catching fish with his bare hands. Ten or fifteen pike were lying in his boat, thrashing their tails about, dying. I was dead already. I lay down with the fish. I knew something. There was something I knew, and that was the very first time I could say, with certainty: I know. The stone shone brighter than the moon. The ferryman was an angel on earth. He had taken my old life away from me and found me a new one. That was what I knew.

"The ferryman took me back to the village. I felt no pain, there was no trace of the blows to be seen—he had healed me. I promised to serve him. The ferryman asked if I was still on a druggy trip, and where I was going to stay. I'd hoped he would tell me. Then I found out that my parents had moved away years ago, but there was a room vacant in the parsonage. The parsonage, of course. I'm still living in that room today."

In his room, Uwe Hirtentäschel yawns. The rain beating on the window makes him sleepy. He clears away his tools. The angels' wings quiver in the oak tree, the half-moons, the oars, the tears. Hirtentäschel sweeps the floor of his studio. He's opening it tomorrow for those who take an interest in art. He has also managed to sell a few things these last years. He doesn't make much money, but it's enough, it's enough.

Children like his little wooden angels. He displays them in the bathtub: twenty little angels in twenty little boats with forty little oars, and if a child shows an interest in the angels, Uwe Hirtentäschel puts his arm in the water and the boats bob up and down.

IN THE YEAR 1658, ABOUT MICHAELMAS-TIDE, THE Well was sunk for the Parsonage, partly for the sake of Convenience, partly to free the Cellar of Water before the Anna Feast, and in the Hole a Piece of Chopp't Wood was found, of the Size of a Hand. Since this Piece of Wood was as much as the Height of two Men down in the Earth, and since the various different Strata of the Soil were distinctly visible, when the Question of how the Wood came to be so deep in the Earth is raised, I can say only that the aforesaid Item must date from before the Deluge.

FRAU SCHWERMUTH'S TELEPHONE RINGS. IT'S Hirtentäschel on the line. He wants to know what she is doing at the moment. Frau Schwermuth is eating mini-carrots and watching *Buffy*. That was what Hirtentäschel thought, and by that he doesn't mean the vegetables and the vampire-slayer, but the fact that it's not Frau Schwermuth in the Homeland House with her flashlight. Just a moment. Someone's in the Homeland House now, does he mean? Yes, now. Hirtentäschel is looking down, and someone is slinking about inside the House. Slinking? Yes, slinking could be the word, anyway not switching on the lights. And another thing: before that, Anna Geher collapsed outside the House, and along came two young fellows, one tall as a beanpole and the other small and stout, and helped her. And before *that*, he could swear, a fox—Uwe?—came out of the House—Uwe, please stick to the point! Can he recognize anyone? Only a silhouette, tall and thin. It's dark, and his eyes, as she knows. . . Yes, Uwe, but you have glasses! Of course he has glasses!—We ourselves are getting impatient now; those two just won't stick to the point, although the point is perfectly simple when the beam of a flashlight, or a flashlight app, is wandering over the wall of a building by night and there's a broken window standing open, although it seems that Hirtentäschel hasn't noticed the window yet.

Uwe, hang on. Frau Schwermuth clears her throat. There's someone at the door, please stay on the line. . .

Sorry, Uwe. That was Zieschke just now. It's all been dealt with. The power went off again. . . no, I've no idea why, maybe mice like before, or the lightning just now. . . No, he'll see to the Homeland House in the morning, I'm only just back from cycling. . . I don't know, maybe something for the auction.

So says Frau Schwermuth, adding that she'll go right over and take Zieschke the key to the fuse box. Yes, no, everything's fine, is it all okay about coffee and cake for Hirtentäschel's talk? Yes, fine. You too, thanks. Thank you, Uwe. Yes. Yes. Goodnight.

Frau Schwermuth clears her throat. Frau Schwermuth eats a mini-carrot. Her pupils move from extreme left to extreme right.

THE STREETLAMP OUTSIDE THE HOMELAND HOUSE isn't working. The gate at the entrance shouldn't be open. Johann shines light in from his mobile. There are bits of glass on the ground. The windowpane is broken, the window's open. Ma made that crochet-work curtain.

He shouldn't go in there; he climbs in. Neither Lada nor Suzi nor his half-elf would have done so. The lights won't switch on. On the other hand, Lada and Suzi and in particular Mustard-Micha would be much more likely candidates to do a thing like that here. A thing like what? Talk about it sometimes, anyway. Not about the Homeland House, of course, what is there to nick in here? Johann shines the flashlight app into the front room. Leaves, not very many of them, are lying on the floor, scattered by a gust of wind. It wouldn't be the first time for Mustard-Micha—just ask Lütti at the fuel station in Woldegk. Micha attacked Lütti twice. A gas gun and an Elvis mask, but as soon as he opened his mouth Lütti knew it was Micha under the mask, they'd sort of known each other for ever, since their fathers left them before they were born, their mothers are still best friends today. Lütti didn't show that he knew who it was either time, so as not to hurt Micha's feelings. A year later Micha organized a booze-up to make things okay and apologized to Lütti. "It wasn't anything to do with you personally." Lütti understood that and accepted the apology.

The booze-up to make things okay was also a celebration of Micha being out of jail. And then Lütti apologized too, because he hadn't meant it personally either when he shopped Micha, but twice was once too many. Naturally Micha also understood that, and accepted the apology.

But seriously, what was there to nick in here? The GDR stuff? Everyone had plenty of that at home. As long as a GDR hairdryer is still getting hair dry somewhere or other, the GDR isn't dead.

The door to the cellar steps is open, a little light comes up from down below. However, the light on the steps isn't working. Johann listens. "Hello?—Ma?"

He shouldn't go down there; he does go down there. A long corridor, with the large door at the end of it standing open. The light is coming from the room beyond the door. The Archivarium. Ma is always talking about her Archivarium. It would break her heart if someone—

Johann knows the room from the 700th anniversary celebrations, when it was nearly empty. Now it is stuffed full of books, standing on shelves and on top of other books, with stacks of papers everywhere. In the corner there is a fine pair of antlers. In the middle of the room there is a table with writing materials, a magnifying glass and even more paper on it.

Best of all is the leather: four gigantic leather wall hangings or whatever you'd call them, made up of separate pieces of leather. Johann runs his fingers over one of them; it is cool. There are signs on it, barely legible characters. A date:

September 1636. Each single piece making up one of the four hangings is written on and dated. It is as if the room had a skin made of leather and writing.

A mouse makes Johann jump as it scurries through the room, disappearing behind a chest. Should he phone Ma, or call the cops at once? But he can't get reception down here. Maybe it was only the wind that broke the window upstairs. But then why is the door here open?

A gigantic folio volume lies on the reading desk, its finely decorated pages charred. Johann takes a photo of the book. The lovely old writing. He really wanted to make sure that the bells were all right. But since he's here. . .

The village was sitting underground, all in a long row, and the earth was cold, and when a chicken began clucking comfortably Barth the blacksmith wrung its neck, and no one said a word.

Suddenly there's a sound like fine sand trickling down. Oh shit. Johann turns round. There's light in the corridor again, a shadow outside the door—he runs toward it—but it closes as he drums his fists on it, shouting.

The display on the electronic lock changes from green to red.

EARLY IN THE YEAR OF OUR LORD 1594, THERE CAME a wondrous procession to Fürstenfelde. Several Carts drawn by Horses and Oxen stopp'd outside the Prenzlau Gate, whereupon men and women jumped down from the said Carts, danc'd and sang and all rac'd about freely, but some lay in Cheynes howling and screaming pitifully, or speaking in strange Tongues.

From out of their turbulent Midst two Men stepped out before the assembled Village, one being tall and one short, both with long Beards and strange forreyn Clothing of fine Fabrick in Motley Hues. Without beating about the Bush, they offered a strange Trade: let the Village bring them, before Morning, all its Dullards, Lunatics, the Feeble-Minded, Fantastics, Deranged and Demented, all those possess'd of Devils and assail'd by Despair, that they be brought to the Northern Sea, where a great sea-going Vessel waited to take them Aboard, as was the Custom, for ever and a Day, the cost being ten Thalers for one such Person.

After this a great Silence fell, into which the Smaller Man cried: We know it is not an Easy Thing to part with your own Kin, yet surely your Lives would be greatly Eased thereafter. See them now making merry, and well cared for, with their own Ilk. And when you think you may fall into Despair yourselves, picture the delightful Sea Voyage they are making!

The Village assembled and debated what were Good and Christian to do. They could not tell, and each made his own Decision.

There was no Peace that Night for the screaming of the Lunatics and the playing of all Manner of Lutes and the like Stringed Instruments. In the Morning the Procession went on, and some, aye, some of us with it.

And if you ever be faring in a Ship on the High Seas, then know that you may at any time meet with a Ship of Fools.

O praise the unfathomable Mercy of God.

THERE IS A SMALL TV SET ON THE CHEST OF DRAWERS
beside the visitors' toilet in the Homeland House. The TV has
an integrated video recorder. We think that is a good, practical
idea, and we are surprised and sorry that such combi-sets are
not so common these days.

What the TV shows confuses us. The TV transmits exclusively the horoscope section of the Breakfast TV program on
Sat 1. Frau Schwermuth records it every morning and keeps it
running nonstop until it's time to close the Homeland House.
The horoscope lady is called Britta Hansen. The village has
known Britta since she was *that* high.

We're confused because the TV is on now, at this time of
day, with Frau Schwermuth doing knee-bends in front of it.

Britta Hansen says: *Think of every star sign as telling its
own story. You are the hero or heroine of that story as you move
past the signs.*

The color adjustment can't be regulated any more. Britta
Hansen's jacket, which is very red anyway, looks as if it were
blazing brightly as she thinks out loud about our star signs.

After reaching the Homeland House, Frau Schwermuth
first locked the Archivarium properly. At least that meant
Jochim the Tinker was in his proper place and couldn't do any
damage. Then she sorted the papers on her desk and stuck a
newspaper over the broken window. And now she is doing

exercises and wondering how to proceed as Britta Hansen, in a very red dress and shiny nylons, devotes herself to the subject of Libra, the Scales.

Venus, forever in love, gives you an unexpected romantic and emotional adventure. Take what she offers, and who can tell, you too could know the magic of eternal love.

A cardboard notice above the TV set says: THE STARS WITH BRITTA HANSEN. Hansen is a qualified astrologer. She draws conclusions about people and their feelings from the position of the heavenly bodies in the sky. The universe is an open book; Britta Hansen translates it into German.

Hardly anyone goes to the visitors' toilet without stopping to look at the stars. That's what happens when there's a flickering screen in a dimly lit corridor. Visitors—people who used to live in Fürstenfelde, old folk, tourists wallowing in homesickness—stare at Britta Hansen's bright red jacket. Many children, seeing the set, have lost interest in the horse-shoeing demonstration in the yard, and have had to be rescued from the nonstop horoscopes by their ambitious mothers, who didn't bring them on a two-hour journey to watch TV but to see a horse shod.

Visitors from outside the village don't know what to make of their encounter with Britta Hansen. Most of them don't like to talk about it. Some think the TV set is part of the exhibition, an everyday item from the GDR, but that's wrong, the TV set is an everyday item from Czechoslovakia in 1988. Very few venture to ask what horoscopes have to do with Fürstenfelde or the Homeland House. It could be that they've failed to understand something, that something has escaped them, and if that something is also to do with the GDR, people often feel very uncomfortable about it. Frau Schwermuth gives the braver visitors one of Britta Hansen's business cards. You can get Britta to describe your own interior landscape for a fee of 100 euros.

This weekend the Sun meets Neptune, there is magic in the air, enough to amount to divine providence.

Even Frau Schwermuth doesn't always understand everything she says.

The soap dispenser in the visitors' toilet hasn't been refilled for two years. If people from the village go to the visitors' toilet they may stop and say, "Ah, there's Britta," to the TV set. But the vast majority don't talk to it.

Britta Hansen's hair is red, although just how red isn't clear. Frau Schwermuth likes it when Britta wears her cowboy hat with a denim shirt and cowboy boots. She is surprisingly often right when she says what will happen in the next few days.

The weekend will be dynamic, heated and fast-moving. Saturday begins in confusion. If you happen to suffer from insomnia, expect a sleepless night. Give all you've got, and you will find the sense in it. That, for instance, is what she predicted on Friday for Cancer, the Crab. Frau Schwermuth loosens up her neck muscles. Her star sign is the Crab.

Every year Frau Schwermuth invites Breakfast TV to the Anna Feast. An outside transmission about the festivities would be great. A fax goes to the TV station and another to

Britta Hansen. Frau Schwermuth always gets a reply from Frau Hansen. Britta would really love to come, she says, but unfortunately she's not the one who makes such decisions, her hands are tied.

At the end of her horoscopes Britta Hansen quotes a proverb, an old saying, or a quotation from some famous person: *If you are going the wrong way, the faster you walk the more lost you will be.*

Frau Schwermuth once said that even as a child Britta was interested in the sky, which is particularly beautiful in these parts. She really wanted to study physics but, fair enough, it turned into something like metaphysics. "Metaphysics between us and the stars."

Frau Schwermuth's eyes glow as she looks at the unblinking screen. Now and then her pupils move to the extreme left and then the extreme right. *All of life,* says Britta Hansen, smiling at Frau Schwermuth, *is a matter of beginning again.*

"Very true," whispers Frau Schwermuth. She switches the TV off and goes down to the cellar. She has a few more questions for the tinker.

Fürstenfelde, Brandenburg. Number of inhabitants: dropping. We have a sign up at the entrance to the village. *Welcome to the Uckermark. The countryside gets beautiful here.* Number of trees marked on the up-to-date walkers' map as "individual trees worth seeing": two.

Whatever you've heard about us that doesn't come from ourselves is wrong. This village is not like what they say in the tourist guides, the books, the demographic studies. If a window gets broken somewhere here, and stands open, we're more afraid of what might get out through it than what might get in.

And you mustn't believe that stupid map: we have a third individual tree worth seeing—the oak in the field on Geher's Farm. They like to leave it out of guides because it's as crooked as backache, and because the field makes no sense for even the most ambitious walker, although the tree is really old and any other 500-year-old oak has a blog of its own.

But the fact is that many people were hanged from that oak tree over the centuries, and we sometimes feel so angry that we'd like to have the whole field covered with cement, not because we're angry with the field and the oak tree, but because apart from Frau Schwermuth no one's interested. There isn't even a plaque about it anywhere.

But we digress.

On such a night as this.

AT WHITSUNTIDE IN THE YEAR OF OUR LORD 1619, a farm worker by the name of Drewes was stabbed. The Murderer ran away, and did not return for Eight Years, but in the end came back of his own Accord, believing that the Crime would have been Forgot. He was taken, kept close confin'd, and met his well-deserv'd End hanging from a Rope.

SO HERR SCHRAMM, FORMERLY LIEUTENANT-Colonel, forester, pensioner, takes the pistol away from his temple and unlocks the car door for the girl. Anna turns the beam of her headlight on him.

"What are you doing with that pistol?"

She dazzles him; it's like being interrogated.

"Hmm, well."

"Put it away."

Herr Schramm puts the pistol away in his tracksuit trousers.

Anna gets into the passenger seat.

"Schramm. Pleased to meet you."

"I know who you are." Anna switches the interior light of the car on and her headlight off.

"Mhm," says Herr Schramm. He rubs his eyes. He feels sad to realize that he is rubbing his eyes, so he asks, "What are you doing out here?"

"Running."

"That's dangerous."

"I'm also getting into cars with crazy guys carrying guns in a field in the middle of the night."

Herr Schramm turns away. There is the night, there is the tree, and there is the field. Anna is looking steadfastly at him. He has bags under his eyes, broken veins on his nose, little hairs in his ears. Herr Schramm looks like someone who doesn't have ambitious plans for his body these days.

"I'm not crazy," says Herr Schramm.

Unshaven, greasy hair. Herr Schramm looks like someone who goes to sleep on the toilet with his toothbrush in his mouth. Who wakes up, screaming, and doesn't know when or where he is. If that were so, at least Schramm would say, honestly, why the nightmare? But what good does that do?

The vest and tracksuit trousers, his unshaven face and general look of decrepitude are deceptive. Over the last few days Herr Schramm hasn't done much, that's all. He washes with a mild, cream soap, without overdoing it. He regularly cleans his house, except for on top of the cupboards, because why bother? He even looks after his little garden the way others might look after a family member—reluctantly and with a sense of duty. All those tiresome little jobs to be done: turning over the soil, weeding, bush tomatoes, birthdays, shopping, visits to old people's homes. His father the drunk had the same little broken veins, it's hereditary. Statistically. Herr Schramm also knows that regularly washing the hair weakens it. It can't cope so well with the artificial effect of the shampoo. That's what happens to a man in general when he lets things go.

Anna takes a deep breath. It works okay. She says, "You were going to kill yourself."

Herr Schramm says, "Right."

Anna says, "What do I do now?"

Herr Schramm tries to start the car, but the engine won't catch.

"When you go running," says Herr Schramm, "I suppose you don't take cigarettes with you?"

"I don't smoke at all."

"Do you have your ID on you?"

"What for?"

"I don't have mine on me. No driving license, nothing. You could get me some cigarettes. Or if not you could fetch your ID and then get me some cigarettes."

"Why don't you go and fetch yours?"

"I won't have the time before I commit suicide."

Anna doesn't want to laugh, but she does, briefly. Her breath immediately comes with difficulty.

"I want to smoke another cigarette," says Herr Schramm. "The tank's empty, and I live out there toward Parmen, while you live here only just beyond the rise in the ground. You're the toymaker Geher's granddaughter, aren't you? We can do it within ten minutes, and then we each go our own way."

Anna shakes her head. No, she is not leaving him alone. If need be she'll take him somewhere. Home, to his family. Does he have a family? Is he married?

Herr Schramm has a family, but you know how it is. And women? He thought about women one last time in the summer, weighing up the pros and cons. Looked around. But at his age, and with his history? And in our village, where few of us say what we feel. Difficult. Widows at the outside. But widows make you think of loneliness in old age. Difficult.

The ferryman told him about the dating agency, where you can pinpoint the pros and rule out the cons. The same as in the army. Herr Schramm liked that idea. And he had instinctively liked Frau Mahlke. How wrong can you be? She simply never got in touch again. He had phoned, asking if he'd done anything wrong. She could tell him, he said. He'd spent a lifetime making either no mistakes or a lot of them, depending who you ask. Today, however, he'd admit to his mistakes, and making another didn't matter now.

Frau Mahlke had sounded funny on the phone. Funny wasn't all right. Herr Schramm couldn't think of any reason for her to sound funny. If she'd told him a reason, that would have been all right. Had he said something? Was he just too old?

Delays in the course of events, she said. She had been beating about the bush. And beating about the bush—maybe that is the only matter in which Herr Schramm is still a soldier. Either you have an order to obey or you don't. Herr Schramm is a critical man when it comes to standing to attention and not standing to attention. Not standing to attention isn't the result of beating about the bush. Wilfried Schramm has never beaten about the bush. Just as he has never bowed to anyone or praised himself, or told lies to hurt someone else. Do right and fear no one. Not standing to attention comes from the fact that he went on his knees to his own mistakes for a long time. Comes from the fact that he told the truth to the disadvantage of others, and the truth weighed heavily. In concrete terms, it comes from the fact that now, in his old age, Herr Schramm stands bending over the engines of agricultural machines all day, if he isn't crawling under them.

Maybe because it is so long before Schramm says anything, Anna remarks, "It smells funny in here."

"That's the little tree." Herr Schramm points to the dangling tree-shaped air freshener. And, "Family doesn't mean anything. That wouldn't do for me or for them now. I just need—" Herr Schramm turns to her again, bags under his eyes, broken veins, he scratches under his collar and leaves his sentence unfinished.

"Okay." Anna is breathing freely again. "We'll do it the way I say. Give me the pistol and come with me. We'll fetch my ID and buy some cigarettes, and then we'll see."

Herr Schramm taps the steering wheel. On average men in Western Europe find themselves in mortal danger once every 13.4 years, women once every 15.1 years. Anna must be about eighteen. He gives her the pistol. The old man and the young woman climb out of the car. "Just a moment," says the old man, and he gets an umbrella out of the boot. The old man and the young woman go over the fields and meadows, down the roads and on into the night.

THE VILLAGE HAS NO WORK TO DO ON THE ROADS by night. The night offers no jobs for anyone. There's no late shift, no hotel, no nightwatchman, no radio DJ, no nocturnal work on a building site. In the village, so the village thinks, no one works for erotic hotlines.

On the roads, the heavenly tree of the stars is hung with moist fruit as blue as night.

By night, only Ulli sometimes earns something at the garage. If there's been a late football match to talk about, or the building of a bungalow beside the lake, or an asylum-seekers' hostel anywhere, then that's discussed after midnight too. Closing time is one at the latest. After one, the owner of the cigarette machine still earns a few euros, but that doesn't count, he's never been to Fürstenfelde, he lives in Ingolstadt or on Ibiza, he'd be surprised on such a night as this. After that the bakery begins earning, but then the time's not night any more, then it's traditionally called the first light of dawn, except at the first light of dawn on Monday, when the bakery is closed.

Night, clouds, violet, the color of the leggings Anna wears to go running along the roads.

On the roads of dear, dirty Fürstenfelde are two elderly, devout Fürstenfelde women, day laborers, they've lived for umpteen years in a hut close to the wall, wet night, hunger and stale air, tallow, racing hearts, lost their men to wars.

Thin soup and bread, it's thin soup and bread or go begging over the border in Mecklenburg, fight gypsies, spend the winter in refuges for the poor as if to shame the Prussian rulers, it's in Mecklenburg, of all places, that they find help in their need. They save for years to go on a journey with no clear aim. They know the legend of the giant who made two lakes out of one here, and they set off south to the giant's mountainous home. They take with them all they possess, which isn't much; their names are Isolde Kerner and Flora Kohl, they are on the road, they have no fear but they are also very much afraid, they share bread and water, going hand in hand, asking their way to the south, where is it, that south, praying, they don't have to say much else. Isolde has lumbago, Flora rubs herbal ointments into her.

The seventeenth century with its wars is over, they travel over scorched earth, they see suffering greater than their own, the bells ring, witches are burnt, idolatry doesn't find itself up in court so often. They talk to those who will talk, they are wary of those who fling insults at them. And many insults are flung; times are not easy. When Flora wanted to claim a day's wage long owed to her by the Kladden woman, the woman refused on account of a broken jug, adding, *you'll get nothing from me, you clumsy whore.* Flora had expected the refusal but not the insult. Then Isolde stepped in front of her friend and invited the Kladden woman to *shave her arsehole.*

So what else? To a man we might say *you sluggard, you whoreson knave.* Or call him a *great oaf,* a *booby,* an *ox.* A

Captain Sharp. And there were variations: *you murdering rogue,*
you clodpole. Women: *sacramental whore* for the pastor's wife,
Polack whore (not necessarily Polish), *foreign whore* (must be
foreign). *Mort, doxy.* On the streets by night you might hear:
Where's that tailor, that furriner, Devil break his neck? Or: *I'll*
ask the Devil to take the parson, I'll have none of them. To wish
the French pox on someone, male or female, was unkind. Worst
of all was to call a man a *rogue of a French whorecatcher.*

On the roads of Fürstenfelde at night there are no beggar
women now. Isolde and Flora defied insults and the weather,
witches and lumbago, they defied the improbability of their
ever having set out on their journey. Two elderly women
holding hands when the fear was too much for them. Sharing
their soup and bread. Some say all they found on the journey
was death. We say you're dead only if you're found dead.

On the roads there's the night that makes us visible, the
streetlamps shine. At the parish council meeting Frau Reiff
recently suggested installing movement sensors so that only
someone who needs light would be lit up. That would save
electricity and money. But you know how it goes. Others who
came to Fürstenfelde recently thought it was a good idea, the
old inhabitants couldn't come to any clear conclusion. After the
meeting everyone praised Frau Reiff for her good idea. We'll
admit that expressing our opinion to the authorities isn't our
strongest point. Then Frau Reiff, perhaps joking but probably
also in earnest, suggested getting everyone born before 1980
to have group therapy to teach them to be braver. But she

hadn't stopped to think that here we're even more afraid of psychologists than of courage.

The wet roads shine by night as if covered with cling film.

After harvest, after threshing, after winter sowing we drive tractors and trucks about the roads by night much faster than the speed limit allows, but that's how it is when you're driving something powerful, loud and shiny and you're sitting high up on it. It's as if when you want to go home after riding high above the fields all day, breathing dust, then on the roads by night you want to show that you're the man, you represent agriculture, you're the one who feeds us, we all have our feet under your table. Then you switch off the engine, you cycle home sniffing through your nostrils all clogged with dust. How good a shower will be.

By night in her gumboots, not satisfied with the progress on her painting: Frau Kranz.

Stung by a midge in the rain: Herr Schramm. "I ask you!" says Herr Schramm. On average midges sting more people with a high concentration of bacteria on their feet than people with fewer bacteria on their feet. Since knowing that, Herr Schramm uses anti-bacterial soap, but all the same he gets stung, only not stung so often on his feet.

On the roads: the huntresses. Frau Schwermuth. The vixen.

By night: music and eternity, how shall we ever find peace?

AT 16 THÄLMANN-STRASSE BY NIGHT: MUSIC. Dietmar Dietz, known as Ditzsche, lives there. Unmarried, always behaves decently to children and animals, a postman before reunification, keeps fifteen pedigree chickens today.

Ditzsche arrived in Fürstenfelde during the Extended Countryside Children's Evacuation scheme, and was never collected. His family here, the Gracedieus, were descended from Huguenots; they weren't bad people. Family is family; better any kind of family than none. The Gracedieus kept themselves to themselves, went on a trip to Cuba every year, took Ditzsche with them once. There was talk: how could they afford it? They died in a plane crash at the end of the 1970s. An end like that somehow doesn't belong in Fürstenfelde, but okay.

A table stands outside the gate to the inner courtyard of the building at Number 16, with a pink plastic box on it. The box is always out there, come rain, come ice, come night. The box contains eggs: ten for two euros. It's a fair price. Ditzsche has good chickens, healthy and well looked after, given special food and the devotion of an outsider. Chickens who smell like proper chickens. They warn Ditzsche of the arrival of a storm or a stranger. They keep quiet when the postman calls.

Every few days Ditzsche takes any unsold eggs out of the box and carefully fills it with fresh ones. This is one of the rare

moments when you can see him outside. The face of Dietmar
Dietz is as pink as his plastic box. Wrinkled, a wrinkled face.
Sinewy arms and legs. Ditzsche's shirts are too big for Ditzsche
in his old age. They weren't always too big. His shirts used to
fit him, and were ironed. His blue-gray uniform suited him
perfectly, which is remarkable when you think how rarely
GDR uniforms suited anyone at all perfectly.

In '95, when city folk rediscovered our lakes, the village
wanted to print new postcards for the holiday bathing season.
The Creative Committee met in the Homeland House to
discuss what pictures to have on the postcards. As well as the
Homeland House itself and the lakes, of course. There were
to be four designs. The third was a horse outside the old town
wall, so that killed two local sights with one stone. When we
came to the fourth local sight we'd run out of ideas. We thought
briefly of giving the church a renaissance, but the majority
were against it. And then the ferryman suggested printing a
picture of Ditzsche's egg box on the postcard.

What a fuss we kicked up.

Ditzsche was a loner, some said, and a loner isn't a good
advertisement for family holidays. And Ditzsche had been in
the Stasi, and thinking of the Stasi puts people off wanting
to enjoy social activities. And so on, and so forth, Ditzsche
this, Ditzsche that.

But then the ferryman said, "Friends: ten eggs for two
marks. That's a fair price, you won't get fairer. And you all buy
them. On the quiet, but you buy them. And it's not as if we

were going to show Ditzsche on the postcard, just his egg box. The egg box doesn't have a past history in the Stasi. All of us here know it. It shows that if you make the wrong decisions, if you lose your job and you're poor and everyone hates you because they all think you were an informer, and you're too stupid to deny it, it shows, like I say, that if life really kicks your arse so hard that you fall flat on your face, and you have diabetes into the bargain, right, well, all that doesn't necessarily keep you from selling very good eggs at a fair price."

The Creative Committee fell silent.

And when its silence was over, we voted on the egg box, but it still wasn't decisive, three against three. So we asked the photographer for her opinion. That was Frau Kranz, because if you can paint you can also take photographs. She didn't hesitate long: "Yes, well, the egg box will do, in fact it's almost original somehow, a colorful, idyllic countryside theme in this bloody dismal road, the egg box is okay."

That was a little harsh of her, but Frau Kranz is like that. Every two years since then, on account of inflation, there's been a new postcard showing the egg box left out by Dietmar Dietz, known as Ditzsche, twice orphaned, the loner, the postman who is still suspected to this day of snooping around looking at people's post, the diabetic whose shirts don't fit him any more, but he has no money or maybe no inclination to buy new shirts, because his chickens don't care about shirts and every day could be his last. But Ditzsche wakes up and gets on with life, and we bet everyone will come to his funeral, the egg box will come too, and most of us will really wear mourning, and the egg box will end up in the Homeland House with the rest of the GDR junk, ten eggs: two euros, with the best will in the world you won't find a fairer price. Recently Ditzsche has hung a friendly-looking plastic hen from the box, by way of decoration.

Sometimes, when you take ten large Uckermark eggs out of the box and leave two euros, or sometimes two euros twenty cents, you can hear the chickens cackling in the yard. If you come to buy eggs at night, you hear music inside the building. It's like that tonight. Tonight there's music in Ditzsche's apartment, and there are shadowy figures behind the curtains, and the soles of shoes moving over the floorboards. Or maybe it's just the curtains moving. Or nothing moves at all. The music is tango or salsa or merengue, here we're not so sure exactly what.

THE VIXEN RUNS STRAIGHT ALONG BESIDE THE water. She picks up the scent of an old female human in the water, one she has sometimes met in the old forest. This human animal can stay peacefully in one place for a long time. Humans don't often act that way. Usually this female's scent is mingled with other fine aromas that the vixen likes to taste: dyer's woad, umber and cinnabar and resin. Now she also picks up the sharp sweetness of fermented fruits, the potassium and manganese of tears. Good. Danger doesn't smell of tears.

The vixen, going farther, soon comes upon a second female human, a large specimen. Close to the place where humans put their dead into the earth, she is walking round three objects on the bank, humming quiet, angry human sounds. The vixen is curious; what's here? The female human smells of carrots, the objects—three dome-like things—have a scent of tin and copper and a third something that attracts the vixen.

The female human sounds as if she wants to have a fight with the domes, but the domes don't do anything. The vixen waits. After a while the female goes away. The vixen circles the domes as the female human did, scenting them. Under the metal she scents ways she has already gone. Prey she has killed. Food stolen from containers that were easy to bite through. She scents the fast dog fox whom she lured to her and tricked in the cold time, and who bit the back of her neck and helped her to feed her cubs at first. She let him think that he had tricked her, and it wasn't her own game and what she wanted.

It's all there. All the aromas she has ever scented. Including her sister's last flight and the dogs that she disturbed. The humans' dogs came so close to the vixen that she could scent their muzzles; they tasted of their masters' caressing fingers. The vixen fled here to the human colony instead of deeper into the undergrowth. The dangerous humans and dogs were in the forest, they wouldn't be able to protect their own earths at the same time. She is still alive, her sister isn't.

Every scent under the domes belongs to a Before. In all of them together, the vixen scents her own survival. It calls her, she wants to free it, she wants to have it for its own sake, she begins digging, wants to get under the domes. The vixen yelps, pants, alarmed and encouraged because under the domes and in the survival there's a scent that makes her think: me.

She wants to tear herself away, must get to her cubs, the chickens are close, she catches an enticing scent of one of her own kind from the largest dome: a fox, a dog fox. She scents his survival, beginning on the moor in a long-gone Before, how his mother vixen disappears, how two young human males feed him, one of them tall, one short, how he follows them without fear, and they follow him. They hunt together, and he entices a vixen, then another vixen, lives in caves and with the humans in human buildings, and he dies in something made of wood and iron that gives him great pain. The vixen learns with him, conquers with him, fears for him—finally runs away from his lifeless existence.

We are confused. Three bells stand on the bank of the Deep Lake. In the middle is the Old Lady, dark and sturdy. The twins flank her, bright and slender, the two moons of a dark planet. A slight sound is the only illusion; the bells are real. A kilo of copper sells for 5.32 euros. The takings wouldn't have been bad.

WE ARE SUSPICIOUS. FOR ABOUT THE LAST THREE weeks a young man has been hanging around the village from late at night until dawn. As soon as Frau or Herr Zieschke opens the bakery he comes in to order orange juice and a yeast pastry with vanilla filling. At the tall counter in the corner where you can stand to eat, he folds his hands as if in prayer.

Frau Zieschke, behind the till, straightens her back.

Herr Zieschke leafs through yesterday's paper.

Not until he has gone do they go into the back of the shop to make sandwiches or do whatever bakers do at the back of their shops.

He wears Adidas tracksuits. A white one with black stripes and a blue one with yellow stripes. Dark dirt clings between the stripes. The shoulder of the blue tracksuit was torn one day, and the skin under it bloody and abraded. Pale, a pale man. His watery eyes are reddened and almost never blink.

Adidas man, people call him.

We know about awkward characters. We know about ruins. We've seen dilapidation before and the shame that goes with all that. But we always know what happened before, and talk about why. Now here comes someone in an even worse state, and he stays out until dawn and no one knows who he is, he gives us nothing to talk about.

Orange juice and yeast pastry with vanilla filling.

After eating his breakfast, he sometimes presses his fist into the palm of his other hand, and his whole torso trembles. Sometimes. He. Rolls up. His. Sleeves. Above his elbows. As slowly as that.

One day it gets too much for Zieschke, who asks him a question. He wants to know something about the young man's past history, maybe a name, a place. The Adidas man reads from the board, hesitantly, like a child.

"We bake. With. Natural. Sourdough."

He divides his filled pastry into small pieces with his fork. He closes his eyes as he chews.

We don't know where he comes from.

We don't know where he's going.

We know what he likes to eat.

After a while the injury to his shoulder has healed up.

BEFORE THE ANNA FEAST IN THE YEAR 1722 A MOST terrible tragedy occurred. The people feared that flax put out to dry would be stolen, so the unwise custom prevailed of shutting up servants or children in the ovens, which still contained the warm flax, and letting them sleep there overnight. That was done with the Geher children, Anna and Andreas. Of the pair, the girl was found dead in the morning, the boy severely injured. The matter was all the more tragic in that the same girl had warned us, the evening before, of vagabonds seeking to steal our bread.

The mother wanted all to be summoned nonetheless to the Feast. It was, however, the saddest we ever held, full of mourning and wrong and not dancing and song.

All honor was paid to the girl.

O mighty and terrible God.

O foolish, foolish Man.

AND HERR SCHRAMM, FORMER (ETC.)—THEN (etc.)—now (etc.)—and also, because he can't make ends meet by (etc.)—is standing in front of the cigarette machine for the second time tonight. On average, ex-smokers are slimmer than smokers. The opposite is commonly assumed. You get fatter if you stop smoking, that's what is commonly assumed. Sigmund Freud's nephew thought up that notion, and you know how good the Freuds are at influencing people. But it's a fact that smokers are more inclined to stop smoking later in life if their bodies stop keeping naturally slim. That undermines the statistics. Getting fat, then, has nothing to do with not smoking, it's a case of an exhausted metabolism. Herr Schramm was never slim and never *very* slim. Herr Schramm was always the sturdy sort.

Coins in one hand, Anna's identity card in the other, Herr Schramm is thinking about those common assumptions.

"What do you think?" he asks, putting the first coin in the slot. "Do people put on weight when they stop smoking?"

"Smoking is good for the digestion, isn't it?" Anna holds the umbrella over Schramm.

"That's commonly assumed," says Herr Schramm, pressing the button for Pall Mall Red. "In reality it makes no difference. In reality you're fat because you eat a lot, not because you don't smoke much. Or else it's genetic." He hesitates with the ID card, scratches the back of his neck with it.

Anna puts her finger to the "In" slot on the machine. Herr Schramm puts the card through the slot intended for it. Nothing happens.

Herr Schramm thinks of things intended to work other things. He thinks of the duty crew of his rocket unit. The man responsible for firing was intended to give the command to fire the rocket. The crew responsible for servicing the starting ramp were intended to service the starting ramp. The C item was part of the A item. The personnel took up their firing positions in the place intended for them. The command to stand down from attention was intended for the close of the maneuver. "Class solidarity and military alliance with the Soviet Army. . . protection of the air space of the GDR. . . the utmost discipline and initiative. . . at the word, stand down!" Everyone was in the clear about his intended task at any time. The wives of the personnel cannot be praised too highly. In the mid-1980s the regiment was severely cut. Lieutenant-Colonel Schramm protested, but what can you do? Rocket technology was mothballed. The main task now was guard duty. My God, guard duty. If Schramm wanted to do it himself, all the same he didn't have to. The last parade on the parade ground was in 1990.

Herr Schramm presses the Lucky Strike button. No result.

Herr Schramm wonders how he is going to get rid of the girl if this cigarette business fails to work again. He presses the West button. No result.

"Why did you want to kill yourself?"

Herr Schramm presses the Camel button. He grits his teeth, his jaw muscles stand out. Still no result.

"I ask you," says Herr Schramm.

Herr Schramm presses all the buttons, one after another. The opponent you best like to beat, so Herr Schramm firmly believes, is yourself. He clenches his fist. Anna's raised eyebrows express alarmed curiosity. He strikes out, stopping a millimeter before he hits the metal of the machine.

When he was in the army, Herr Schramm often went swimming. Early in the morning, over to the Güldenstein and back. On the way out, swimming fast and furiously. Touch the Güldenstein, breathe deeply. On the way back, swimming slowly and thoughtfully.

"Have you done something bad?"

"Seems to me I've never done anything, ever, but get hold of cigarettes."

The machine shows the amount of money fed into it. Maybe the bullet harmed the electronics. It's always the electronics. Herr Schramm presses the button to get his money back. No result.

"You were a soldier, weren't you?"

"I never led anyone into battle. Did marksmanship only in Kazakhstan, for practice. What we were doing here was to keep the skies safe."

"The skies?"

"And there was always technical stuff to be serviced and something to be cleaned. Think of that. Think of cleaning anti-aircraft rockets."

Anna stares at him. Searchingly. Yes, you could say that Anna looks at Herr Schramm searchingly. She stared searchingly at him in his car, and when she fetched her ID from the farm, and when he asked if she knew that the Russians had shot dozens of people in the field under her window.

"Belorussians," Anna had replied, staring searchingly at him, and she does it again now as he leans his head against the vending machine. If someone intends to kill himself, you keep staring at him.

"Don't do that," says Herr Schramm without looking up.

Anna goes on staring. She fetched her asthma spray from home, for emergencies, and also her phone, just in case. She doesn't want to use it yet. The rain is slackening.

Herr Schramm walks away. At the graveyard, he turns down to the lake. The path is steep and muddy. Anna tries to keep up. Herr Schramm doesn't mind about the ground and the weather. The name of his father is one of the names on the war memorial in the graveyard.

There's something unusual just past the graveyard: the bells on the promenade. "Well, I ask you!" says Herr Schramm. "What's all this, then?" He looks at the bells. The falling raindrops make them ping softly. Anna still has eyes only for him.

"Do you keep having memories tonight too?" she asks.

"I," says Herr Schramm, "always keep having memories."

Since Anna found Herr Schramm in his car, they haven't met anyone. Now she can guess at the painter's light some way off, against the background of the otherwise dark lake. Only Anna doesn't want to share Herr Schramm with anyone else now.

"Why do you ask?"

"I won't be here any more on Monday."

"Going away. Mhm."

"I keep remembering my time here and wondering what I'll miss. I think what I'll miss most is not spending my youth somewhere else."

Schramm taps the bells. Puts his large hand on the curved casing of the Old Lady. "We once," he says, stroking the bell, "had an Uzbek general visiting."

"Visiting the rockets?"

"Visiting the rockets. He stayed for five days, and after that the unit was never the same again. Everything was going downhill anyway, the economy and so forth, but that wasn't it. That man, Trunov was his name, spent those five days living with us the way every one of us would have liked to live. When he had gone, everyone fell back into the same old rut, and our morale went off with the General to Uzbekistan or somewhere else."

"I'd like to understand that if I could."

"Yes, but I don't know what it will sound like. . ." Schramm smells his hand. "Right, listen. You can't say that a place or a general is—" Schramm shakes his head. "Trunov told us to lay out a kitchen garden. We didn't have to do as he said, but we did. We even gave it a name."

"The Trunov Garden?"

"The Kitchen Garden of Comrade General Paša Trunov. It grew wonderful peppers year after year. My word, it did."

Herr Schramm coughs, but it could have been a laugh. He crouches down. "Hey, come here. See that?" He points to the ground near the bells. "Someone got stuck here. Those are the tracks of tires."

"So?"

"Put two and two together."

Anna isn't feeling in the mood for riddles. Only now does she seem to see the bells. She doesn't think them very interesting. Herr Schramm turns away too. He wants to show Anna something, and gets her to climb the wall.

"So now?" says Anna, from on top of the wall.

"Story time," says Herr Schramm.

Once upon a time there was   called Jochim

An old tinker ~~mmmmmmmmmmmmmmmm~~ who lived in ~~mmmmmm~~ Fürstenfelde. He was a poor man, who didn't own much except for a little cottage: a cooking pot, a plate for his food and so that he could make music on it with his spoon, in addition to two jerkins, one to wear and a spare one, and an old-fashioned top hat, which he kept on even when he was asleep. People regarded him with suspicion, as they do when someone would rather talk to himself and his headgear than to other folk.

the tinker   Kiecker Forest

One day ~~he~~ goes to collect dry branches in the ~~Kiecker Forest~~ to provide himself with firewood for the winter. On the way back he takes the shortcut over the fallow field on Geher's farm, ~~mmmmmmmmm~~ and as he stops to ~~mmmmmm~~ rest under the ~~mmmmmmmmmmmm~~ oak tree, he thinks he feels a branch knock the top hat off his head.

When he picks the hat up, he finds an apple underneath it. In surprise, he picks it up, rubs the peel clean on his jerkin and bites into the apple. His teeth meet something hard. Next moment half a tooth is lying on his tongue, but instead of the core he finds a golden ring. The tinker curses, but a tooth is a tooth, while a ring is a ring. He puts it on one of his crooked fingers and picks up his firewood.

With the bundle of branches on his back, he goes home to the village. On the road, several old women stand gossiping with each other. They never have a good word to say for the tinker, even when he has done his work well.

Suddenly they scatter, screeching. Stupid women, growls the old man, they ought to know me by now.

Outside the church, he comes upon several laborers mending a door. They never miss a chance to play a trick on the tinker, who once had to wade into the lake to rescue his hat.

When they ~~were aware of~~ saw the swaying bundle of branches coming toward them, they turned pale with fear, left their work and took refuge in the church.

~~They must be drunken minds~~ They've been drinking, thinks the old man. He goes to his cottage and throws the bundle off his back. Then he makes an open fire in the kitchen to warm himself.

Before long the villagers are ~~gathering~~ assembling outside his cottage. The first comers press their noses to the little windowpanes in curiosity. That is too much for the tinker. He goes outside and snaps at the people, "What are you doing here?" ~~But no sooner has he spoken than they start screaming.~~ No one takes any notice of him.

The old man wonders what it is that makes the people run away from him ~~.~~ or fail to see him. Can it be to do with the golden ring on his crooked finger?

He ~~wanders along about upset in a daze and wonders~~ goes into the village ~~to see a neighbour and asks what the matter with the people is~~ and now he hears, to his surprise, that the people were horrified to see a great load of branches floating along above the road without anyone carrying it.

Then it dawned on the old man that it must be to do with the ring from the apple. And sure enough—it makes its owner invisible.

The honest tinker made ~~one~~ good use of that fact. He ~~supported be~~
~~knew quite well~~ no longer went about his work mending pots and pans. ~~and~~
~~knew what was the ringing for~~

~~As soon as he knew what should say to his village and~~
~~all people's doings again~~ He got his food from
other people, especially those who used to
mock him and spoke ill of him. An old
maid, who had once broken off her
~~all her be soon part that was very and so much the~~
friendship with him, because of his big head,
~~never was put with those of his strength there was but say~~
died of fright. That almost made him feel
sorry. It didn't bother him that he
couldn't talk to anyone. In the past hardly
anyone had ever listened to him, nor taken
what he said seriously. Very few in the
village noticed the absence of the old tinker,
and when and how he disappeared entirely
no one can say, only that for another
whole year people had less food than usual,
but since no one really suffered hunger on
that account, they put it down to
kindly spirits and spoke no more about it.

THE VIXEN FOLLOWS THE SCENT OF CHICKEN down the lighted stone path between the human earths. There could be danger lurking anywhere here. One is already lurking. A human male. The vixen catches the scent of his shoulder: the injured flesh. He is standing still in front of an earth that she likes to visit herself. Inside it humans do what humans most like doing: they make one thing into other things. They make large, firm, crisp things out of wheat dust. And sometimes, not often, but they are delicious, those things are put out behind the earth, where the vixen waits for them, not often, but they are worth the wait.

She makes a small detour round the human male. This time the makers of things out of wheat dust haven't left anything out. But the vixen catches the soft scent of chicken feathers behind a row of boards by the next-door earth. She investigates the boards until she finds one slightly raised from the ground. She slips through. A spacious place with the wooden henhouse in a corner. The hens are dreaming. Their sleep is mild with rain.

BEFORE YOU BUILD A CHICKEN RUN, GET TO KNOW all you can about both chickens and foxes. Find out about the instincts of chickens and the stories of the fox.

The Durdens had always been short. Nothing could change that, no wise women or stretching apparatus, no marrying tall people, no hormone treatment—and the last of the Durdens living here, first name Heinrich or Heini, known as Tiny, Fürstenfelde's last Mayor before the fall of the Wall, was only 1.45 meters tall.

We didn't think Durden's stature was worth mentioning. A joke here, a bit of teasing there. It bothered him considerably. It influenced his footwear, it left its mark on what he thought and did, to wit his efforts to wield influence and authority, and it had him always striving for higher things. He had failed as chairman of the Agricultural Production Society under the GDR, he had failed as a husband in three marriages. So he tried his luck as our Mayor.

If you are building a chicken run, you must realize that you are keeping the chickens 100 percent in, but you can't keep the fox 100 percent out. If he gets in the chickens are at his mercy. The enclosure that was built for their protection becomes a condemned cell.

Durden took up the office of Mayor in '84; in '85 the Schliebenhöners went to the West, the only ones here to do so. Did the former event have anything to do with the latter? No one expressed suppositions out loud. It was just that since taking office Durden had gone on and on to the Schliebenhöners about the idea of a house swap. They had a large house but lived alone, and Durden lived alone, but all the same he wanted a big house.

A month after the Schliebenhöners had disappeared, Durden moved in. Their big house had a balcony with a view of the Great Lake, and a kitchen garden surrounded by blackberry bushes, and a large lilac looming over it like a roof. A cherry tree adorned the inner courtyard. The Schliebenhöners had not sold their goat, so that no one would suspect anything.

If you are building a chicken run, make sure that the chickens have enough space to run around and amuse themselves, and if they have dark feathers that they have enough shade in summer. Chickens also need a place to which they can withdraw when the life of a chicken gets to be too much for them. If you are building a chicken run, build the fence at least 1.50 meters high or higher. Anything less will be child's play to the fox, not an obstacle.

The Mayor made himself at home. He harvested the garden produce, fed the goat, forged signatures. After his mayoral work was done, he drank beer on the balcony and looked at the sky more often than the lake. He knew he was seeing stars that had been extinguished long ago, and that weighed on his mind. Was it a sign? And if so, what of?

If you are building a chicken run, make the entrance tunnel go in a zigzag, with short straight bits and sharp angles, so that a chicken can get along it easily, but not a fox. And get a dog with a nervous disposition.

The circumstances of Durden's move were dubious, but we and the time were not yet mature enough to point out such a thing in public. Furthermore, the village had worse problems than the Mayor's house-moving: to name just one, liquid manure trickled down from the arable fields into the lakes, making their ammonium content twelve times more than was permissible. Children ran into the water and came out itching. Blue-green algae increased and multiplied like rabbits. No one in the Agricultural Production Society was interested in that; even Durden had once tried mentioning the matter, and got nothing but promises.

There was one small comfort. The pike-perch from the Great Lake were sold in the West. People were annoyed about that, rightly so, but not quite so annoyed when the business of the ammonium content came out, and of course we didn't wish severe nausea on anyone over there—but even a Wessi, we thought, can take a little bit of nausea if there is any.

If you are building a chicken run, use sturdy, close-meshed wire netting. You don't want the fox to be able to climb it or bite a hole in it. Fix the lower one-third of the netting properly to a low concrete wall that continues underground, preferably for half a meter down. The fox digs fast and well. Don't build the little wall too high; chickens need light, and should be able to see what is on the other side of the wall. Artificial light makes them nervous.

Durden had a garden makeover. He wanted more tidiness, more pumpkins and melons, fewer blackberries and indeed fewer berries in general, because berries are kids' stuff. He didn't like the goat, but he kept her because she licked his hand even when there was nothing in it.

One day he went with the local branch of the Small Animal Breeders' Association to the district show in Sarow, and saw Dietmar Dietz, known as Ditzsche, win the crowing contest with his Dwarf New Hampshire rooster, which crowed 151 times within an hour, and then win the green victor's ribbon too in the Dwarf Chicken class, with a blue-porcelain colored fowl that had feathered feet.

Now Durden wanted dwarf chickens too.

Ditzsche thought it was a joke, but Durden's eyes were shining. The Mayor wandered past the pens. Feathers shimmered in the most wonderful colors, and he pointed in silence to one of the fowls now and then, if he particularly liked it.

Ditzsche tried to dissuade him: it took a lot of time and trouble, he said. Breeding pedigree chickens called for care, good rearing and, yes, love.

Good rearing, said Durden, reaching out to a hen, would not be any problem. And after today he felt any amount of love for these proud creatures.

Ditzsche didn't like to hear chickens called proud. Their swelling breasts, raised heads and erect bearing are physical and not mental attributes.

The Mayor stopped outside one pen with a solitary rooster in it, blue-black, with a golden back and a bright red comb, stalking thoughtfully about in circles. The little man linked his hands behind his back and walked round the pen, instinctively imitating the bird.

"An Old English Dwarf Game Fowl," said Ditzsche.

"Old English," whispered Durden. "Game Fowl," he whispered. "How many hens does a rooster like that need?"

The rooster stared at Durden, or the sky above Durden, and fluffed up his plumage. The decision was made.

If you are building a chicken run, think about electricity. However, remember that an electric shock will irritate the fox but not drive him away for ever. Foxes do not give up before they have reached their limits. Count on needing at least 3,500 volts. The electric wiring is fixed on the outside of the enclosure. Only chickens that leave it are endangered.

Durden wanted to put up an enclosure for his chickens. Ditzsche offered to help him, and warned him about the fox. Then it must be secure, said Durden. Ditzsche told him about keeping chickens, told him about the fox. Durden drew a plan. Ditzsche improved the plan and got hold of the materials. They built the enclosure together. Two days later the chickens were delivered. Three of them were killed the following night.

When Durden discovered the massacre in the morning, he summoned Ditzsche and demanded an explanation. Ditzsche examined the scene of the crime. The chickens had been killed in their henhouse. The fence was intact, there were no holes in the ground. Then Ditzsche noticed the goat. She was grazing close to the fence; Durden had tied her up to its corner post overnight. Ditzsche studied the animal. He found reddish hairs on her back. He showed them to Durden.

What the hell did that mean, Durden asked.

Ditzsche smelled his fingers. "Fox. The goat is too close to the fence. The fox used her as a springboard."

Durden, lost in thought, repeated the word "springboard" several times. In an even voice, rather too even a voice, he then asked why Ditzsche, with his alleged knowledge of the subject, hadn't taken this eventuality into account.

Ditzsche had no answer. A surviving hen clucked quietly. Durden compressed his lips; his chin was shaking. "How are they ever going to trust their home now?" he whispered, as if he didn't want the hen to hear him. "They'll always be thinking they hear a beast of prey outside. Instead of the hand that feeds them they'll expect the jaws that eat them. Those chickens," said Durden, clutching the wire netting of the fence, "can never be happy again."

Once your chicken run is up, let two roosters fight for the hens. The winner will protect his hens all the better the harder he had to fight for them. He will warn them when danger threatens, and the hens will take refuge in the henhouse. If a fox threatens the hens, the rooster will sometimes save their lives, but often he will not.

Durden refused to pay Ditzsche even for the materials. In the village he told everyone how that idiot had cost him three pedigree fowls, and blamed it on a goat. He didn't tell the story himself, of course. He had other people do that for him.

The gossip did not win out. Foxes eat chickens, full stop. If I were a fox, said the village, I guess I'd find pedigree fowls particularly delicious. Instead of talking about Ditzsche, people discussed possible ways of fox-proofing a chicken run. The ferryman said, "Ditzsche is above suspicion when it comes to chickens," and the ferryman's word had always carried more weight than anything the top brass of the village said. The matter was forgotten. Except by Ditzsche.

Once your chicken run is up, sprinkle plenty of pepper round the fence. Put human hairs in the netting at close intervals, rub your sweat on the fence. Urinate regularly near the enclosure.

Durden once joined us when we were drinking at Blissau's. It was late, some of the customers were falling asleep at their tables. Durden began talking about his chickens. He could hear them clucking all the time, he said, even now. They complain, he said, they're feeling sorry for themselves. They're not happy.

The little man was remorseful. He ran his hand through his hair, ordered a beer and didn't drink it. We comforted him, because everyone deserves comfort after midnight. We said the chickens aren't sensitive to feelings. They don't regret anything.

They ask only for the necessities. Durden either listened or he didn't. He lay down to sleep at home, and in his mayoral dreams he heard the Dwarf Game Fowl clucking.

The fox came back. Durden watched him. The fox slunk round the enclosure in broad daylight, provocatively slowly. The rooster led his hens into the henhouse. One of them stayed outside it. The fox put his nose up against the fence here and there. Scraped the ground a little with his paws. Then went away without success. The goat was standing somewhere else now.

Would the Mayor have intervened if the fox had got in? We'll refrain from making assumptions. Next day Durden gave the chickens away to the others in the Small Animal Breeders' Association, keeping only the hen who had stood her ground.

Ditzsche said: if a chicken is fearless, that doesn't make it brave.

After the fall of the Wall, Durden wanted to join the Free Democratic Party and stand for Mayor again. When Ditzsche heard about that, he went to Blissau's and told people there about Heinrich Durden's letter to Hans Modrow. Ditzsche was landing himself in the soup. Because how did he know about that? And then again: it surely wouldn't have been the only letter he had opened. The informer's revenge on the local politician. Some of them at Blissau's sounded almost flattered to think an informer could have been spying on them. Ditzsche said he wasn't an informer. He didn't say he hadn't read the letter.

In his letter, Durden had fulminated against the Church and argued for the continuation of the Stasi in another form. He was saying all that, he claimed, on behalf of the village. Although the village didn't know the first thing about it. What else was in the letter hardly mattered. No one writes letters in our name. Durden never stood as candidate for any post in Fürstenfelde again.

Ditzsche lost his job. To this day we don't know whether it was only Durden's post that he read, or everyone else's too.

When you have put up your chicken run, prepare the chickens for battle. Arm them with iron spurs overnight.

Heini "Tiny" Durden died in 2005. The inscription on his gravestone says: *His Star Is Extinguished.* The Schliebenhöners have come back and are living in the big house again. The chicken run is also inhabited. Not by pedigree fowl, by good healthy chickens with golden plumage. The vixen prowls round the cherry tree. And beside the chicken run, a wheelbarrow stands.

IN THE YEAR OF OUR LORD 1618, UPON THE NINE-teenth day of May, six suns were seen in the sky here.

JOHANN IS KEEPING HIS COOL AGAIN. BUT SERIously, who wouldn't have screamed (briefly, anyway), on finding himself locked up in the cellar? A few minutes later Ma turned up. Again, he should say; Ma turned up again. When he heard her voice, of course he was relieved at first. And then she didn't let him out.

Ma. Honestly.

Ma misunderstood everything that Johann said, or ignored it, and asked him questions that he couldn't answer through the door. Who was behind the break-in, where were the others? In the end she threatened to take Johann's top hat away if he wouldn't cooperate. Johann thought that was almost funny.

So then she went away, and he shouted after her, but the leather skins swallowed up the sound of his voice.

Ma called him Jochim. Johann knows who Jochim is: a character out of those folk tales. Ma read him the story of Jochim when he was little. And he read it to her when she was depressed.

Johann runs his finger over the booklets on one of the shelves, pulls one out, leafs through it. The Tinker's Ring. Jochim turns invisible, people are scared, he decides against invisibility in spite of its terrific plus points, *The End*. Hmm. Ma tells it differently. Jochim stays invisible and annoys the people who always used to make fun of him.

Ma scared Johann more than being locked up here.

But Johann is keeping his cool again. He climbs on the chest and reaches his arm, with his phone at the end of it, up to the ceiling. No network. He clears books away and pushes the chest over to the opposite wall. Still no network.

Johann is keeping his cool again. He has time. There's light here, there are books, and under the table is a can of Cola Light, still half full. Johann starts reading.

AFTER PRACTICING INIQUITY MANY A TIME IN THE Uckermark with their Attacks, Robberies and rascally Conduct, doing heinous Deeds against God, the Law and all that is Meet, Right and our bounden Duty with evil Intent, causing Uproar and manifold Violence, and last of all, in the village of Lychen, turning a Church into a Stable, keeping Beasts therein, moving the Altar and the sacred Vessels into that same Stable and forcing the Priest to preach there, those notorious Thieves, Deceivers, Agitators, Smugglers and Footpads Hinnerk Lievenmaul and Kunibert Schivelbein, the latter being otherwise known as Long-Legged Kuno, were taken and deliver'd up to the Uckermark High Court in Prenzlow, on Saint Andrew's Day in the year of Our Lord, 1599.

The presiding Judge was His Worship Justice Joachim von Halvensleben.

Lievenmaul and Schivelbein spoke in their own Defense.

Besides the well-known Case that had come before the Chamber not long since, concerning the Matter of whether the Flight of the aforesaid Rapscallions were an unpunished Crime or no, on this Occasion a new Plaintiff, Count Poppo von Blankenburg, accused the Defendants of stealing nine Thalers from him in a false Game while attempting to abstract a Barrel of Beer from his Cellar.

Lievenmaul and Schivelbein let it be known, firstly, that there had been no False Game, Blankenburg himself being False through and through, more particularly his Hair, which much resembled a Besom Broom—but by all that was holy, the Count play'd a very poor Game.

The Defendants were reprov'd by His Worship for such scurrilous Talk.

Secondly, the Defendants could not, said they, have stolen the Thalers from the aforesaid noble Lord, as they did not belong to him. Rather, the Thalers were the property of the town of Fürstenfelde, as laid down by Law in the Ruling of 1514 whereby one Thaler per Cartload of Crayfish—nine in all this Year—was to be paid into the Town Coffers, and not therefore into the Coffers of Herr v. Blankenburg, albeit that Noble Lord took the money Year after Year. A second Verdict had indeed been given, but by a Court so influenced by Herr von Blankenburg that the Trial had turned out in such a way that not just the Plaintiff, but also the Judge, all seven Jurors and every other Person attending the Courtroom were involv'd. The People of Fürstenfelde had to accept this outrageous Miscarriage of Justice, they being threaten'd with Guns and other Engines of Murder, and not wishing to end like the Mayor of Göhren, who defended himself and was beat to Death in Unexplain'd Circumstances. They—Schivelbein and Lievenmaul—swore before God and the Court that they had returned the Thalers and the Beer, save perchance for two Pitchers of the latter, to the folk of Fürstenfelde.

And as for all the other noxious Deeds with which they were charg'd before the Court, they would plead guilty to only one, namely running away from the Tower in Prenzlow after they were condemned to Death the previous Year, but this could credibly be seen as the Work of two Desperate Men.

All their Talk, however, was in Vain, likewise Schivelbein's plea that they had never hurt any Person corporeally. Sentence of Death was therefore pass'd on these incorrigible and habitual Offenders.

His Honor acceded to their request to determine the Place of Execution themselves, intending no doubt to placate the Common Folk, with whom the Condemn'd Men stood in High Regard, since they reliev'd only those who, they thought, deserv'd it of their Possessions. So the Condemn'd Men chose to die in their Birthplace of Fürstenfelde.

AND THE VIXEN LEAPS, TAKING OFF FROM AN OLD idea, on such a night as this the chickens are making a noise in the henhouse, her first leap is not enough, again, again, and again, she does it but she lands hard and clumsily, limps, the vixen limps to the henhouse, the chickens inside are scraping the ground with their claws, there is no gap in the wood of the henhouse, the vixen scents that a human was at work on it, she scratches at a little metal thing with her left paw, the wood opens, gets inside, a tunnel, her right paw hurts, it's cramped, she can hardly get round the corners, the warmth of the chicken, droppings, little feathers, blood, the walls are closing in on the vixen, it's so tight she can't turn round, zigzag, can't manage the corners, this will give her nightmares, and the vixen sneezes. The vixen sneezes, and somewhere inside the nightmare labyrinth a chicken sneezes too.

On, and now the chickens at last, beating their wings violently, singing, scratching, just a moment, just a moment, the eggs, there, there and there, the first breaks, it isn't easy in the confusion, just a moment, there's a lot of noise, she kills one chicken, tears its head off to make it a little quieter, the second egg, careful now, she takes it behind her teeth between her tongue and her gums, it's all right! There it is, it breaks, yolk, lovely yolk, with yolk in her mouth she kills another chicken, impatient now, the last egg, the last egg gets trodden underfoot, who, the vixen looks round, the chickens are wagging their heads, and then—then the rooster wants to fight, the rooster pecks the back of her neck hard, deep, and blood, her own blood, runs, stings, the vixen has dust in her eye, keep calm, out of here, her right paw hurts, the back of her neck, but most of all her eye, it isn't dust, the large fowl is pecking at her, out, out, zigzag, she's in flight now, this is the vixen in flight, her eye hurts, bothers her, she climbs on the wooden henhouse, heaves herself over the woven metal, lands on her injured paw again, her mouth full of feathers, yolk, and the night is full of blood, on such a night as this, the night is blind in one eye.

ANNA IS SHIVERING ON TOP OF THE WALL. THE rain has slackened off, but the wind is stronger. The trick of it, Herr Schramm explains, is to squint slightly, like with those colored 3-D pictures, and in the end you can make out a heart or a rocket in them. Anna doesn't know about 3-D pictures, she knows about 3-D films and 3-D printers, and Herr Schramm is surprised that she doesn't know about 3-D pictures, it's not really a question of different generations.

But squinting doesn't help—Anna still can't make out the Güldenstein. "I thought," she says, "it was only a fairy tale. A farmer, a donkey and a stone shining like gold. I think someone drowns in the end. The farmer?"

Herr Schramm is an upright military man with poor posture. Herr Schramm is so thirsty for a cigarette, so thirsty, and every second without one is a second in a hot desert of salt.

A bat swoops over the promenade.

The stone exists. Herr Schramm knows that, Herr Schramm doesn't need to explain what he knows to the girl now. It lies in the water just off the little island with the barn on it. As children they used to go out to it on a wooden sledge, when there was thick ice over the lake. It was best at night, because they weren't allowed to go out then.

"I didn't know you came from here."

It was best at night, because then the Güldenstein shone.

And Herr Schramm, Lieutenant-Colonel, forester, pensioner, points out into the black dark as if there were something to be seen there.

Anna can't see anything.

All the gold we'll ever have touched in our lives, says Herr Schramm, was made in an exploding star. The Güldenstein shines like gold. Not by day, not in the sunlight. By day it looks like any other stone. But on starless nights. Herr Schramm looks at the clouds. Ologists of some kind came to see it. Geologists, biologists or suchlike.

"And what did they say?"

What would you expect? Algae, moss, parasites, fungi. At least: a ferryman once lived on the island with the barn on it. Not much is known about him today. He was just a ferryman. It's known that he once didn't want to work on the day of the Anna Feast. Day of rest. The times were hard enough, you wanted to drink and sing and not spend three hours going round the lake on foot and back by night. Half of them would never have arrived. Well, so they gave the ferryman a barrel of beer, and then he did it.

"Super story."

Not the one that Herr Schramm wanted to tell. He wanted to tell the story of the light that the ferryman always carried with him, even by day. And after he had brought his last passenger ashore, he went back to his hut on the island and left a lonely little light burning all through the night.

"A lonely little light?" Anna giggles.

A lantern or some such thing. Listen, will you? People asked: why are you doing that? Who is that light going to guide? Why don't you save your oil? They knew he wasn't a rich man.

I always have a light to spare, the ferryman said. Without a light you're nothing and no one. Only the light makes you human. Of course that's just some sort of saying, but think about it.

Anna and Herr Schramm do think about it.

Anna says, "But it's still not as great as all that."

As a child Herr Schramm went out to the Güldenstein on the wooden sledge when the lake had a thick layer of ice on it. Preferably by night. He wasn't supposed to, but he did all the same. Preferably with Imboden, with Hanno, with Eddie, and Anna's grandpa was with them too.

Yes, so now you see. Now his granddaughter is suggesting to Herr Schramm that they could go over there together when the lake freezes.

Herr Schramm clears his throat. Turns to Anna. She has switched that stupid headlight on. For goodness' sake, switch that thing off for a moment. No wonder Anna can't see anything.

Anna does as he says.

Herr Schramm turns back to the lake. All those things that the Güldenstein is supposed to have been. A huge lump of gold. A treasure. A star in the sky of the black lake. A lighthouse for anyone in need of warning and guidance.

Algae and moss. The downfall of the greedy farmer in the folk tale. A story of which Schramm knew, back then, that he would tell it to someone one day. Anna, listen: there's no story. Once upon a time there was a ferryman who always had a light with him. And when he was dead a stone began to shine.

Once upon a time there was young Wilfried Schramm. He sat on a shining stone and smoked his first cigarette. Wasn't very good at it. Shivered with cold and excitement. Bats rose from the islet and flew over the lake. At the time he thought, *bats meandered.* Not the right word for a bat, much too slow. And from the stone, Fürstenfelde and its lights, on a slant and long-drawn-out, looked like a huge ship that had run aground sometime and couldn't float itself again. Generations of idiots on it who wouldn't give up, and new idiots keep getting born and dying there too. Some do all right, some don't.

Anna says nothing. Anna squints. Above the ash trees over there?

On average, the suicide rate is higher in countries with a good standard of living than in poorer countries. More men than women kill themselves everywhere. Except in China. On average the rate in the GDR was one and a half times higher than in the West. Herr Schramm can't believe that was just to do with the GDR. More a question of tradition; look at the Rhineland where everyone is Catholic and hardly any of them kill themselves.

Herr Schramm believes in moss and algae, not reincarnation and magic. China, for goodness' sake. Herr Schramm thinks it makes no difference whether you come from China or Fürstenfelde, whether you were a ferryman or a shipwrecked sailor in the past or now—for a while your light will shine. Shine ahead of you. Maybe shine for no one, maybe for someone. The Güldenstein.

Anna doesn't have to get a clear view of Herr Schramm's face to see it. The torrent of words that washed over his usual taciturnity surprised her. Now he's brooding again. Tired. Maybe tired.

Now there are squelching steps in the mud, and a light coming closer. A broad shadow emerges from the darkness of the graveyard, a flashlight in its left hand, what is presumably a pistol in its right hand—unless it's only a joke that a woman says, "Hands up!" to the old man and the young woman.

Presumably we now have two weapons here.

BE HEROIC

Learn to run fast, swim far, climb high (but be cautious), learn what is fitting for a woman and what is fitting for a man, and then do what you want to do. Learn (if you like) what you are told is not suitable for you.

Be heroic in your endeavors. Know what you want from life, and don't wait for it to happen but set out deliberately to get it. Don't pursue happiness, pursue success (take your time).

Be heroic in what you think but not thoughtless in what you say. The time is always right for thoughts, but there is a wrong time for words. Know that time and respect it, and then your thinking will not have been in vain.

Be heroic in what you do. If it will injure others but will be to your advantage, don't do it (unless the others injure you). If it will be to the advantage of others but not to you, then the deed must be a very good one (and the others must be worthy of it). If it will be to the advantage of others and you too, then do it, but know that you will never be able to satisfy everyone.

Be heroic in your judgment. Trust in the word of God, the judgment of a knight, the ruling of a judge. But listen also to the sinner's repentance, the penitent's excuse, the complaint of the guilty, the defense of the accused. And then decide (they will lie to you).

Be heroic with questions. Be heroic and say when you do not know the answer, and be heroic enough to ask for it. But ask your questions in such a way that you are not trying to please someone but only want the answer. Never answer for the sake of speaking but for the sake of the answer itself.

Be heroic in keeping order. Know morals and manners so that you can change them (know your rights as well as your duty).

Be heroic in society. Offer help and take it (know to whom and from whom). Care for the weak in their time of need, challenge the strong to act for those in need. If there are quarrels, do not think who is to blame, think how to settle and solve them. But do not land yourself in need if it means helping others out of it (make sure you know another solution).

Be heroic with your memory by admitting honestly what has been done.

Be heroic and know that heroes cannot always be heroes; there are many other things to do.

III

ON THE 29TH DAY OF SEPTEMBER IN THE YEAR 1722, I received a message from that unhappy mother who lost her little daughter so cruelly in an oven, the same child having bravely warned the village before of thieving vagabonds. I did not know why the woman should send for me in her hour of need, but I did not hesitate. Perhaps I might be able to offer a little comfort in the great sadness that her terrible loss had brought upon her and the village.

Many a house in Fürstenfelde has stood empty since the war. Those who fled the place come home only gradually, and many, may God have mercy on them, will never return. I am afraid for the village, I fear that devastation threatens it, and it will be deserted like others in the country round about.

My grief grew greater when I came to the woman's little house, and found more misfortune. The building seems to have suffered from a fire recently, and was patched up in makeshift manner against the weather. The fire has thrust its blades deep into the wood, leaving black wounds.

I found the mother in a wild fallow field full of weeds, under an oak tree. She was tall, thin and all in mourning, motionless as a figure in a woodcut. She spoke without any greeting, without looking at me, her voice hoarse with sorrow. It was not I to whom she spoke, hers was a message about the conduct of life intended for a child. That child would never receive her message, it was her dead daughter to whom she called. To the mother, her daughter was not dead, and so she spoke as if she herself were going on a journey and leaving her child at home.

Her words went through my throat like a ploughshare. They cast my thoughts into turmoil, except for reflecting on the cruel fate that can befall certain human beings. I left the place without a word, taking what the mother had said with me. I am sure she wanted me as a witness to carry the story of her child out into the world, and may God help me, I will do so.

ALL THIS IS RATHER TOO MUCH FOR US. FRAU Schwermuth raises her gun, as a sign to the others to come with her. The light of her flashlight wanders angrily between Anna and Herr Schramm. Anna has her arms in the air above her head like someone in a film. She is blinking.

"Anna, get down off that wall."

Anna does as she is told.

"Right, now both of you come over here to me. You too, Lutz."

Lutz? What Lutz?

"Come on, Johanna, are you crazy?" Herr Schramm isn't taking orders any more. He doesn't move. He sits enthroned, tall and warm, above the grotesque outline of a woman in a helmet threatening him. Or does he just sense the chance of a happy ending for him at someone else's hands?

Frau Schwermuth shines her flashlight in his face. "I won't repeat that again."

Herr Schramm sighs. Hard to say whether it is a sigh of resignation or a sigh of annoyance. Anna's expression is more easily interpreted. Let's call it determined. Determination tenses her muscles, takes Herr Schramm's pistol out of the kangaroo pouch in front of Anna's raincoat and points it at Frau Schwermuth.

Determination: "Drop that gun."

Well, well. Herr Schramm is beginning to feel as if he is the only one not crazy tonight. "I ask you!" he whispers. He takes a step aside, placing himself in the line of fire between Anna and Frau Schwermuth. The Wild West in Fürstenfelde. On such a night as this.

"I knew it, traitor!" Frau Schwermuth shows no sign of being about to give up. She has caught the tinker and made sure the bells are safe, now it's *her* turn. "Anna, lower your crossbow!"

As if taking your own life wasn't hard enough, Herr Schramm now has to save two others. "Right," he says. "Right." And: "Johanna, please. What's going on? This makes no sense."

"Lutz, my dear Lutz, won't you see it or can't you see it?" Frau Schwermuth is breathing heavily. "The girl will give us away! She'll murder us all, all of us!"

Herr Schramm has no statistics ready at the moment to deal with something like this. "Johanna," he says calmly, "my name is Schramm. Wilfried Schramm. And this is Anna. Granddaughter of Geher the toymaker. She's not going to hurt anyone. Isn't that so, Anna?"

Anna nods, which isn't very satisfactory in the dark, so Herr Schramm repeats his question in a louder voice and gets a loud "Yes" back.

"No, she can't help it!" Frau Schwermuth's voice breaks. "She has to give our hiding place away. Fürstenfelde will be looted, no one will survive! But if we lock her up we'll survive! Help me, Lutz, or you'll be the first to die. It is written! Every child knows that!"

Herr Schramm as a child had *Struwwelpeter* read to him, that's all he remembers. He has no idea what Frau Schwermuth means, but he does fear that her shaking voice and wild remarks bode no good.

Behind him, Anna clears her throat. "She," she says, swallowing, "won't—I mean I won't give anyone away." She is trembling all over, tries to calm down, tries to remember what her grandfather. . . "I can shoot, though. Twice. In the eye, twice. Two crossbow bolts. I won't give anyone away, I'm. . . saving people. That's how it is. Lutz—" She doesn't finish her sentence.

Herr Schramm knows that even someone with nothing to lose can lose time. He runs at Frau Schwermuth.

She is aiming at Lutz. Her big body sways in time to a song that only she can hear. Her pupils wander from side to side.

IT WAS IN THE YEAR OF OUR LORD 1636 THAT NEWS of the marauding Soldiery outside Fürstenfelde set the Village in an Uproar, for this was not the Troop of any Army, but that accurs't roaming Gang of discharg'd Mercenaries without Means, once enemies of One Another, now going through the Country with Fire and the Sword, leaving Death where they found Life, and nothing but Ashes where Houses once stood.

The People knew plundering and enforc'd Contributions all too well, whether by Swedes or Imperial Men made but little Difference. Rumors of the Cruelty of this Rabble, however, bore Witness to such barbarous Terror that many even fled with little more than the Clothes on their Backs. Those who stayed, perhaps eighty of them, Women, Children and the Aged, had been too weak to flee, or pray'd and hop'd that all might yet be well.

Old Lutz, which same had fought many a Battle in the Past, rail'd against those who resign'd themselves to their Fate rather than find a Hiding Place. The History of Man, said he, was the History of those who had hid well. So said the old Soldier, and furthermore he bade all who lov'd their Lives to follow him. Almost all did as he said. Lutz took them to the Passage hid Underground, dug out in Olden Days by two Thieves to get into the Cellar and rob Provisions. They could stay here, said he, without the Knowledge of Any, until the Danger be past.

The People had brought down Possessions and Nourishment, Chickens and even a Calf. The Dogs had barked, and were left behind. The Villagers sat in a long Row beneath the Earth, and the Earth was cold, and when a Fowl began to cluck Barth the Blacksmith wrung its neck, and none said a Word.

Old Lutz stayed up above, not for his own Sake. One young Woman had not wished to hide, but had placed herself with a loaded Crossbow on the Walls as if to drive off the Enemy. Lutz did not know her. She had arrived only a few Days since, being wounded in the Field and separated from her Regiment. She had been succour'd and tended here, and now she wish'd to show herself Grateful.

Down at the Foot of the Wall, old Lutz drank and squinted up at the young Woman. She was trembling, holding the Crossbow in the Crook of her Arm like as if it were a Babe. When the old Man said that most here had a good Hiding Place, she dismiss'd that without many Words, and kept silent Watch for the invisible Foe under Cover of Night. The Wind was already blowing with the smoky Smell of Death on it, and there was Fire and Screaming in the Darkness. The Mob was approaching over the Fields.

Lutz had found out her name: Anna.

WHO WRITES THE OLD STORIES? WHO ERECTS A memorial to fear? Who traces the furrows for sowing seed with a rake?

Who tells us what we ought to know?

Who tells us what we know?

Who tells us what? We.

Who tells on us?

Who tells?

Who?

A fire comes and it's all gone, all of it.

Who writes the story of the fire?

Let's say a young woman is standing on a town wall, and she is armed. No, let's not say "standing." Let's say she "steps from foot to foot on the spot in the cold." That tells us about the weather too, and if someone is stepping from foot to foot on the spot, we get a sense of time passing. Let's say, instead of "armed," that she has "a crossbow in the crook of her arm." That's better. And ahead of her is the enemy in the uniform of the night. Uniform of the night!

Heroes need names. Let's call her Anna.

Down at the foot of the wall, old Lutz says, "Anna, one thing troubles me in this hour. I have never spoken loving words and meant them."

What? Yes, what's that supposed to mean? No idea, it's written like that. However, it does us good to hear the old man's rough voice. He is drinking beer, perhaps leaning on a rusty halberd. But the girl says nothing. Such a crazy thing to say, and no reply? No, the enemy is advancing. "A movement," calls Anna, loading the crossbow with her bolts. "They're coming!"

Old Lutz warns Anna not to shoot. "Put the bow away, girl, come down from there." At that distance and in the dark, she won't hit anyone anyway. Even if she does, she can't win this fight. There are dozens and dozens of them coming, and she is alone. "That's enough heroism. Join the others, girl, disappear. You can yet be loving in your life, go, Anna, disappear!"

Who writes the old stories? Who decides who will be hit by the bolts? Bolts? Surely they all had muskets at that time. Anna has a crossbow, full stop. She takes aim, she shoots. The first bolt hits the leader of the rabble in the left eye, goes through his brain and kills him then and there. With the next bolt she hits the second man, who is carrying a banner with no crest on it, only dried blood, in the right eye and kills him too then and there. As quickly as those two fell, the attackers draw back.

David versus Goliath. Hmm, no. We don't like that. Why not? Why is Lutz hiding the people? It would be more exciting if they were really in danger. And this is all going too smoothly. Suppose someone else comes along? For instance, someone from the village who thinks Anna is a traitor. Thinks she is one of the rabble who has smuggled herself in to find out whether an attack is worthwhile, whether the village can defend itself, and so on. Let's say the Mayor. Yes, him. He tells Anna to put her crossbow away and come down. Right, but if she is really a traitor then the Mayor needs a weapon, or she will shoot him. Okay. He has a. . . a wheel-lock pistol. What's that? *GEO Epoch* magazine about the Thirty Years' War describes it as the best handgun of its time. We're always learning something new. Okay. Anna comes down. We need another twist in the story now. Right. It's a fact that Lutz trusts her. He stands between her and the Mayor, who aims his pistol at Lutz. Right, we already know about that.

Who writes the old stories?

Who takes that job on?

FROM OUR VANTAGE POINT AS WE HOVER ABOVE the scene, it looks as if Herr Schramm is working magic. Both his hands are outstretched, one to Frau Schwermuth, he's almost touching her, the other to Anna, and they are both of them aiming their pistols at him.

My word, thinks Herr Schramm. But he has already seen that it's not a real pistol in Frau Schwermuth's hand. A sort of pistol, yes, but he doesn't mind water, he's all wet anyway. However, Herr Schramm also thinks that if this were on *Crime Scene* you could bet on a minor character with strong feelings shooting him in the shoulder now, or shooting Frau Schwermuth in the forehead or the knee.

Anna is clutching his pistol in both hands.

Frau Schwermuth sobs.

What looks to us like magic is the fact that Herr Schramm slowly lowers his arm in front of Frau Schwermuth, and in a synchronized movement Frau Schwermuth lowers her gun with the yellow dolphin on the barrel.

Then Herr Schramm says Anna's name and the name of his favorite place. "It's all right, Anna," says Herr Schramm, "in winter I'll take you to see the Güldenstein." And he lowers his other arm, while in a synchronized movement Anna lowers hers.

Frau Schwermuth bursts into tears.

Herr Schramm clears his throat. He finds tears in connection with the Prussian spiked helmet really embarrassing.

"Johann." Frau Schwermuth looks at him pleadingly. "I think Johann. . . in the Archivarium. . . we must. . ."

Herr Schramm offers her his arm. She gratefully links hers with it. Anna is trembling all over. Herr Schramm thinks of ruffling up her hair, but she must be too old for that, and also she is wearing a cap.

On such a night as this, the Güldenstein shines a little more brightly.

SOMEONE. SOMEONE WRITES THE STORIES. Someone has always written them.

AN EXCERPT FROM THE ACCOUNT OF THE TRAV-
eling barber-surgeon and dentist, Johanness Michael
Harthsilber, of a girl who fell sick of a ravenous hunger. This
occurred in the year 1807, in the little town of Fürstenfelde
in the Brandenburg Mark, and was written down by Herr
Harthsilber.

The girl was twelve years old, and small of stature. She
hardly ever played with children of her own age, being weak
and sickly in other respects as well, but regularly attended
church with her father, a blacksmith. Her mother had died
at the girl's birth.

It was on the second day of the New Year that the girl felt
a great *appetentia* for food, which soon assumed such proportions that her father, in his concern and uneasiness, sent for
me. I found the girl in an unusual *conditio*! Her forehead was
burning, she was sweating, etc., yet when she was not asleep she
kept calling for food. But her stomach would not accept any
thing, and the girl vomited it all up again. Before my eyes, she
devoured a large chicken, bones and all, a loaf of bread and a
piece of butter, putting it straight into her mouth with her hand.
In addition she drank milk and beer, and poured rye flour down
her throat, but all of this came back up and out of her again.

I tried to prohibit her from eating, but a very strange thing
happened: when she was not fed as she demanded, the girl bit

her own finger! I told her father to tie her down to her bed, which he did, being full of love for the poor little soul. The child screamed as if in pain, and begged us for food.

The *casus* was hard for the blacksmith to bear, and in these circumstances I must praise his generosity and hospitality in entertaining me in his own home as well as I could hardly expect at the best of inns. In thanks I shaved both him and his brother in the same way as I shave gentlemen of a certain age and station in Berlin, with a little pointed beard and a slender mustache curving to left and right!

We now gave the girl nothing but vegetable broth, which could not diminish her craving for food. She drank the hot broth straight down, without caring that it burned her throat, and immediately called for more.

On the fifth night, a terrible thing occurred. The girl freed herself from her bonds, and gnawed the flesh from her own hand and arm, so that much blood was shed, and the bare bones were exposed. Before God, that was the worst sight I ever beheld.

In spite of all her bleeding, the girl was still alive. She demanded an apple, which was surprising, for she had not cared what she ate before. Her loving father hurried out and came back with apples. The girl took a bite out of each and then said, in her fever, that these were the wrong apples. The fruit that she desired was to be found in a fallow field run wild, under a solitary oak tree. Once again the father set out, so he was not obliged to see his little daughter die in convulsions and pain. He did not, however, find an apple where he had thought to do so.

I left that poor, sad village not without a troubled mind myself, in fear of God, and thanking Him that He does not show that same countenance to all His flock.

HOW'S THINGS?
   Can't complain.

JOHANN'S LIST OF TOP CANDIDATES FOR HIS FIRST time ever:

1. Wiebke, daughter of Herr Krone. Unfortunately her father is always sarcastic, and a butcher too (dangerous mixture).

2. Andrea from the eco-café in Parmen. Tricky, because eco people have to keep so many rules.

3. New on the list: Anna riding her bike in her dress with spaghetti straps.

After two hours of solitary confinement, Johann is beginning to feel bored. He opens the chest that he pushed to the side of the room earlier. There is a single book in it, wrapped in cloth, old and thick. Instead of a title it has a cross on the cover.

Johann sits on the table, takes a sip of Cola. It is a church register, or maybe a chronicle. The first entry dates from 1587.

Johann leafs on through it.

In the year of Our Lord 1615, in the Month of June, the Following took place. After Konrad Köhler wasted away, losing his Hair and his Power of Speech, and then perish'd of his Sickness and lay Dead, his Mother suspected a young Maidservant, Anna Meier, whom he was said to have reprov'd once, and so the Meier Girl was taken Prisoner, and confess'd under Torture that she was to blame. According to the Sentence pronounc'd on her as a Witch in Brandenburg, she was torn to Pieces with Six pairs of hot Pincers, and then burn'd at the Stake. This Execution took Place on the Eve of the Anna Feast, and was of unusually long Duration, for a violent Storm was raging over the Village, with much Thunder and Lightning.

4. Or maybe Jessie from the Landshop supermarket would be a better choice? MILF. Experienced, an older woman, wears those Crocs shoes with holes in them. Lada says women over thirty who wear Crocs are particularly randy. Jessie is married. Married women, says Lada, are even randier. Lada says they're like war veterans who still want to prove their worth on the battlefield.

THE FERRYMAN ONCE SAID THAT THERE IS SOME-
one in the village who has more memories of other people
than memories of his own. The village immediately felt sure
that he meant Ditzsche. But we think he could have meant
other people.

Ditzsche checks the egg box. There is still music playing in
his apartment. He takes the coins out of the box, counts the
eggs. Eight euros, and Piazzolla's Argentinian music playing
indoors. Ditzsche: a thin man, sinewy. He closes the lid of the
box, taps out the rhythm of a few bars on it.

We don't know what to make of Ditzsche. What is it that
the night finds interesting about him? The fact that he's always
a loner? The loneliness of an old man? But we have Herr
Schramm for that. Ditzsche never seems seriously bothered
by being alone. Not with his chickens, not with his music, not
with our letters. Maybe that's it? The postman as an informer.
On the other hand: nothing was ever proved against him, and
he himself has denied acting on anyone's instructions. And
certainly he denied reading our letters.

Dietmar Dietz is like an earworm, a catchy phrase from
a song you hardly know. A song of which you remember just
that one memorable line from the refrain, and very likely
you get that wrong (betraying the village, passionately keen
on dancing, clucking chickens, shy with other people). The

tune won't let go of you, you hum and whistle along with it, you don't even know whose song it is.

Ditzsche disappears into the yard and checks up on his poultry. The vixen is lurking in the darkness outside, the limping vixen, blind in one eye now. She has probably caught the scent of the eggs. She crosses the road and gets up on her hind legs, forepaws propped against the table, nose against the box. With one leap she is on top of it.

The song is the song of those whose aim doesn't go wrong. The song of the driven and unforgiven. Even hurt, even in a spin, we and the fox both want to win. The song is unorthodox, the song of a fox, the song of a fox who opens a box.

FRAU REIFF LETS HER CAT OUT AND WAITS WITH her hand on the door, out of curiosity or civility, for Anna, Herr Schramm and Frau Schwermuth to be within hearing distance so that she can wish them a good evening. "Still out and about so late?"

The trio, as if in chorus: "Yes."

A few years ago Frau Reiff bought the old smithy, renovated it with the help of friends and the village, and now has a pottery workshop there. We think it's the most beautiful house in all Fürstenfelde.

What do we mean by beautiful? Nicer than the neighboring houses. The sun comes in, the house stores up the warmth, it has a history, that kind of thing. One very important point is that Frau Reiff did much of the renovation herself. It has its own garden, another plus point. For instance, think of all the extra vegetables that can be given away to neighbors who don't have any garden! Or her family in the city, who can be persuaded of the advantages of a country life by having their mouths literally stuffed with those vegetables to silence them. Something else that matters is what kind of a person you are. If you have a nasty character, the facade of your house is nasty too, that's what we say here. Who's going to praise someone's hedge if they don't like the hedge's owner? We also think Frau Reiff's house is beautiful because Frau Reiff is not to blame for anything. Or not so far as we know, anyway.

Beyond the front gate there is a spacious interior courtyard. Beyond that you go through the former barn with its hayloft (which can be hired for events, hay and all) and you reach the apple orchard. Among the trees there is an old kayak, there's a swing for the children of the wind, and the cat is now exploring among the trees.

The dwelling house is on two floors. The rooms are bright and warm, the walls plastered with loam and love, as the saying goes. All the materials were local. Nothing artificial, instead you catch a glimpse of pine cones, pebbles and other natural things that have made their way into the materials, some ideology as well. Visitors like to pass their hands over the walls, and Frau Reiff likes to see that.

Frau Reiff has three children. Three girls or three boys?

A broad staircase leads up to the first floor. The steps are paler and lower in the middle than on the outside; that comes of the weight of time. Halfway up the staircase there's a circular window looking out on the interior courtyard where Frau Reiff entertains the participants in her *raku* workshop. Depending on the group dynamic and the air temperature, they sometimes sit out here until late at night, and sometimes someone points at the circular window after noticing movement on the stairs.

Those are the children. They climb up the outside of the steps, because the old wood complains more loudly in the middle. That's on account of the weight of time. The calm and restless children of the exiles who found shelter here. The strong and restless daughters of the last smith to work here before the war. The thin and restless sons of the Fahrin and Besekow farming families who owned and cultivated their own fields. Before them others; we don't know about them any more. At night all children are thirsty.

If a guest asks whether Frau Reiff has any children, Frau Reiff says either: yes, three sons, Janek, Karol and Izydor; or: yes, three daughters, Martha, Anna, Elisabeth; or: yes, three sons, Albert, Georg, Lennart. She has become used to it, it makes conversation so much easier, and she doesn't have to explain what she can't explain. It's true, as well: in a way they are all Frau Reiff's children, they live under the same roof. Frau Reiff leaves a glass of water out for them at the foot of the stairs in the evening.

You can deny only what exists.

Frau Reiff's workshop is in what used to be the servants' room of the smithy. The smell of clay and smoke clings persistently to everything. The unfinished pottery and the ceramic dust remind most women visitors in their fifties of a film with Patrick Swayze—we can't remember the title at the moment—in which Swayze and his great love make a vase before she dies. Or after she has died?

A visit to the workshop also increases the likelihood that the following remark will be uttered: I'd have loved to learn how to do something with my hands like that. Or: I'd love to learn, etc. Or: one of these days I'll learn, etc. Frau Reiff's pottery courses are booked up well in advance, anyway. People come from all over the German Republic north of

Kassel. When the students stop for a break, they like riding on the swing in the apple orchard when there's a couple taking the course, or when two of them have come a little closer to each other in the workshop. Someone always asks about the kayak. Frau Reiff doesn't know the answer. The kayak has always been there, she says, and she likes having a kayak in an apple orchard.

Others like the dry-stone wall round the garden. Frau Reiff tells them that whenever something worries her, she goes out into the fields until she finds a stone, it must be roughly the same size as her worry, and then she brings it here, puts it on the wall, and her worry immediately gets less. The lady who is the archivist here, she says, has told her that a smith did the same thing hundreds of years ago. She likes to think that her own worries are stacked on top of the worries of a man who lived in this place so many years before her.

Frau Reiff has made the stable into a showroom. Pale blue vases, pale blue dishes, pale blue mugs standing on small pedestals, monuments to the skill of her fingers. Sometimes there's a price on them, sometimes there isn't. Much of what she makes is not for sale. We could claim that those are the most filigree pieces. But what do we know? Perhaps Frau Reiff just likes them, and it's a good thing not to let what you like go.

Sometimes Frau Reiff sits at the foot of the stairs, and the children come down to drink water. Their fingers slide through the glass and close in a gesture of drinking, with nothing in their hands. Frau Reiff offers them bread as well, but they all leave the bread alone, except for a girl with greedy hands that can't catch hold of anything. Finger by finger, then her arm, then her foot, the girl eats herself instead.

Frau Reiff's apple cake tastes all right. If mankind were on the brink of annihilation and had to rely on homemade dishes, the people of Fürstenfelde would all survive, you'd be surprised, but you wouldn't be surprised for very long because we'd survive you.

Frau Reiff comes from Düsseldorf, which of course is a very long way off geographically, but in other respects as well she's not one of us. We may distinguish between those who come here from outside and the old inhabitants, as people do everywhere; the difference is that we make no secret of it. Those from outside have to take part in the life of the village, must commit themselves, must make their mark, although not with too much enthusiasm, because that in turn makes us skeptical. They must show concern and not just want to live their own nice, comfortable lives.

Frau Reiff did nothing at the old smithy without letting the village know. She sits on the parish council, and is in favor of street lighting and movement sensors. That could save us a good deal of money. Like us, she thinks windmills are beautiful, and like us she thinks wind turbines are ugly. Frau Reiff has made her mark all right.

Among other entertainments at the Feast, there will be African harp music at Frau Reiff's. Everyone will be there, apart from Rico and Luise. If she wasn't one of us, only casual customers would come to hear the harp music.

On the other hand, if you think about it for any length of time, those children can't be the children of exiles. None of them stayed in the village and died here, and if one thing is obvious about the subject of ghosts, then it's that they are not necessarily known for haunting places where they spent a few months once as children.

There's a plow stuck deep in the ground among the apple trees, as if it had fallen from a great height. The steel roller attached to the plow is a little rusty. The village asked what the plow was for. Frau Reiff said everything was staying put.

There were mud floors in the house in the old days, heating was by means of a ceramic stove. Polish forced laborers slept on the floor in front of the stove, and later on German refugees. All of them caught and cooked pigeons. They were put in the same camp in Fünfeichen, not far from here, but at different times. They slept under the same roof, separated only by a little time and history.

Frau Reiff doesn't know the life story of the plow.

She has a long day ahead of her. After the children have had their drink of water, she sees to the cat. He scurries out of the garden and into the house. Frau Reiff takes the last apple cake out of the oven; she has made six for the Feast. She drinks tap water from the hollow of her hand. The cat winds round her legs, purring.

A characteristic of *raku* pottery is the fine cracks that form at random as the glaze cools. They never run the same way. Like breaks and cuts in our life stories that become a part of them. The glaze of *raku* pottery melts at 800 °C to 1,000 °C. Frau Reiff is experimenting with mixed colors, but pale blue predominates.

ON THIS NIGHT THERE ARE MISDEEDS ON THE roads but no injustice. Error but no mistakes. A court of law but no verdict. A wind still blowing but no rain falling now.

It is Anna who asks questions once she has calmed down a little. Nothing surprises Herr Schramm any more. Frau Schwermuth is sniffling, her pale forehead furrowed with anxiety. She has wedged the spiked helmet under her arm. Her answer to the first question was that she wants to get back to the Homeland House as quickly as possible; she's afraid she has locked her son up in there. And to the second she replied that of course she knew what the matter with her was, but she couldn't explain why it was so bad tonight of all times. It was the stories' fault. They kept her awake when her medication made her tired and fat. But the medication kept the lid on the stories. The stories and the characters populating them.

Anna stares at Frau Schwermuth as hard as she has been staring at Herr Schramm all night. She thinks of the field on Geher's Farm. Of the characters populating it. Of those she imagined in the field as a child when she couldn't sleep. Anna says she can imagine how Frau Schwermuth feels. Frau Schwermuth says that's nice of her, but no one can imagine what she can imagine, no one. Then Frau Schwermuth says: I am empowered to call the night by its name.

Anna asks no more questions. Herr Schramm thinks about that "I am empowered." And how he has never said a sentence beginning "I am empowered."

The name of this night is tide, flood tide, now it is ebbing, let's see what has been washed up. We will go walking among the flotsam and jetsam, taking care not to step on anything! Frau Schwermuth has such long, beautiful eyelashes, and when she blinks waves of darkness break.

Frau Schwermuth goes into the cellar first. She quickly taps in the code and opens the door. Faint light. Books, notebooks, paper, on the shelves and in stacks. Thick folio volumes, loose pieces of parchment, the leather skins.

"Aha," says Herr Schramm. Herr Schramm is not all that fond of reading.

There is a little light up near the ceiling, the machine beeps, regulating the temperature. It's cold. The leather on the walls shimmers and moves. It's a skin of stories growing on us.

Johann is sitting on the table with his feet on the chair, a fat book on his lap. Beside him is his bell-ringer's top hat. Johann is freezing. Frau Schwermuth drops the helmet, swerves neatly round the mountains of paper, clasps Johann's legs, sobs. Johann puts his hand on his mother's back.

"Come on, Ma." He doesn't sound cross. It does no good when Ma is in this state. "It's all right, it's all right."

So much paper, and not a handkerchief anywhere. Frau Schwermuth touches Johann's cheek. Is everything really all right? No, but it will be. And how about her? No, and it probably never will be.

The pages of the book on Johann's lap are finely decorated, the print is like the print on the label of the 𝔘𝔫𝔣𝔬𝔯𝔤𝔦𝔳𝔦𝔫𝔤 energy drink. Johann closes the book.

Frau Schwermuth utters a short, sharp scream. "Johann! Haven't you been wearing gloves?" She has her voice back. "Heavens, don't you see what that book is?" She conjures a pair of white gloves out of the air, takes the book away from Johann and puts it carefully on the desk. The cover is charred at the edges. She opens it, her pupils wander from left to right, thunder rumbles in the pages.

On the 23rd Day of September 1613, the Spire of the Church here was struck by a Thunderbolt with a most dire and dreadful Noyse, so that a Bell in the said Tower was split in Twain, and two Houses and a Barn full of Grain caught Fire and were Burn't to the Ground.

Frau Schwermuth closes her eyes, breathes in and out. She has sat here hundreds of times, reading and digging under what once was for signs of today, indicating plans that the past has made with us, with her.

Johann takes her hand. Frau Schwermuth opens her eyes. She looks round at the visitors: Schramm and the girl—both deep in the leather. They are searching too. Herr Schramm is caught up in the 1970s, Anna in the more recent past. Frau Schwermuth wipes away her tears. She wants to go home.

Herr Schramm speaks first when the quartet are back in the fresh air. "Listen, Johann, got any cigarettes?"

And Johann might even have some if Ma wasn't here. She is standing by the broken window that she has covered up with newspaper. And naturally there is something that we can only hope Frau Schwermuth doesn't notice: almost all the broken glass is lying outside, almost none of it inside.

"What shall we do about the window?"

Herr Schramm says, "I'll see to it."

"The Feast mustn't be spoiled."

"Johanna, I'll do it. We'll take you home."

That isn't necessary, says Johann. Frau Schwermuth nods, and links arms with her son. Anna and Herr Schramm watch them go: Johann thin as a stalk of maize, and with his hair cut to match, standing out to left and right like, well, maize leaves. And she—she's Frau Schwermuth.

As they walk away she says, in a rather subdued voice, "Jo, you must do a few things for me tomorrow. I can't."

"What are they?"

"First there's the anti-Fascist bike ride at twelve."

That's when he has his bell-ringing exam, says Johann.

"Oh." Frau Schwermuth stops. "I don't think anything will come of that. I know it sounds funny now, but your bells are down on the banks of the lake. . ." And so on, we don't have to listen to it all, we know those two are safe together.

We take a historical interest in Frau Schwermuth and those like her, those with her kind of head. She's had her hair done specially for the Feast. Now it's been flattened by the spiked helmet. She puts the helmet on again. Johann puts on his top hat. They turn the corner and leave our night.

AT THE ANNA FEAST IN 1929, THE SHOOTING GUILD was photographed outside the house of the new champion marksman, Herr Werner Schramm. Unfortunately the picture is not a success. You can't tell one face from another, our uniforms look like dressing gowns, in fact it is a disaster, that bastard Schliebenhöner who took the photograph ought to be horsewhipped out of the village. The photograph, plus frame, costs five Reichsmarks.

ON A CHIPBOARD SURFACE SURROUNDED BY human earths and dogs' dreams, the vixen crouches in front of the container which, she knows, holds eggs. Her pelt is sticky with rain, she tastes her own blood, her paw hurts.

The vixen touches the container with her paws.

The vixen scratches its sides. Its top.

The vixen bites the container. The vixen jumps on the container, makes herself heavy, jumps and jumps and hurts herself landing, jumps and jumps and jumps. The vixen pushes her forehead against the container like a little bull. She can't get any purchase on the wet surface.

On top it is paler. She bites the pale part. The pale part moves, the dark part doesn't. The vixen waves her brush. The vixen tugs at the pale part of the container. When she lets go, the pale part snaps up. The vixen pushes her muzzle under the pale part. She lifts her muzzle, and the pale part rises. The vixen gets the idea.

The vixen is not alone.

Two male humans are leaning against the rock opposite, watching her tussle with the egg box. The vixen stops, one of them comes closer, is so close that he is within arm's reach of her, nearly there, but the vixen can't pick up any scent, no, couldn't say where he came from or went. He and his friend are loners, but they have no aromas. She stays put. The other young male human gets into the metal box that carries humans overland, a box, a box faster than any fox. Rhythmic sounds swing through the air. The vixen waves her tail in time with them, can't help it.

The first male human reaches his tentacle out to her, its claws spread. The vixen gets behind the container, ready to retreat, her injured eye throbbing with pain. But the human just picks up the container.

She's a killer on the road.

The human calls in a quiet human tone. Her urge to flee disappears. At last the vixen scents something in his call. She scents speech in the sounds of the human who has no scent. He is calling gently to her.

A small male human comes out of the earth. The container is marked with his scent.

A fire going cold.

He croaks, goes toward the vixen, but the one without any aroma goes to him, calls something, the small male human stops. Good. The vixen gets up on her hind legs, propping herself on the container, the scent of egg wafts out, she tries to haul herself up by the edge of the container, slips on the wet wood, won't let go and hauls the container over with her. Its contents fall toward her. Eggs break on the stone, she can already scent the little male human's boots, she growls,

A barrel of a gun

snaps at him, no—snaps at a shell that has fallen out of the container, digs her teeth into that hard but fragile shell, runs for it with her brush held low, is off and away,

A villain on the run.

The startled, small male human and the vixen's accomplices are left behind.

Well played, clever robber girl, we say.

ON THE 27TH DAY OF APRIL IN THE YEAR OF OUR Lord 1611, a female Wolf in Cub was taken in our Trap on the fallow Field at Geher's Farm. Thereby was great Harm averted, for ten Wolves would have wreaked Havock among our Cattle.

DIETMAR DIETZ SOON CALMS DOWN AFTER THE theft of the eggs. He acknowledges the fox's clever wit, and the young men agree with him. They fall into conversation. The two young men ask about the Feast, saying they've heard that there's good dancing in Fürstenfelde. Ditzsche sets them right: there's good dancing anywhere people can dance well, he says. The two of them appreciate his little boast, they say goodbye and wish the old man good music forever when he dances, which is what he likes to hear.

Ditzsche will dance, will swivel his hips without letting it look suggestive. He will smell of aftershave and Frau Reiff's apple cake. Surrounded by the stony faces of senior citizens dancing the polka, any kind of passion looks extreme.

Many of the older folk have forgotten about Ditzsche or even forgiven him. Not Imboden, who can hardly control himself when Ditzsche turns up anywhere. But last year Zieschke played a piece something like a tango, and Frau Kranz danced with Ditzsche to it. She and Zieschke were already here when Ditzsche's close relationship with our post was revealed.

But between ourselves: haven't you ever imagined, for instance on a walk and when the postman has just disappeared into the entrance hall of a building, what it would be like to take a handful of white letters out of the yellow box on the yellow bicycle, or get on the bicycle yourself, ride away, and spend the day immersed in the lives and bills of other people?

These days, with the Internet, doing such a thing would be less interesting than in Ditzsche's time. These days we all write emails. Well, here in Fürstenfelde not all of us write emails. And other people read our emails too, viruses and Americans read them, but that doesn't bother anyone much. Back in the past only Ditzsche read other people's letters. And the Stasi, but perhaps here it really was only Ditzsche. Although everyone knew everything about everyone else anyway, and still does.

Some day, when Ditzsche is no longer around, Fürstenfelde won't dance so well. Imboden isn't getting any younger either. Dietmar Dietz speaks lovingly to his chickens in Spanish some-times. Maybe he learned to dance in Cuba, maybe he learned at the People's University. And maybe he doesn't dance so well as all that, but someone once said with conviction that he did, so it became the truth, how would we know? Usually it's not so much a case of what's really true as what people think is true.

When he was delivering letters, Ditzsche sometimes forgot himself and did a little dance. Everyone likes to see someone who may be bringing good news forget himself and do a dance. And maybe Ditzsche was dancing for joy because he already knew the good news.

Out of a pension of 534 euros a month, Dietmar Dietz spends nearly 300 euros on his chickens. When Ditzsche is no longer here, there won't be a single pedigree chicken left in Fürstenfelde. Chickens will just be chickens. If you've ever seen specially beautiful chickens, if you've ever seen Ditzsche's pedigree Kraienköppe chickens stalking about, you'll know what a loss that will be.

But it's a comfort to know there's someone among us who understands rare creatures, or creatures hitherto entirely unknown here, whether he's a biologist, a geneticist or a chicken-breeder. That someone, in Herr Schramm's words, has a talent for the creation of what's new and the preservation of the norm. Such a talent that Breakfast TV phones Ditzsche and calls him "Herr Dietz," asking about his availability, and Herr Dietz hesitantly cracks a joke to the effect that he must look in his engagements diary. The Breakfast TV people say it would have to be a Saturday afternoon, and Ditzsche replies, "Then come to the Feast and you'll really have something to see, not just my chickens."

When people still went walking on a Sunday, Ditzsche would open his inner yard and let the chickens out of their enclosure. The people out walking wanted to see the chickens, and the chickens wanted to be seen; they stalked around and children clapped their hands. Ditzsche stood to one side, doing something or other, and no chicken ever left the yard. That's all over, and the chickens didn't stalk, Ditzsche would say, the chickens just had rather prominent chests and tall, elegant figures.

Even then, Ditzsche left his home only to go to work, to get things for his chickens, and to shake a leg dancing at Blissau's. In spite of all his dancing partners, nothing ever came of Ditzsche's acquaintance with women.

"Ditzsche, you're as stiff as your chickens," the ferryman once said, and Ditzsche replied quietly, "My chickens aren't stiff, but you're a layman, you wouldn't know."

And stiff wasn't the right word for Ditzsche, either. Abashed was more like it. Except when he was dancing, Ditzsche looked abashed the whole time. And you can't stand the company of someone who's always abashed for long. As soon as the music stopped, Ditzsche looked down at the floor. Didn't know what to do with his elbows and his shoulders, never asked a woman a question. And that's no good, women have to be asked questions.

After that business with Durden and his act of revenge, Ditzsche lost his job and disappeared for a couple of years. Some said he was taking more dancing lessons in Cuba. Others said: you always want people to be doing something special, but on the whole people don't do anything special. We've seen Ditzsche climbing scaffolding in Prenzlau.

He came back in 2003, but there's very little to be said about that. Durden had retired, the old bigwigs wore new suits, the polka was still in fashion and was now joined in popularity by the metal band Rammstein, equally simple in principle, and they're both all right. What didn't function in the past still didn't function, or functioned in a slightly different way, and functioned either better or worse, depending on your attitude to past history.

Dietmar Dietz functioned as usual. He began rearing a new breed of chickens. If he really did read our letters, people in the village may have shown him that they knew it, but he himself didn't get to know anyone better than before.

He will open his inner courtyard for the Feast. The enclosure will be clean, the chickens will shine beautifully in the sun. Outsiders will pay them compliments as if there were no tomorrow. And in the evening Dietmar Dietz will dance, well and unabashed.

THERE'S STILL TIME TO PASS BEFORE THE FEAST, but it won't be long now before the first light of dawn. The Adidas man has stationed himself outside the bakery earlier than usual; perhaps he thinks the Zieschkes will open sooner today. He keeps his head bent, rubs his hands either in anticipation or because of the cold. He is wearing the white tracksuit this morning. One trouser leg is hanging in tatters, as if a beast of prey had caught him there.

We're too tired for suspicion after such a night as this. Never mind what we think of the Adidas man. All the clothes he needs are those two tracksuits, and all the nourishment he needs is orange juice and yeast pastries with vanilla filling. And those are all the words he needs to order them in the morning. Not everyone needs a history of his own.

Lada has never met the Adidas man before. Now he and silent Suzi come out into the road, both looking as if they haven't had enough sleep. Until a moment ago they were playing games of chance on their computers to stay awake. Lada is still wearing his Shell overall, Suzi runs a comb through his hair, the dragon scales on his forehead sparkle in the light of the streetlamps. The plan is: the sooner they clear up Eddie's place, the sooner they can start celebrating. They light cigarettes. Simultaneity, comradeship, happiness.

Yes, and there's that character in his tracksuit outside the bakery. Lada's mother once confessed that she was afraid of him because he really didn't laugh, ever. Maybe Lada is thinking of that now. Thinking that a fear of his mother's is standing there, and he should have dealt with that fear long before this; he signs to Suzi to wait.

The Adidas man rubs his hands again, even after Lada positions himself between him and the shop door. After he has said something. Has repeated it in a louder voice. Has asked something. Suzi taps Lada's shoulder, walks his fingertips over it in an impatient gesture that says, "Let's get going!"

Lada puts his forefinger under the Adidas man's chin and raises it. He wants to look into his eyes. Those eyes are cornflowers. He doesn't blink. He's a field lying fallow. Lada's words pass over the field like wind. The way Lada is now, Lada is an arsehole.

Silent Suzi takes his arm. Draws him away. Helps the Adidas man up. And as he does that the Adidas man, with blood on his lip, whispers something in his ear.

Lada kicks the lamppost. The lamp goes out.

Strangers seldom come to us. They seldom stay.

Strangers who spend some time with us seldom stay strange.

We seldom make friends with the strangers, even if they do spend some time with us.

We're social. We're anti-social. We're open-minded. We're suspicious. Who likes being bothered? No one.

The slats of the Venetian blind clatter. Frau Zieschke's calves, apron, bosom and friendly round face come into view. The doorbell jingles generously. The baker's wife looks confused by the small assembly outside. The Adidas man smooths down his hair, as if all the fall had done was disarrange it.

Frau Zieschke hesitates. He can come in if he likes, she says, but it will be a little while before the baked goods are ready to serve.

Cornflowers, Adidas stripes, we don't know his name, we don't know what he can do. The Adidas man goes into the shop. With blood on his lip, he goes straight to the corner table and stands there. Frau Zieschke puts a packet of paper napkins in front of him.

A paper napkin is dabbed on a wound.

Frau Zieschke nods to her son outside. The boys move away. She puts coffee on. The Adidas man has dabbed his split lip dry and presses his fist into his other hand so hard that the knuckles show white.

The baker's wife gives him a cup of coffee. With a biscuit on the saucer.

He breaks the biscuit in his fingers.

He closes his eyes as he munches.

We don't know where he comes from. We don't know where he is going. A stranger is eating and drinking in our bakery.

UNDER A BEECH TREE ON THE OUTSKIRTS OF THE ancient forest, the injured vixen lies on damp leaves. Mist glows above the fields, enveloping the human earths. The vixen takes short, fast breaths. The little container is lying in front of her nose; she scents eggs, eggshells but no yolk yet. She gets up, limps farther into the forest with the container in her mouth.

The badger catches the vixen's scent and follows her, enquiringly; she has something that he likes, so he follows her. The vixen knows about the badger. Knows about his speed and agility and his bite. But he won't dare. The badger scents blood on the vixen, scents chicken, scents the eggs. It would be better for him if he could also scent her determination. She isn't going to let him have her catch without a fight. The badger overtakes the vixen and stops. The vixen trots toward the badger. The vixen is calm.

There is movement in the mist: the wind carries an aroma out of the forest, an aroma that displeases both the vixen and the badger. It surprises her, almost frightens her. The badger forgets about the eggs and strolls away, but the vixen calls a single clear, long-drawn-out warning, and runs on as fast as she can. Bitter and over-sweet: carrion and droppings, a member of her own family never before scented in the ancient forest. Wolf.

Reaching her earth, the vixen lets the egg container drop. It opens and an egg rolls out. She ought to have many more eggs here for her cubs. She barks softly, calls several times in quick succession. They don't come to her. She whines, she scents blood, scents wolf, snarls, she scents beech, ash, moss, blood, blood, worm, human, she scents the eggs, herself, the cubs, she scents the earthy honey of her coat, crawls into the earth, scents roots, scents play, scents cubs, can't find them anywhere, picks up their tracks, scents wolf, here, here, here, she scents stars, night, time, death, the vixen freezes rigid with her jaws wide open, snarling, calling, whining, it's over.

The vixen eats the eggs. Devours the eggs. The vixen barks. The vixen curls up in her earth. Licks her injured paw.

BATS SWIRL THROUGH THE AIR RETURNING TO their caves. Wild boar, full-fed, grunt. The screech owl lands softly, sings tu-whit tu-whoo.

LADA WOULD LIKE TO APPEAR ON THE TV PROGRAM *You Bet!* With this particular bet: he bets he could tell, from the way a streetlamp is made, where exactly he must kick it hard to make the light go out. He bets he could get it right with nineteen out of twenty streetlamps, although only those made in Berlin, Brandenburg and Mecklenburg-West Pomerania.

Silent Suzi is trying to tell Lada something. "Was strange man say me something."

"He's nuts," says Lada.

Suzi shakes his head, nudges Lada impatiently, repeats his gestures.

"Hey, Suzi, what are you getting at?"

Suzi points to his trainers.

Lada doesn't look at them, he is too agitated. He would have liked to wait for that punk to come out of the bakery again "so as to show him that he couldn't cross the line." Now he says, "Tell you what, Suzi, people think that guy is done for. Ex-druggie or some such, like Hirtentäschel, only done for. But he isn't. Because did you see how he landed? If you're done for, you don't catch yourself up like that. If you're done for you just fall down."

Suzi shakes his head and rolls his eyes. Indicates that he wants Lada to watch his mouth, forms the words with his lips and repeats the gestures.

"There that strange man say me something."

"The guy told you something?"

Suzi nods.

He crouches down and touches the road. They have reached Eddie's workshop.

"Road?"

Suzi shakes his head.

"Ground? What is it, man? Suzi? Asphalt?"

Suzi nods. Asphalt. With his lips and his hands, fingers spread, he mouths the words "something" and "under."

"There's something lying under the asphalt?"

Suzi nods.

AND A FLINT AX WAS FOUND IN A STONE GRAVE.

And a pair of tweezers was found in a tumulus grave; the tweezers were decorated at the broad end and were probably for plucking out the hairs of a beard, so it is assumed that the dead man had a well-groomed one.

And in a Slav grave a meerschaum hand spindle was found, and a coin in the dead man's mouth to pay the ferryman who would take him over to the next world.

And in another grave, the grave of a dead child, there was a hammer and a ceramic rattle. The hammer head was inside the rattle. If you shake a ceramic rattle, it makes a sound.

And when the promenade was flooded in 2004, they found the grave of a warrior who had been buried with a whetstone and a bone ax, so that he could face his enemies with a sharp blade for all eternity.

And in the year 1739 an edict was issued against *Gypsies, Vagabonds and other such Traveling Folk*, who were a thorn in the flesh of the local aristocracy, since *any Person who knowingly gives them an Abode* was threatened with a fine of 1,000 thalers. The village communities were also charged with taking travelers into custody. Once *a Rabble of Gypsies* came to Fürstenfelde. The men claimed to be horse-dealers and musicians, the women to be soothsayers. Their children moved fast. Their tools were the *horsewhip* and the *crystal ball.* The *Gypsy gallows* of Fürstenfelde stood on *the ground of a field lying fallow.*

And Maria Wegener once protested against the exclusion of joiners and carpenters from the local guilds. She had been unable to prove that they were rightfully born of *four grand-parents from Fürstenfelde,* and were thus worthy to work in our *workshops and guilds.* Frau Wegener was a wood-carver. She had done carvings for the door of our church, but they had gone up in flames, so no one knows if they looked good. Count Poppo von Blankenburg had commissioned Frau Wegener to carve him a yew-wood spoon. It was beautiful, a fine spoon with a broad bowl and an elegantly curving handle set in silver. Yew is slightly poisonous, but probably no one died of using the spoon, in fact you would have had to eat the spoon itself. A valuable spoon like that was left as a bequest when the owner died; as he passed away, it passed on. Von Blankenburg, our agricultural machinery mogul, keeps the yew-wood spoon that he inherited in a glass display case. Magdalene sometimes eats her muesli with it.

Maria Wegener's favorite tool was a *knife with a carved box-wood handle and a bone ferrule.*

And broken shards of Germanic and Slav origin were found in a rubbish tip, in the same stratum, with fragments of a comb made from deer's antlers under them.

And when diggers were working on the primary school, the building workers found an underground passage beneath the asphalt.

And one grave was that of a woman of about fifty, with two rings as worn on the temples in late-Slav costume beside her. Her head and feet were weighted with stones, probably to prevent the dead woman from returning. Anthropological examination made the reason for that obvious. Her skull showed bony excrescences as the result of benevolent tumors. The woman, who was found in a petrified condition, had a horn six centimeters long over her left eye. It may be assumed that her family were afraid of her.

Fürstenfelde is registered as an archaeological site.

THERE ARE A GOOD MANY HOUSE CLEARANCES IN our village. Lada is in charge, and has five people working freelance for him. When Suzi doesn't have to be at Gölow's, he helps out. The two of them make a good team. Lada doesn't listen, and Suzi doesn't mind how many words he hears. On Monday it will be the turn of Anna's house, and now it's the joiner's. Eddie's house. Eddie has been on the list since January, but Lada didn't want to do it too close to his death, because when it's our joiner, who has paneled half the village's bedrooms, you don't, as part of the village, go straight to remove the paneling from his own bedroom, not even if his daughters keep phoning to ask what's going on, why hasn't the job been done yet? And you don't break up the joiner's furniture without drinking to him one last time with the other old boys, or drinking to something else entirely, but having a drink as a memento is what matters. You don't just say, here, 170 euros per ton of mixed scrap. And by the way, what are you going to do with all his tools and his old machinery? At first the daughters said they didn't mind what became of it, but then Lada hinted that it might be worth getting some of it valued, and suddenly they did mind what happened to the tools and the old machinery.

The only person who can use the machinery is probably someone about as old as Eddie. The joiner was still sitting at those machines until the end, the joiner was a real glutton for work. Many of us lie in his coffins, they were good value, sometimes the base of the coffin was part of a cupboard, while for Herr Geels, our trained angler, his old boat was just the thing, it looked great, not a classic form, but it looked like a boat. Well, not really so great, but that's how Geels had ordered it, and he had no objection; he should know, because he'd be lying in it himself in the end.

Of course there were some complaints as well, there's always a bit of shrinkage. As they say elsewhere. We don't say so. We say: anyone too mean to go to a trained joiner can't complain if something doesn't quite fit later.

But anyway, the joiner was a glutton for work. You could call him in the middle of the night and he'd come round, repair your TV set and watch Breakfast TV with you, or take the set away if he thought it was no more use. Our joiner was also an electrician. Many say he was a better electrician than a joiner.

And in retrospect maybe he wasn't such a good electrician either, if you take the Archivarium as an example. It was Eddie who installed the electronic lock, and then the code sometimes didn't work, or the door hummed so that Frau Schwermuth complained she couldn't concentrate, or it was left open, like tonight.

A glutton for work, our Eddie was. When he was dying he made his own coffin, a nice one, cherry-wood, he liked the smell, that's one of the little things that we all know about him. Another is that our joiner kept everything, as Lada and silent

Suzi are now realizing. Not because he was a sentimental man, indeed the joiner was exactly the opposite, he was an optimist. He thought he'd be able to use it all sometime, down to the last nail. His three daughters are none of them sentimental; they none of them stuck it out here, and we know we ought to put that more positively. The three of them thought their future chances would be better somewhere else, and now one of them is divorced, one is working in a *dm* drugstore, one has a son with learning difficulties, and we don't feel glad or anything nasty like that. Well, maybe we do a little, because they never came back to see their father's house, the house of their childhood, after his death, and because they told Lada everything could go, just get rid of it. Get rid of it! We didn't like their way of sticking to their point for no good reason. We didn't like their wholesale refusal to separate what was important from what wasn't important, because yes, we're sentimental, we are. The joiner had kept all that stuff for us. Materials that he was planning to make into things sometime and sell them to us, or things intended for us although so far no one wanted them, and finally things we'd broken that had ended up with him. Sometimes Eddie brought us back our own radio sets decades later, with a serious expression and not without pride. Of course we didn't want them any more, so he kept them. And were the old radios just to be thrown away now? The workshop was full of radios up to the ceiling, along with electrical goods and parts of electrical goods, plus music cassettes and video cassettes, toasters, hair dryers, old issues of *Playboy*. Silent Suzi is astonished, his entire head plus the back of his neck, where the dragon keeps watch to make sure no harm comes to Suzi, is rigid before this infinity of raw materials, implements, tools, dust and history, our own history included, wood in all phases of its aging, cast iron, aluminium, rust, yes, there's a lot of rust. Eddie always had something better to do than tidy up. When we shot down the Yank aircraft in '45, Eddie was first on the scene, clambering up on it to pick up what he could carry—from the depths of the shed, Suzi salvages the propeller. A hundred and seventy euros per ton of mixed scrap?

No, Eddie wasn't sentimental, but we are, we're sentimental, and the Feast is a kind of deadline; our joiner liked to be active then, to the last he built the bonfire, letting him do it was something of a risk, but nothing too bad ever happened. He also had a little stall for the children, and spent all day burning their names or whatever they wanted into wood. Often they wanted an animal, and it didn't look particularly good now, but you could tell roughly what family of animal it was, usually a fish, a catfish with whiskers. Lada has a piece of wood like that at home, with *Robert likes horses* on it, which had been the case at the time. Lada remembers the tool Eddie used, if he can find it Lada has plans for the tool.

We carry Eddie's workshop round in us. In our lips when we open and close them, with its pincers. Our hearts throb to the hammer blows coming down on thousands upon thousands of nails. So much that was mended didn't stay mended.

We keep the broken bits in us, the useless things, the things that have served their purpose.

Lada and Suzi are in the house now. Plastic window frames. Man-made fabric wallpaper. Extremely colorful plush sofa. Massive farmhouse table. Homemade furniture stands next to wooden paneling from the GDR, and stuff from the cheap furnishing stores of the post-unification period. The carpets stick to the floorboards, and you can follow exactly the route the joiner and his wife and their three daughters took round the carpets in the house over the last thirty or forty years: kitchen—front hall—sofa—corridor—bedroom. The carpets smell.

The daughters are coming in the afternoon. They're staying the night in Carwitz. People say it's lovely there. They say: Hans Fallada. We say, Carwitz is in Mecklenburg, and Hans Fallada treated his wife badly.

Lada would have liked to open the workshop today for people who felt curious or sentimental, and clear it only after the Feast. The daughters wouldn't agree. Either all the stuff is gone by the weekend, they said, or we'll give someone else the job. They didn't even sound annoyed any more.

Eddie could watch Western TV before most of us had a TV set at all, but he had better things to do. Eddie was a jack of all trades. We'll be bumping into him at the Feast. Someone will say: you don't see the likes of Eddie any more these days. Of course that's not right. It's only that we won't be seeing that particular Eddie any more.

Lada and Suzi assess Eddie, figure Eddie out. Muster their arguments for negotiating with the daughters. Judge how much of Eddie can be broken up, and what they will buy from the daughters for how much. Let the Homeland House have a few things? Suzi agrees.

They put gloves on. Lada and Suzi break up Eddie. A hundred and seventy euros per ton of mixed scrap. No more sentimentality when Lada takes the first door off its hinges. He'll rope in Rico and Mustard-Micha later for the heavy things. The skip fills up, the skip may wake the neighbors or it may not. We want to see it, we won't get sentimental when Lada runs his fingers over the door to the workshop. Eddie made it himself, of course, curved sections of tropical wood, where did he get it? Probably straight from the jungle. And Lada nods, because he knows it is extremely good work, good enough for him to wonder briefly whether the door would fit into his own leisure-time cellar.

Lada measures it.

Lada and Suzi are a good team. After three hours of taking things apart and dragging them away, however, they know the job won't be done as quickly as they thought. And Suzi will soon have to go off to do one or two other things, seeing to Gölow's pigs, for instance, so they slow down, smoke outside the workshop, eat jelly bears, drink 𝔘𝔫𝔣𝔬𝔯𝔤𝔦𝔳𝔦𝔫𝔤. The sun rises in the mist, Lada's angular, shaven skull is shiny with sweat. Lada stubs out his cigarette and sets off in search of the drawers containing Eddie's tools, Eddie's materials. He finds what he needs: a tool like a soldering iron, a saw and a piece of wood, it may be maple, from which he saws a small plaque, 30 x 30 cm. Lada writes on the plaque. The point of the tool is glowing. He calls Suzi, come here a moment, holds the tip of the tool out to him, touch that. Suzi shows Lada his middle finger. Lada burns what he wrote into the wood with the tool. Suzi reads what it says and is pleased. When Suzi is pleased it looks splendid, Suzi's impressive black eyes shine, the dragon stretches in satisfaction.

The trace of the burning is dark brown on the light wood.

Lada's underarm musculature.

Lada's many talents. He could be an Eddie one of these days.

Lada's words, the words that Lada thought up.

AND HERR SCHRAMM, FORMER LIEUTENANT-Colonel in the National People's Army, then a forester, now a pensioner and also, because the pension doesn't go far enough, moonlighting for Von Blankenburg Agricultural Machinery, is driving the Mammoth 6800 silage chopper through the village, where the majority of inhabitants are asleep, and he is driving at 40 k.p.h., and the Mammoth 6800 silage chopper isn't the quietest of machines. The Mammoth 6800 silage chopper is 350 horsepower, and that, thinks Herr Schramm, is quite enough to answer all the questions that a silage chopper can be asked in the course of its life.

The silage chopper is Herr Schramm's favorite agricultural machine. At Von Blankenburg's he was all for it from the first, you might say responsible for it. It had been Schramm who collected it from its previous owner, and the journey was a special one too. From Schwerin to Fürstenfelde, along country roads all the way on a mild spring afternoon, rapeseed in flower, insects coming to life, and Herr Schramm up in the cab, his cigarette packet almost full, maybe he'd have a beer, two at the most. Herr Schramm doesn't drink and drive.

Nice country roads, a nice speed of 30, in fact the Mammoth can easily do 50, but there's no need to go so fast on a fine spring day, it would just be gaining time.

Herr Schramm is an upright military man with poor posture. On that spring day Herr Schramm has responsibility and a purpose and in addition a talent for steering wide vehicles which he had to use often enough in his days of army service in Wegnitz, and he liked doing it when the bright young sparks of the motor division criticized the big, broad SIL truck, saying that pig of a SIL would never go through the gap. Lieutenant-Colonel Schramm would get into it, and the pig of a SIL passed neatly through the gap, even after Schramm had spent an eventful evening dancing in the barracks.

Herr Schramm smoked and looked at the fields of rapeseed, and beyond the rapeseed at the wind turbines. Wind turbines infuriated Wilfried Schramm. Not for the aesthetic reasons held by many others; aesthetic reasons are not good reasons at all. But because the rotor blades kill bats. Quarter of a million bats a year. Twelve of them per turbine.

His anger didn't last long. Herr Schramm had cigarettes and a road three meters wide, he blinked the indicator when the road ahead was clear for drivers to overtake him.

Built in the year 1994. Four-wheel drive. Air conditioning. Kemper chopper head. Herr Schramm helped to get the Mammoth into shape. Helped? Initiated the process, delegated some of it, lent a hand himself. Overhauled the electrics of the reversing and grinding units. Carefully repainted the flaking paint, sky-blue. Built in a radio. But you can't do anything about 4,000 working hours on the clock. There were newer, better, more sophisticated models than the Mammoth 6800 now. No buyer was found, even after the price was cut.

Herr Schramm is a loyal man, but not clingy. What you have you have, what you can't have, you can't have. But when he had heard the day before yesterday that there was a buyer after all, and he of all people was delivering the Mammoth to the buyer in Neubrandenburg on Monday, it cannot be said that Herr Schramm exactly jumped for joy.

Herr Schramm sits in the sky-blue cab of his Mammoth 6800 thinking, what do I mean, why am I calling it *my* Mammoth? The Mammoth rattles and bleats its way along the roads at the end of the night. Anna is sitting beside the tall man, bobbing about like a Christmas tree decoration.

Herr Schramm is a critical man. He has objections to easy access to such things as weapons, pornography, political parties and cigarette machines. Herr Schramm thinks of Martina (nineteen, Czech Republic). Manicure! That's what it's called, that's the word. Martina had well-manicured fingernails.

With a skillful turn, Herr Schramm brings the Mammoth to a halt beside the cigarette vending machine. The Mammoth and Anna breathe a sigh of relief. Anna asks what is going to happen now, but she has a good idea what will happen now. They have hardly spoken since leaving the Schwermuths, Schramm gave monosyllabic answers to Anna's questions, so after a while Anna stopped asking them and just trotted along with him to the place where the agricultural machinery was parked, feeling helpless yet somehow not helpless, because she was still with him and he was still with her.

"Right," says Herr Schramm. He makes the 350 horse-power engine roar. It wasn't really necessary, but it sounds good if you like the noise. "Here we go."

Herr Schramm rams the cigarette machine.

Anna squeals a little, but just because of the jolt.

Herr Schramm goes into reverse. When the Mammoth 6800 is reversing, you usually hear that beep-beep sound. He has disabled it, he doesn't want to warn anyone. "Right," says Herr Schramm, and he rams the cigarette machine again, and this time the bar in front of it gradually gives way, bending, and Anna screams but also laughs a little, because how could you not laugh?

Herr Schramm rams the cigarette machine, and it's not just the horsepower, although of course that does its bit, but also—one would have to reckon on that—several tons of weight exerting persuasive influence on that little bar, and if one thing is clear, then this is it: in the long run a cigarette machine like that doesn't have a chance against Herr Schramm and a silage chopper with a Kemper chopper head, and the fifth or sixth time that metal meets metal it works. The bar breaks like a bar breaking, and the machine falls to the ground like a machine falling to the ground. Well, there aren't many similes available; it doesn't happen very often.

"Terrific," says Anna.

"There," says Herr Schramm, switching the indicator on.

We don't know how to tell the next bit. At the moment when Herr Schramm switches off the engine, there is a curse from the upper floor of the boarding house opposite, and someone says, "I don't believe it," and at the boarding-house window appears the sleepy head of—we don't believe it either, we can't say her name—

"Frau. . . Mahlke?" cries Herr Schramm incredulously, and if there is one thing that for decades Herr Schramm has not been, and never will be again after tonight, it is incredulous.

"Wilfried?" says Frau Mahlke at first hesitantly, and then, reasonably enough, sounding annoyed. "Wilfried, what are you doing there?"

Of course that is not a very good question, thinks Herr Schramm, because it is fairly obvious what he is doing, and he says so too. "Well, getting some cigarettes."

And in the first faint light of dawn Herr Schramm, former Lieutenant-Colonel in the National People's Army, then a forester, now a pensioner and also, because the pension doesn't go far enough, moonlighting as a mechanic, a driver and a cleaner for Von Blankenburg Agricultural Machinery, sees the color and light of Frau Mahlke's eyes (green and glowing), which remind him of the meatballs, the hot summer's day, the best day of the whole summer, and he sees the color and light of the Mammoth 6800 (sky-blue and shiny), which remind him of the journey from Schwerin, the best spring day of the spring, a day when he did something he could do, did something he wanted to do, and this girl stayed with him, wanted to save his life without knowing what his life was like, yes, thinks Schramm, it's all right after all. And from upstairs Frau Mahlke calls, "Come on up and I'll roll you one," and it is so improbable that she is calling that, so improbably improbable that she is there at all, that Herr Schramm can only shake hands with Anna, give the Mammoth a pat, and then run to the door of the boarding house, although it will stay closed until Frau Mahlke comes down with the key.

IV

WE ARE TOUCHED. JUST AT THE RIGHT TIME FOR the Feast, one of those who have moved to the village, namely Frau Reiff, has tracked down our four oldest post-cards and had them reprinted on good cardboard. The Homeland House can sell them and keep the money. Frau Reiff has given us the originals for the auction.

1. *The War Memorial* in the Friedhofshain: the year is 1913. It is an eagle on top of a rectangular column tapering toward the top. You can see the gravestones indistinctly behind it. It records the names of the dead in three wars: 1864, 1866, 1870. In the corner it says *Greetings from Fürstenfelde.*

It has survived the World Wars. The list of names from those two wars, as you might expect, is longer, and stands on extra stones beside the column.

2. *The Shooting Range* shows Fritz Blissau's beer garden. The year is 1935, the village is celebrating the Anna Feast. The village has put on its Sunday best and is wearing a hat. Except for Gustav. Gustav is eight. But Gustav's pudding-bowl haircut looks like a hat, so it fits in. A young woman is coming up from the left in the postcard, carrying a tray laden with drinks, although everyone has a drink already apart from Gustav.

Those are good years. There are 400 more of us than today. We leave the village from two railway stations and drive around in fifteen motor cars. Optimism procreates children. Gustav's parents can afford a proper haircut for Gustav. His father is the pastor, his mother is a secretary at the telegraph office. The country people nearby regard us as townies. We believe in work and the Fatherland, we have work and the Fatherland, we wear bows in our hats. We are living in a condition of blissful ignorance. After the war we'll be going around barefoot.

There's a canopy of chestnut leaves above the shooting range. Gustav is sitting at his table alone. His father wanted him to be in the photo, and had to persuade Blissau, who doesn't like to see children running round among his guests and his jugs. Gustav likes running round. He wants to be a geographer, like Hans Steffen. The Nuremberg Laws are six days old. The tablecloths are white.

The village looks at the camera. Only the young woman stares at her tray of drinks: please don't let there be an accident now. It does us good to see you all looking so tense because of the photographs, while at the same time we can tell that you really feel relaxed.

Herr Schliebenhöner releases the shutter.

A bee settles beside Gustav's hand. Bells ring. The sun seems to be shining above the chestnut leaves.

3. *The Windmill*: a beautiful tower with wide sails. Two cows are grazing in front of the mill. In the viewer's imagination, the wind is blowing and the sails are going round. No one is indifferent to windmills. In the course of his life, every fifth male Federal German citizen will try to understand exactly how a windmill works.

Nothing is left of the mill today. The people in the new buildings hang out their washing to dry where it used to be. Silent Suzi's mother hangs out her bed linen. The Bunny logo flutters in the wind and rain.

Windmills are windmills, washing lines are washing lines. The village doesn't say: oh, if only the windmill were still standing. The people from the new buildings are glad to have washing lines outdoors; their apartments are small.

But we'd like to talk about mills. There were four of them here. One was demolished in 1930, only the lower part of another still stands and is used as a second home at weekends by a married couple from Hamburg. The third dates from the six-teenth century. The feudal lord, Count Poppo von Blankenburg, was not at all happy about the flour it produced, and sent miller after miller packing. Finally he decided to try his luck as a miller himself. He took on three young miller's men to help him, gave the priest living quarters in the mill to protect it from the Devil, and also hired a wise woman who promised to drive away mealworms and any ghosts haunting the mill (§ 109 of the Procedure for the Judgment of Capital Crimes, the Holy Roman Emperor Charles V's statute introduced in 1532, made it easy to distinguish between harmless and harmful magic). Finally he gave orders for three virgins to be brought to him. History does not relate what they were meant for.

The result was disastrous.

The priest and the wise woman went for each other first metaphysically, then physically. The miller's men seduced the virgins, or vice versa, and when the village had no flour left at all, not even bad flour, its people assembled outside the mill to ask what was going on. The Count appeared at a window, shivering and shouting. How, he asked, was a man to get anywhere with a mill that felt like a human being and just didn't fancy grinding flour?

"Talk to it kindly," called a small voice from down below through his ranting. "Be nice to it." The speaker was a girl with blue-gray eyes and short blonde hair. The nobleman fell silent, and the farmers, the laborers with their pitchforks, and a fox who had come to see what there was to be seen here were surprised too. But then the people agreed with the girl. Perhaps they really thought it would help, but more likely they just wanted to hear how their Count went about beguiling the mill.

And he did it, too. He immediately turned to the mill's shutters and began praising them lavishly. What beautiful shutters over its windows, whether they were open or closed! And its sails! So large and useful. And so on, although here we must point out that no one would know the story today if Frau Schwermuth hadn't discovered it.

In the place where Poppo von Blankenburg spent a day flattering a windmill, bewitching it, whispering sweet nothings to it, until in the evening he heard a sigh—perhaps it was the mill, perhaps it was the wind—whereupon he found that he could grind such fine, pure flour that at the Anna Feast, which was soon celebrated, the villagers hardly touched any meat once they had tasted the bread; in that place a wind turbine stands today.

The fourth mill, the one on the postcard, was demolished by Belorussians in the last days of the war. It then occurred to them that flour wasn't a bad idea, and they put the mill back in running order. The bread, which had a sour flavor, tasted wonderful to anyone who could get hold of any. We can still hear the grinding sound of the mill. We remember Alwin, the miller's man here in the war. He had crooked teeth and could do conjuring tricks, he made the coins brought by servants coming to collect the flour disappear, and days later they found a coin in their bread, what a surprise! Alwin had to stop that game when matters of hygiene were taken seriously. After that he always guessed which card was the King of Hearts. The Belorussians shot him outside the mill. His name was Alwin, he had crooked teeth, and he could do conjuring tricks.

The mill itself had a name, but it got lost among the rubble.

It was demolished in 1960 and carried away, bit by bit, to our gardens, our walls, our cellars.

4. *The Promenade*: lined by ash trees as it still is today, so there's not much change there. The lake on the left, the town wall on the right. A bench between them. Shady. Shade is the theme. A young woman and a young man are sitting on the bench, holding hands. She is in white, with a brooch on her collar, he is trying to follow the fashion for mustaches. The year is 1941. Hardly anyone wishes you "Good day" now. Either it's "Heil Hitler" or you don't give a greeting at all, but in a public place like the promenade no one would like to appear discourteous.

An ordinary sort of couple. Not too good-looking, not too elegant. Hands perhaps a centimeter or so apart. We say they are a couple because we know how it turned out; they almost held hands that day; there was a wedding, and nine months later along came Herrmann. Only they weren't in love. Not on the promenade, not in the bad times that were coming and fired up many a relationship. They stayed together, yes, and they didn't bother each other. You could say they behaved to one another all their lives like their hands on the postcard, just about to touch. If you look closely, you can see that the young woman on the promenade is suppressing a yawn.

Two people under the ash trees on the promenade. Two people who wouldn't have spent their lives together but for the promenade. If Herr Schliebenhöner hadn't stopped them separately and asked them to pose for a photo on the bench, they'd have passed each other a little way up the promenade with a shy "Heil Hitler," and that would have been it.

You would have been able to see the ferryman from the promenade. And the women in Frau Kranz's first painting. Three bells are resting under the ash trees beside the lake. Perhaps they like it on the promenade.

That well-lit promenade. That subsidized, undermined promenade. Ah, those mice who scurry over the tarmac. A little refuge for those who may be in love, a forum for pro-letarians, a place for Anna to run when she goes running, a country road for satnav devices. That eternal promenade. Our promenade.

ANNA COMES UP FROM THE PROMENADE, RUNS past the new buildings, past the Gölow property, turns along the former railway embankment, puts on a spurt at the dilapidated railway station where, as we remember it, the morning train from Prenzlau let off the first guests coming to the Feast.

Anna approaches the fallow field. Not even the oak tree has survived such a night as that intact. Anna is tired. She would be home in two or three minutes, but she wants to look at the oak tree. The tree slants up into the mist, its branches touch the ground to left and right as if they were growing straight from the soil. Anna climbs over the fence and makes her cautious way through the bushes. The field doesn't care about caution, she can hardly move along, gets her clothes caught in the undergrowth, does not get impatient.

Lightning has split the oak tree, breaking it open from inside. It is white; white timber. Let's imagine that the air smells of smoke. The ground is churned up, a narrow grave as if the lightning had turned the soil. Or as if someone had been digging.

Two pale skulls lie in the earth. The yellowish-white of hungry teeth. Anna has only a few meters to go, in a week's time her term begins, she's going to study marine technology in Rostock, she wants to design ships; she'd like the ships that she designs to be built so that other people can steer them over the seas. She bends over the skulls, is going to pick one of them up, puts a twig into its eye socket, and a hand comes down on her shoulder.

We would scream. Anna keeps calm. The skull slips off the twig and is caught by a stranger's hand in mid-flight through the air.

"Good catch in this light," says the tall, handsome one, grinning at the skull.

"They never had a Christian burial rite," says the small, sturdy one, crouching down at the side of the grave. They are Anna's rescuers from earlier in the night. Anna takes a deep breath and shakes the hand off her shoulder.

"What are you two still doing here?" As long as you can say the right words in a firm voice, you have nothing to fear.

"We thought we wouldn't go before telling ourselves hello," says Q, examining the skull and cleaning soil out of the holes in it with his forefinger. Henry plucks leaves off his companion's coat. They have cigarettes with them, and cans of beer. Anna declines to drink with them—oh, come on! No.

Q gives Henry a light; the flame shoots out of his thumb. Henry dips his hands into the grave like a surgeon into a patient's body, bones clatter, he brings out the second skull. Q holds his to his cheek, as if he wanted to show Anna the likeness.

"The oak tree," says Anna. "Frau Schwermuth once told me people were hanged from it."

"We come into the world innocent, we may go to our death sinners."

"The rope showed that we weren't always winners." They laugh. Anna doesn't. They clink the skulls together. To the dead! They drink. Henry offers his skull a sip too.

"Who—" Anna hesitates. "*What* are you?"

Q takes off his coat and puts it round her shoulders. Henry walks over to the grave, rhythmically opening and closing the lower jaw of the skull he holds with a clatter, Q joins him, they are actors now, and this is the last act. Not Anna but the grave is their audience.

They speak in unison, thoughtfully: "We—we are what you would be: worldly-wise, carefree are we. Power, a dig at you as we're leaving, honest avengers wanted for thieving. We are the fury of ancient songs, wild as we go about righting wrongs." Softly at the end: "We are two who will endeavor, with our necks in the noose, to sing for ever."

Henry puts his cigarette between the jaws of the skull. The field crackles, as if familiar with fire.

The cigarette goes out. They put the skulls carefully back in the grave. Pile the earth over them with their bare hands. Anna takes Schramm's pistol out of the pocket of her jacket, and lays it in the grave too. Helps them.

They escort Anna to the farmhouse, take off their caps, bow politely to her; their farewells do not take long, and then they are off, two dissimilar figures going cross-country through the Uckermark, one tall and slender, the other short and strong.

WE ARE EXHAUSTED. THE BIRDS HAVE NO CONSID-eration for us. The dawn twilight, the tiles, the stones in the fields: all clammy. Suzi takes a detour along the side of the lake. Mist hovers over the water. Frau Kranz is packing up her things. Suzi offers to help her. No. The old woman wades through the reeds. She shows Suzi the painting. Her lips are bluish. His glance wanders from left to right. He goes closer. Frau Kranz wants to know his opinion.

Suzi points. "I—artist—not." Suzi smiles.

Frau Kranz points to herself. "Artist—not."

Suzi, slightly embarrassed, shakes his head.

Below the ruins of what was once Schielke's farmhouse there's a fridge stuck in the muddy ground, with a can of tuna still in it. Suzi smiles. Seen from here, no Fürstenfelde exists. Of course the mist will lift, the weather will be fine for the Feast, but at the moment there is no village, there are no stories, no wonders and marvels. There's Suzi and a path along the bank of the lake, lined with blackcurrant bushes.

That Suzi—blonde as a child, black-haired as a man. Back straight, Suzi. His father drank the bitter blackcurrant juice. Back straight, Father. His father's life before the new build-ings went up: herding sheep. Many incomplete sentences at breakfast. We'll leave him out of it for now. Suzi smiles.

Magdalene von Blankenburg does yoga under the linden tree on the bank in the morning. It may be too wet today.

Yoga trousers, best trousers. Suzi can make out the hunting lodge behind the bushes, the little turrets rise into the mist like something in a fairy tale, that's what things look like when a blue-blooded aristocrat says what he wants. Suzi combs a strand of hair back from his forehead.

Suzi's father took him to work with him. They drove around. Father in uniform, a tank like a diver's on his back. Little Suzi waiting for his father in strangers' living rooms. His father always taking everything people offered.

Silent Suzi climbs the fence. He puts his arm cautiously into the bushes. Waits. Spider on the back of his hand, tiny spider. Suzi's father caught flies out of the air. Suzi pees in the lake. It is getting warmer under the blanket of mist.

Any good-looking woman looks even better with a Baroque hunting lodge behind her. The sight of Magdalene: compensation for dragging things about at Eddie's. Blonde, her eyes blue-gray. Could be one of us. The lake is buzzing. Insects guessing something. Guessing storm. Yoga mat. Yoga trousers. Yoga braid. Yoga book. Not a yoga book, but Hugo von Hofmannsthal.

Magdalene does the greeting to the sun. Suzi doesn't know that is what it's called. The mist disperses. The only complete sentence his father said to Suzi was: "Now, tell me the whole truth, Suleyman, no lying." The last image: his father in a denim shirt, jeans and camouflage rucksack, with the bitter, loving smell of blackcurrants coming from his mouth. Money for maintenance arrives now and then, sometimes a letter. All okay. Suzi smiles; the sun is here.

Magdalene ripples softly in the sun. Suzi forgets his mother, forgets Gölow, Lada, Father, Suzi is the main owner of all the time in the world. Magdalene is reading now. Pretending to be reading. The air still isn't warm, but pleasant enough. Suzi takes off his sweater, sits on it. In his undershirt. Magdalene knows about Suzi. All those times he goes fishing here. When they once meet by chance in the ice cream parlor she says hello, but he does not reply.

Suzi is whistling, barely audibly. A mouse comes out of the reeds, nosing around. Suzi puts a jelly bear on the grass. The mouse snaps it up.

A minnow jumps in the lake. Something glittering lies in the reeds. Two mice scurry from there to here. Suzi smiles. Gives them another jelly bear. Whistles. They bring him the glittery thing. It is slightly bent, a little crown like those the beauty queens wear. Only prettier. Prettier, of course, because it is Magdalene's.

Good.

The mice have gone away.

Good.

Suzi goes over. Gives Magdalene the tiara. Magdalene reads aloud to him. Between sentences he feels her gaze on him, on his undershirt, his dragon, his hands, his cheeks and his temples. Now and then he closes his eyes to feel it on his eyelids too, along with the sun.

Hugo von Hofmannsthal smiles.

FRAU KRANZ WAS WELL EQUIPPED, BUT THE CHILL of the lake and the cold wind have seeped into her old bones, slowly freezing her hands and her memories. Frau Kranz is frozen through, remembered through, and in a bad temper, and it is not surprising that she is dissatisfied with her picture.

And now here's Frau Zieschke into the bargain buttonholing her outside the bakery, in an elated mood. Lord almighty, it's much too early for cheerfulness, but Frau Zieschke is one of those whose emotional streaks reach out in all directions. She is waving the *Nordkurier* like a soldier with a banner after victory in a battle: Frau Kranz is in the paper, a whole page! With a photo! In the photo Frau Kranz is smiling, although now she can't remember any reason for smiling and surely Frau Zieschke isn't going to read it all out loud to her in the street! Frau Kranz pushes the baker's wife back into the bakery, and there a way to calm the woman down occurs to her: she shows Frau Zieschke last night's painting. Yes, that, she says, is how it will be for the auction. It works: Frau Zieschke's enthusiasm disappears.

"Oh," she says.

Frau Kranz takes the newspaper and asks the baker's wife to make her a hot milk. She does feel a little curious. She skips the introduction with her biography and career, because she knows all that. She merely skims the central part, with the

description of her hairstyle and the way she smokes a cigar.
She shakes her head over the lavish praise of a picture she
can't even call to mind from its description. She reads only
the conclusion properly.

*Ana Kranz does not see herself as a painter of local scenes.
She doesn't like to be linked with a particular countryside and
its culture. However, her paintings do show local scenes—the
countryside of our Uckermark. They show our memories, even
those that we first know we have only through our image of them:
our childhood, the young faces of our parents and grandparents,
the work and everyday life of three generations in the eddies of
time. Kranz's paintings are no less than journeys into the past.*

*Ana Kranz is not a painter of local scenes. She is our painter,
and a painter of this place. We wish her well on her ninetieth
birthday, in deep gratitude for her work in our homeland.*

Slushy, but never mind, thinks Frau Kranz. You can forget
the rest, and your birthday isn't until next Saturday.

She escapes the bakery with the arrival of the next customers. Frau Kranz can tell that the weather is changing from
the pain in her joints, but above all from the blue sky. An old
woman on her way home. She had made herself pretty for
the memory, and it had been no use; you can't fool memories.

Frau Kranz has failed with her picture of the night. She is
a little sorry for the sake of the village. Frau Schwermuth and
Frau Zieschke and the Creative Committee were expecting
something special for the auction. Hirtentäschel even wanted
a preview of the picture so that he could say something about

it. There isn't much to say about this painting. Frau Kranz had seen that in Suzi's beautiful eyes, in Frau Zieschke's eyelashes that stopped applauding for a few seconds.

She had wanted to paint more than what she saw and knew, but she knew only the six women, and she saw only the gray of the night. On such a night, she had tried to imagine what the village would see if it were in her place, and she hadn't the faintest idea.

At home, Frau Kranz drinks elderberry juice, cleans her teeth and lies down in her bed, with the picture of the night leaning against it, and the picture of the night is gray and bleak. She closes her eyes. Through the window, the sun paints on her face what the sun sees and knows.

A sun like that also shines on Frau Kranz's favorite picture. Yes, we think she does have a favorite, although she denied it to the journalist when he asked her. The name of Frau Kranz's favorite picture is:

THE ROMANIAN OUTSIDE THE CARAVAN FOR
Romanian Harvest Workers on the Country Road out at Kraatz.

The Romanians pick apples and strawberries for five euros
an hour, they harvest lettuce, they cut asparagus. Some come
back year after year; you might think they had made friends
in the village. They eat ice cream at Manu's, one of them
sometimes goes to Ulli's for a beer and might recite a poem
in Romanian, but they marry elsewhere, in their towns with
musical-sounding names, in Baia Mare and in Vişeu de Sus.

A few years ago caravans for them to live in were placed on
the country road out at Kraatz. Wheaten-yellow, a hotplate, a
window with a wide view over their place of work, the fields; an
estimated fifteen square meters, an estimated 240 euros, four
beds for an estimated six persons, no smoking; they all smoke.

And last year: neo-Nazis from this area except for our own
two, Rico and Luise, who had overslept and missed the gath-
ering. Campfires, togetherness, barbecues near the caravans,
music, pogo dancing and fun with the wobbly caravans, and
at some point in the small hours of the morning the police.

Afterward the words *Rumänen raus*, Romanians Out, were
to be seen in large, slanting letters on one of the caravans, but
kind of in a quiet voice because they were sprayed in white on
a yellow background, and because the exclamation mark was

missing, and it stayed like that for some time until one morning a sleepy Romanian climbed out of the caravan, looked at the slogan for the time it took him to smoke a cigarette, fetched sticky tape and toilet paper and made the "r" in *raus* into an "H," adding a hyphen after *Rumänen*, so that it now read Romanian-House. It didn't take him a moment, he cleaned his nose, sat down on the little flight of steps in front of the caravan and ate a bread roll.

That is Frau Kranz's favorite picture. That is Frau Kranz's Romanian. A small man with a receding hairline, tracksuit trousers, undershirt, breakfasting in front of his house, the morning sun. A tattoo on his upper arm: the letters B and D in a heart, and the year 1977.

We think that is Frau Kranz's favorite picture because she dedicated it to the Romanian and gave it to him. She never usually dedicates pictures to anyone. And now it is hanging somewhere, maybe in Baia Mare, maybe in Vişeu de Sus: a morning in the Uckermark in 2012.

ON THE MORNING BEFORE THE FEAST THE VILLAGE does not walk three times round the field, reciting a secret saying; it does not sprinkle grain at every corner for the birds to eat, instead of stealing from the field; the village has forgotten the secret saying.

A troop of girls adorned with brightly colored silk ribbons do not pace out the fields, they do not shout and make a noise to tell field spirits and kobolds: we're here, keep away, even winter belongs to us. The girls are not accompanied by young men singing, and the old folk do not wait companionably at the village inn for the return of the young, ready to begin the Feast afterward with a dance round the bonfire.

The village has not pinned nosegays of pinks to its breast, and does not sit amicably together singing the old songs, nor does it say whether it rained the night before the Feast:

"If St Anna brings us rain, heaven's blessings come again." It's all one to the village whether it rains on St Anne's day or not, no one whispers *so help us God, Maria, holy St Anne, so help us God* these days, and St Anne's day is really in July.

The first thresher has not made the Anna Crown, and the crown, interwoven with flowers, is not placed on the head of any girl not yet promised in marriage, nor interwoven with thorns to lie on the head of any woman who has made a pact with demons. No wearer of a crown will dance round the bonfire or burn on it, and white-clad children do not flit between the festive tables, the rakes are not adorned with colored ribbons, and the colored ribbons don't flutter in the wind. Sometimes there isn't any wind.

THE SENIOR CITIZENS ARE AWAKE. IMBODEN IS doing his morning exercises: 1–2–3.

Frau Steiner is saying her morning prayers. Frau Steiner's golden teeth, her white hair: how people stared at her when she was a young woman. Her hair was red then, and she preferred to be alone with her cats, or out and about in the Kiecker Forest looking for herbs. Difficult, difficult. So Frau Steiner joined the faithful and took care to be seen more often in human company. Soon fewer people stared, apart from the men, because she wasn't bad-looking. Today her hair is white and there is indifference in her eyes.

Frau Steiner is delivering advertising leaflets for Netto and Saturn and such stores. She once even shopped at Globetrotter in Prenzlau herself, when a pair of walking boots that took her fancy was reduced in price. She still likes to be out and about in the ancient forest. From five cats at first, she now has fifteen, but today you are considered no worse than crotchety with so many cats.

If she isn't careful the red roots show at her parting.

Frau Steiner has survived three husbands; each of them died after exactly nine months of marriage. Difficult, difficult. Anyone could work it out in retrospect. Anyone could say something, meaning something else.

But no one says anything else, only: poor Frau Steiner. Three husbands, no children. Devout. Has to deliver leaflets.

We are the only ones who hear her morning prayer. And it isn't a prayer, or it is one that you must say in a whisper, shaking as if you were feverish. The cats mew; they are hungry.

> *I am fighting with mine ire, with she-demons I*
> *conspire.*
> *May the first demon heed him, may the second demon*
> *lead him.*
> *May the third demon charm him, may the fourth*
> *demon harm him.*
> *May the fifth demon bind him, may the sixth demon*
> *blind him.*
> *May the seventh bring him to me and make him wish*
> *to woo me.*

Frau Steiner puts her lips to the head of a little stone figure in her hand and closes her eyes. It is a statuette of St Anne, mother of the Virgin Mary and patron saint of widows.

The senior citizens stretch. The senior citizens shake out their pillows.

THE VILLAGE WAKES UP COFFEE MACHINE BY coffee machine. Eggs are hard-boiled, anglers collect their catch. Ditzsche cleans himself and the chicken run, looks under the wings of his chickens. The bakery has given away free coffee, has sold orange juice and yeast pastries with vanilla filling, only Frau Kranz has gone off again without paying, but maybe the milk was meant to be free too.

There are no bells ringing for prayer. The acoustic heralds of the Feast are the sound of drilling from a power drill and the engine of a bus revving up—the wheels, stuck in the mud, are doing their nut. Lada is responsible for the drill. Lada knows he shouldn't be doing what he is doing, but Lada often knows that. Lada is drilling holes in the commemorative stone beside the holes that already exist. Before long the first windows are opening for protests to be uttered. The classic protest is that the drill makes too much noise. Lada either can't hear the protests, or he hears them and he couldn't care less. He has worked through the night, he's wearier than the protesters, and an exhausted man is always right.

Otherwise the village has little to protest about. A new day is beginning, and no one has died. Even though pistols were involved. Herr Schramm hasn't shot himself or anyone else. Frau Kranz hasn't drowned.

Fürstenfelde in the Uckermark, number of inhabitants: no change.

There have been cases of breaking and entering, one or two, we're not sure how many, but nothing was stolen. All is well, in that we still have what belongs to us. What happened in the Homeland House? Broken glass, and an electricity failure, and since Eddie is dead we can't blame it on him any more. The police don't like calling us to say there's nothing to tell us really.

The first guests soon arrive. Some satnav devices show Friedhofsweg and its extension the promenade as a fully negotiable road. There's supposed to be a large car park about halfway down. That, of course, is often seen as a huge joke. The Sat 1 transmission bus, for one, can't confirm that the Friedhofsweg is a fully negotiable road. Unless you're a mountain bike. The Sat 1 transmission bus can't confirm the existence of the car park either, or that at best the lake might be it. The Friedhofsweg slopes steeply toward it. On the right the graveyard wall, on the left the town wall, straight ahead the water. Nowhere to turn. In rain the ground is saturated, the bus can confirm that all right. The wheels, the reverse warning tone hovering over the monument to the fallen, beep-beep-beep, bats fly up. Britta Hansen in her Norwegian pullover is in the passenger seat. She has warned the driver, let's call him Jörg, about the road, but only half-heartedly because it's ages since she was here. Her grandfather is with us for ever, lying next to the road in the soft ground. "I get so damn melancholy when I'm here," she says. Jörg has other problems. Jörg changes up a gear. Beep-beep-beep.

Not twenty meters away, by the water, the bells watch the large vehicle. The bell-ringer didn't set his alarm, and that's a bit of luck, because the bells are not at home—he can sleep his fill for once. Johann has decided to take his bell-ringing exam. Pa will look after Ma that long. But somehow the bells must be hoisted up again. He didn't want to worry the bell-ringer, so he texted Lada, and Lada answered at once: "Sure what you paying." And straight afterward: "We do it this way I help you then you come to Eddie's place and help me for free." And a few minutes later: "And my golf out of the lake okay."

Ulli has got hold of the sliced sausage and opened the garage. He has decorated the platters of meat with cocktail umbrellas. They're practical because of the toothpicks. Now the platters are waiting on two stools, and it's too early for sausage. However, the drinking has begun. Ulli is discussing the matches of the day with several pensioners from the new buildings. The ritual is the same every Saturday. Ulli acquires the betting slips, lectures his audience on the odds and the most interesting matches in short and poetic terms:

"Hannover away

won't get very far

against Borussia Dortmund."

Then they mark up their slips and dream. Today he also gives the pensioners a scratchcard. The sound of coins scraping is in the air.

Ulli has known people to win, and sometime there'll be another win. Down below here the Feast has begun; it's the same as usual at Ulli's. Almost. He is washing yesterday's glasses. Normally the guests wash their own, sometimes there's a little queue at the sink. The men give each other tips on the best way to do it (how much dishwashing detergent to use, *this* is the best technique with the little sponge, how to dry glasses and so on).

Imboden comes in, mildly excited. Has Ulli seen it yet? Seen what yet? Right, then Ulli must come with him, but first they both need a beer to bring along, there's something to celebrate.

It's the commemorative stone. A small wooden panel is hanging from it. So now Ulli reads Lada's wooden panel before Imboden's happy eyes. The betting pensioners have joined them too, people are already drinking to Ulli. He feels both slightly pleased and slightly embarrassed because of what the panel says and drinking to himself like this, although what the panel says is true:

JUAN STEFFEN OPENED PEACE NEGOTIATIONS IN
SOUTH AMERICA
ULLI OPENED THE GARAGE IN FÜRSTENFELDE.

Ulli nods, everyone nods. Now what? Well, nothing, the day goes on.

Imboden goes to Frau Reiff's. He has a date to meet the bell-ringer, they're the old guard; in the past Eddie would have joined them. There's coffee and apple cake and a lecture. They both like lectures; it would be nice if there were lectures here more often, but this is okay.

Imboden tells the bell-ringer about the panel, the bell-ringer tells him about his injury. What they don't say is more exciting. The bell-ringer doesn't say that he does not want to be the bell-ringer any more, just Gustav, and Imboden doesn't say he's been at the garage again. Both have much the same reason: they're ashamed. Imboden knows Gustav doesn't think much of the garage. He's bothered about the kind of people you get there. In principle, the bell-ringer doesn't think himself too refined for anyone, but on the other hand he doesn't think he's the unrefined sort. But most of all, he notices when Imboden's been drinking. In principle he has nothing against that either, but he'd prefer it if Imboden drank with him. That has nothing to do with the kind of people they are, it's just that then he could keep an eye on Imboden better.

After the lecture (a hobby diver showed slides of things lying at the bottom of our lakes, for instance a bazooka and a washing machine), the old men make plans for the rest of the day. Any time now, at twelve, the bell-ringer should be supervising Johann's bell-ringing exam. He has decided it won't take place. He would have to ring one of the bells, and he can't. Nor does he want to. He doesn't know how he is to teach the boy. The anti-Fascist bicycle ride is to be at twelve too. Imboden must be there; as father of our Deputy Mayor, Frau Zink, he can't boycott it.

At this point we ought to make it clear, anyway, in case anyone gets the wrong idea, that strictly speaking it is a preventative anti-Fascist bicycle ride, because while racism etc. has been known not so far away, of course, here it hasn't had any public profile since the war, except maybe at Ulli's recently, when Özil didn't sing the national anthem again, and some people thought that meant they can't be glad when Özil scores for Germany: only a man who sings his country's anthem can score for his country. And we think they think they really aren't glad, but that's not so, because they were definitely glad when things were close and Podolski decided the game.

Anyway, Frau Schwermuth had the idea of the anti-Fascist bicycle ride, and expected twenty participants. At twelve noon there were eighty waiting outside the Homeland House. There was whistling, an IG Heavy Metal banner brought along by a joker, several people who came cycling especially from Prenzlau and Woldegk.

At five past twelve Frau Schwermuth still isn't there. We don't expect her to turn up. But then a bicycle bell rings, and Frau Schwermuth has exchanged her spiked helmet for a cycling helmet and zooms down Marx-Strasse, laughing: "No braking, come on, everyone, follow me!"

On the whole we can say that the anti-Fascist bicycle ride was a success, but also not entirely a success, and not because after three rounds of the village it was over, but because Rico and Luise weren't even awake at twelve.

The Templin Cycling Group joined in the third round. They did a time trial in our honor, Templin—Fürstenfelde—Templin. General ringing of bicycle bells by the anti-Fascist cyclists, general waving by the time-trial cyclists, because they don't have bells, every gram of weight is one gram too many, Frau Schwermuth briefly got into the slipstream of a sporting cyclist. Everyone was happy.

The event finished at the parsonage. Frau Schober had baked three cherry cakes for the cyclists, which of course was nothing like enough cherry cake to go round. Hirtentäschel made a speech lasting half an hour about the anti-Semitism lurking in the midst of bourgeois society, often in the guise of criticism of Israel. At the end of his talk Hirtentäschel gave three sentences as examples of how to criticize Israel *without*—intentionally or unintentionally—saying anything anti-Semitic.

Frau Schwermuth is happy. Happy about the cakes, the cyclists, the applause for Hirtentäschel. But however often, like her, you don't eat cake, you still don't snap at friends and guests, and you don't leave an occasion that you've organized yourself early—unless you're not really happy and don't want other people to be worried.

Out in the road, tears come to Frau Schwermuth's eyes. People are out walking, opening the open doors of the craft shops, clattering the lids of biscuit tins. The village asks itself questions, the village shows its talents. She just wants to get home quickly. Frau Schwermuth passes her hand over her eyes.

The day smells bitter of coffee brewed for too long, sweet with the cinnamon dusted over apple cake, and bitter-sweet of horse dung. Outside the Homeland House the blacksmith is patting a horse, trying to calm it down. The two of them are surrounded by a fierce group of about a dozen girls. The girls want the big man and the big animal to do something fascinating, they've been promised that will happen.

Someone calls Frau Schwermuth's name. It is Zieschke at the window of the Homeland House. He looks harassed, sounds grateful. "My word, Johanna, good to see you," and can she take over for him there? They all want something from him, and he doesn't know his way about the place very well. He also has to prepare for the auction.

Frau Schwermuth blinks her tears away.

It is very busy in the Homeland House. A Californian pensioner is in polite competition with a party on an excursion from Neubrandenburg for the use of the only table. He wants to spread out his ancestors in their Leitz file folders, they want to spread out their picnic wrapped in silver foil.

Frau Schwermuth sits down. Her desk, her timetable, her own Leitz file folders. The Californian pensioner asking, "Are you the one to help me with my ancestry?"

Breakfast TV is there. It didn't like Ditzsche's inner courtyard as much as the courtyard of the Homeland House, with its old ceramic stove and the well, so the TV show asked Ditzsche to bring one of his chickens and be filmed here. It's all the same to Ditzsche; he has shaved, put on his smallest shirt and tucked it into his trousers.

It was not entirely all the same to Zieschke for Ditzsche, of all people, to be giving an interview in the Homeland House, but there you are: TV is TV, and this is the "Travel Fever" slot of the program. Maybe someone will come out with a case of Fürstenfelde-fever, anything that sets it off is fine by us, even if it comes from Ditzsche and his chickens.

Frau Schwermuth doesn't hear what Ditzsche is saying at this moment. She closes the cellar door behind her. There was only one possible answer to the Californian pensioner's questions: "We have that in the basement, let me get it for you."

Silence is requested in the inner courtyard. The camera is running, and Ditzsche can start talking, with his hen in his arms. The woman presenting the "Travel Fever" slot of the show smells of shampoo, and that calms Ditzsche down, because he thinks he too smells of shampoo, so they have something in common. At the end of the interview he asks to make a private remark to viewers; it is about letters and the Stasi, and he may think it is being transmitted live, but the program won't go out for a couple of days, when Ditzsche will be seen for all of five seconds, plus another three for a close-up of his hen. The private remark, thank God, will have been cut, and all that's left will be, "My name is Dietmar Dietz, and here we have a German Dwarf Reichshuhn, color: black and white Columbia."

However, the horoscope slot went out live. Britta Hansen greeted viewers from her own part of the country, and closed the horoscope this time with a quotation from Schiller: "He who does not venture beyond reality will never conquer the truth."

No cellar here is so deep that you don't hear the sound of our bells. Soft and harmonious—the Old Lady seems to be in a good mood—their chimes tower above Fürstenfelde. Your son is ringing them, Johanna, and we know he will pass the exam, or rather we don't know it but we would like him to. After all, it's fabulous to show how you can excel in the field of useless activities. We ought to think not about why we do them, but about just doing them—and as for being useful, who can judge what is and what isn't useful anyway?

Take the example of the anti-Fascist cyclists and their helmets: they have now assembled in the church forecourt, Hirtentäschel is showing them his angels and telling them his story, and Frau Steiner is making eyes at Herr Hirtentäschel, she has her own way of doing that kind of thing, Hirtentäschel can't concentrate properly, and anyway many of the cyclists are still wearing their cycling helmets, because once you've put a cycling helmet on there is no important reason to take it off until you go to sleep, unless the straps are rubbing you. And many people may say, what's all this about the cycling helmets, they're no use if you're not riding your bike! Well, that is the parallel with the bells, because it's a fact that the cyclists paid no attention to the bells at first, but now their heads in the brightly colored helmets are raised, and a powerful, hard, then fine melody peels away from the traditional chimes—yes, all right, melodies don't peel, they peal, but do listen, Johann is just playing something, a little tune, *his* little tune, and the cyclists are immediately enthusiastic, and what, may we ask, is more useful than something that makes people enthusiastic? Johann is ringing all three bells on his own, which is difficult, you really need a ringer for each bell, but the boy has paid attention, and likes doing it, and generally that's all you need to be successful, and Johann's hands aren't soft any more, he is wearing his bell-ringer's top hat, that's the way to do it. Lada and Suzi are up there with him, eating jelly bears. Lada looks down at his village, and then Lada spits out a jelly bear, it flies through the air, and there, now you see what we mean: it can sometimes be useful to wear a cycling helmet even when you're not riding a bike.

The sound of the bells dies away, the tune is over.

The cyclists hesitate. They don't know whether the bells of Fürstenfelde always sound so great, because if so applause is somehow inappropriate, you don't applaud when someone makes a delicious sausage sandwich every day. The old bell-ringer relieves them of the decision by beginning to clap heartily, and once someone has gone first it's easier for the others to follow.

Frau Schwermuth is back at her place in the Homeland House. The bells to which her son gave a voice are still echoing in her ears, she hardly listens to the Californian. She is only glad that he really does mean our Fürstenfelde, and not, like his countryman from the States who once visited the Homeland

House, the Polish one. It was sad, because Frau Schwermuth had to tell the man that he would probably have to go to Boleskowice in Poland. "Many, many have lived here," she told the other American in English, "peasants, counts, witches and thieves, but no Mennonites. Trust me, I would know."

Yes, she would definitely know.

IN THE YEAR OF OUR LORD 1599, ON THE EVE OF the Anna Feast, a mighty wind raged in the morning, doing great Damage to the Houses, raising Roofs and blowing down Barns. A great Quantity of Partridges was also driv'n into Town, and the Wind struck them down in the Streets, causing folk to run away in Alarm at the first, but they soon thought better of it, catching such of the Fowl as did not fly away and roasting them for a Festive Dish.

It is not for Us to say whether this was a Sign and a Wonder portending the strange Events of that Feast. On that Day the notorious Robbers and Malefactors Hinnerk Lievenmaul and Kunibert Schivelbein, known as Long-Legged Kuno, were to be Burnt to Death. The Date when the Condemned Men were to be given over to the Pyre had been announc'd long since, by ringing of all the Bells, and such as had come to see the Show were eating Partridge, the Flames already lick'd round the Calves of the Evil-Doers, when the Wind rose once more, carrying Sparks into the town, which same then caught Fire.

O ye Elements, keeping uncanny Fellowship with the Uncanny! Great was the Confusion and *Perturbatio*, in the midst whereof Lievenmaul and Schivelbein took to their Heels. Many said it seemed as if the Blackguards were dissolv'd away into Smoak!

Worse Devastation, thanks be to God, was averted, in that only four Houses burned down. When the Smoak was blown away, and the Thieves had fled, some cried out that 'twas not the Seed in the Pyre made it burn, as had been thought, but the Robbers' Friends intending to free them. Others again accused the Authorities in Prenzlau of building the Pyre poorly, in such fashion as to endanger them: for the said Authorities, by wishing to see two men die by Fire, had killed nigh on a hundred. One man, Bartholomeus Schutte by name, claimed to have seen a Fox with a burning Brand in its mouth. This said Fox then trotted into the Smithy, which same burned almost entirely to the Ground. What we may make of that, only the Brandywine can tell.

For this time, howbeit, the Robbers were free again, and not all would say they were not glad of it.

In the Chaos, however, as the Flames were extinguished, the Malefactors perpetrated another Robbery, in that they stole our Bells, which the Bell-Ringer had zealously rung to announce the Execution, and after that the Fire. The said Bell-Ringer was bound with ropes and placed in the Belfry, with the Stipulation that no Bell be rung until the last Word were spoken.

The Bells were found by the Deep Lake. It is Suppos'd they were too heavy for the Skiff when Hinnerk Lievenmaul and Kunibert Schivelbein, known as Long-Legged Kuno, were convey'd by our Ferryman over to the other Side.

V

ALL THAT WAS PRELIMINARY SKIRMISHING. THE Feast proper begins with the auction by the Deep Lake. Only after that is music played, and Ditzsche dances, only after that does the village tuck into the food. The pigs are already being turned on the spits, there'll be drinking and burning, of a witch or a dummy, it all depends.

Frau Kranz seems a little distracted; maybe she's tired. She is sitting in the middle of a bench where they are drinking beer, and is soon surrounded by friends and neighbors. Gölow brings her water, Imboden kisses her hand; he's not very good at that, but he insists on doing it, so fair enough. Again and again someone joins her, touches her—she doesn't like that, but tolerates it—asks how she is, asks about her picture. She is sitting here, she says, so she is all right, and the questioner will soon see the picture. It is still leaning against the beer table being used for the auction, draped in a white sheet. It is at least twice the size it was last night, but not many people know that.

The atmosphere is relaxed; a pig wanders among the benches, spontaneous verses of "Sound and Smoke" are sung, people sing along, there must be some 200 people here, we know many of them from the night just past.

The pig is the one that got away with its life, and since we are speaking of pigs: after last year's mini-pig, Gölow has brought something special with him again. The carved wooden figure of a piglet with a human head has been in the possession of his family for many generations. It is a good fifty centimeters long and stands thirty centimeters tall, and Gölow has always liked its friendly face. Only recently has he discovered the signature: *Wegener* is carved under its right-hind trotter. Research—on the part of Frau Schwermuth—has informed us that the piglet must be some 400 years old. There was a woman woodcarver of that name in Fürstenfelde at the time, and a story about the piglet exists, would Gölow like to hear it?

Zieschke opens his beer and is glad so many people have come. He particularly wants to welcome Frau Kranz. Ladies and gentlemen, says Zieschke, friends. He unveils the painting; the sheet drops to the ground.

THE PEOPLE ARE STANDING UP TO THEIR KNEES in the deep lake and do not move. No one is swimming, no one has wet hair. Are they afraid of the deep water? The air is still, no wind. The lake is smooth as if under a thin coat of ice. The sun is bright. Two young men are watching each other, hands in the water, ready to start spraying it up in the air. Their expressions are mischievous, their muscles immaculate. A third, over to one side, is watching them, wearing a large pair of brightly colored bathing trunks, his thin arms wound round his torso like wire. He is waiting for the game to begin, and something tells us he is the one who will be sprayed by the other two any moment now. Johann, this must be Johann, and the other two, tattooed with wolves and dragons, are Lada and Silent Suzi. Not far from them are three men with brown old-age marks: the bell-ringer, crooked and thoughtful; Imboden in his sun hat; and Eddie! Eddie is alive, Eddie is holding a screwdriver in the water as if to loosen up the lake a little. Who else have we here? Someone playing a fiddle, that's Zieschke, not a note can be heard. Herr Schramm over here, Herr Schramm is smoking. His head thrown back, the tall man is enjoying his cigarette. Frau Schwermuth is here as well, fat and white and strange as the limestone cliffs on Rügen Island. A Hawaii pattern adorns the wraparound skirts worn by her companions, who turn cheerfully to look at Anna, amused, as anyone would be who could manage to walk *on* the water. Anna is in a one-piece swimsuit, swimming cap, goggles, with her broad back, beautiful as anyone concentrating is beautiful, a little like a professional swimmer before the start. We are determined, relaxed, rapt in reverie. This is Fürstenfelde. Someone with water wings is juggling, four colored balls in the air suit the sunny day well. That's Hirtentäschel. He wants to be seen showing his skill, although he would certainly say he's doing it just for himself, it's meditation. Oh, Uwe, it's all right to show off what you can do for a change, instead of always going on about what you once were. Who else? Frau Steiner is reading Frau Schober's future in the tarot cards on an air cushion; the future doesn't look good for Frau Schober. Ditzsche, off to one side, is alone. All right; several are off to one side and alone. Silent Suzi's mother, Manu from the ice cream parlor, Poppo von Blankenburg. Ulli, however, has two families—the drinkers from the new buildings and his own, including some who like boozing a lot, but no one overdoes it. A man with a red bald patch and the words *GEO-Special Alaska* over his stomach, that can only be Gölow. A delicate-looking woman lies on the air mattress beside him. Then there's her and her and him and him, Frau Reiff in the old kayak, some nudists playing volleyball. It's as if people were sprouting out of the water everywhere like plants, wherever we look. This is Fürstenfelde. The ferryman is there as well, look, on the landing stage: his beard, his long hair, his cape too warm for the eternally fine last day of the year. He's squinting at the others, what is he planning to do? His Fürstenfelde is the one reflected in the shallow water. Is he calling someone to cross the lake? He takes his time. It can wait, it must wait, we still have so much to do. There's a light on in the ferry boathouse. And the longer we look, the darker it gets, it will soon be night. The Güldenstein is glowing. The people are still here. Herr Schramm must be enjoying a cigarette that lasts for ever.

Right at the front: Frau Kranz—we recognize her by her easel—with a tiny movement, the only movement, in her right arm.

And then Zieschke bangs his beer bottle on the auctioneer's desk, and the auction begins. Who'll bid me ten?

We are glad that Anna probably won't be burnt. Standing by the bonfire, she raises a burning brand in the air and bids ten euros, but we outbid her, we bid twelve.

MY THANKS TO

Christine Marth, Martin Mittelmeier, Maria Motter, Thomas Pletzinger and Katja Sämann for their perception, wit, investigative talent, encouragement, and all their support for my work on this book.

MY THANKS TO

the inhabitants of Fürstenberg, Fürstenfelde, Fürstenwalde, Fürstenwerder and Prenzlau for their information and hospitality, and also to their respective museums and associations of local history for the historical insights. Their church registers and chronicles, and the accounts by Lieselott Enders of the history of the Uckermark, have been important sources for the present text.

SAŠA STANIŠIĆ was born in 1978 in
Bosnia and Herzegovina, and currently lives in
Germany. His award-winning debut *How the
Soldier Repairs the Gramophone* has been trans-
lated into 32 languages. *Before the Feast* was a
bestseller in Germany and won the prestigious
Leipzig Book Fair Prize.